"Like *Where the Crawdads Sing*, Spreier's *Resurrecting St. John the Rancher* takes place in our nation's rural environs and speaks to numerous social issues, engaging the reader through a variety of plot twists, a multigenerational cast of characters, and a mystery that isn't unraveled until the very end. A compelling read."

—Peter Prichard
Author of Amazon international bestseller *Have a Positive Impact During Uncertain Times*

"Spreier's vivid storytelling makes you think you may already know these people and leaves you wondering if you ever really know anyone. His midwestern town of Creekmore is like Wendell Berry's Port William sprinkled with cayenne pepper."

—Tim Krause
Author of *Finding Theo*

"Revel in the tale of an unlikely saint in *Resurrecting St. John the Rancher*, a story that touches significantly on the cultural, social, moral and religious experiences of twenty-first-century rural America. Spreier's characters are quite recognizable, yet their uniqueness unfolds as they address the challenges of living authentically in their own time and space. His subtle theological overtones add to the suspense and open a deeper understanding of why people do what they do."

—John B Larrère
Author of *Executive Prayers* and *The Retirees' Prayerbook*

"*Resurrecting St. John the Rancher* will continue to haunt you long after you turn the last page. Filled with unforgettable characters on an epic quest of personal redemption, it is a novel that will make your soul smile."

—Rick Lash
Author of *Once Upon a Leader*

"A charming, engaging story of death, life, love, faith, and values. A witty veneer of pointed irreverence fails to mask a core of underlying faith, even in the midst of failures and mysteries. Spreier's depiction of small-town life is friendly and honest and makes one think about the many things that divide—and unite—our communities."

—Steve Brookshire
Founding member of Pass the Plate Book Club

"A rare combination of good, old-fashioned mystery and wow-worthy psychological and spiritual insights. Spreier pulls you in literally on page one and does not let go until the very end. His protagonist, Scooter, is a flawed, perplexed, yet endearing Everyman who grapples, as so many do, with a history of toxic influences. As a therapist, I smiled easily as I read how Scooter used the odd circumstances of his mentor's demise to put to death much of his own religious and psychological nonsense. This book made me ponder my own inner journey, and if that was the author's intent, he succeeded greatly."

—Les Carter, PhD
Author of *When Pleasing You Is Killing Me*; YouTube influencer, Surviving Narcissism

"Rarely could one find a more intriguing, finely honed cast of colorful characters than in this honest, multilevel mystery emerging in a small rural town. A couple of decades after their happy high school days, former friends find themselves on opposite sides in Scott Spreier's sprightly novel of love, jealousy, faith and death."

—Darwin Payne
Author of *Quest for Justice*

"A fast, enjoyable read unabashed in its take on thorny issues, such as religion, sexuality and death. *Resurrecting St. John the Rancher* lays bare one man's journey to spiritual, psychological, and relational healing. Spreier has a way of bringing hope and laughter into depression, self- judgement, and the damnation meted out by others."

—Michele Blaker

Resurrecting St. John the Rancher

By Scott Spreier

© Copyright 2022 Scott Spreier

ISBN 978-1-64663-771-3

Published by

◣ köehlerbooks™

3705 Shore Drive
Virginia Beach, VA 23455
800–435–4811
www.koehlerbooks.com

RESURRECTING ST. JOHN
THE RANCHER

SCOTT SPREIER

VIRGINIA BEACH
CAPE CHARLES

For those I've loved ... and hurt.

We're comfortable in Hell because we're familiar with the street signs.
    —Unknown

. . . it is possible for one who is a solitary to live in the crowd of his own thoughts.
    —Amma Syncletica

Maybe stalking the woods is as vital to the human condition as playing music or putting words to paper. Maybe hunting has as much of a claim on our civilized selves as anything else.
    —Steven Rinella, *Meat Eater: Adventures from the Life of an American Hunter*

Is the penis a muscle or part of the brain?
    —A breakfast table debate between Wilson (age five) and Mary Lu (age eight)

1

I'LL NEVER FORGET the day I found John. It was a crisp High Plains autumn afternoon. Buck and I were hunting eighty acres of grassland ten miles south of town on the old Marshall ranch. The fading western sky, wispy and subtle hued, told me nightfall and winter were not far away.

I had just nailed a young rooster that blasted out of the knee-high little bluestem. It was a long, going-away shot, difficult for a mediocre sport like me—the sort of shot you see on those celebrity hunting shows, where professional athletes and country music stars blast dull-witted, pen-raised birds out of the sky with fancy guns and well-bred dogs whose training costs approximately a year's tuition at a state university.

I complimented myself, as there was no cameraman or audience to witness the feat, only Buck, who, inspired by the novelty of me hitting something, charged off to retrieve the unlucky victim. It should have been the perfect end to a perfect day. Man and his best friend sharing a special moment, both relishing a successful hunt and the joy of working together as God intended. Except that Buck disappeared down a small, weed-choked draw and didn't return.

"Bird, Buck. Find the bird."

No dog. No bird.

"Buck, you silly dog, get the goddamned bird!"

Nothing.

I hit the button on his shock-collar. Still no dog.

I began to worry. Buck seldom acknowledges my insults, so that didn't faze me. Nor was his refusal to retrieve unusual. He's only half bird dog and that half is pointer. I trained him based on a book I picked up at a yard sale and a couple of TV shows on the Outdoor Channel. But the first tiny jolt from his fido-fryer usually brings him charging merrily back, bird or not.

I started for the draw but stopped suddenly. There, dancing among the dying sunflowers and goldenrod, was what looked like a skull. Not the grinning skull of a pirate tale, but a rather ironic one.

I shouldered my twelve-gauge. But instead of commanding the specter to halt, I just stood there, mouth agape, squinting and blinking and wondering why my mind had picked this otherwise peaceful moment to take me over the edge.

Suddenly, the skull grew a furry, wagging tail as Buck burst out of the tall grass with it in his mouth. He came to me, sat as he was trained to do, and proudly deposited his find in my shaking hand.

It was a human skull, picked clean but intact. And oddly familiar. Its ironic smile should have offered a clue as to whom I was holding, but without eyes its persona remained infuriatingly vague—much like the sense that overwhelms you when you cross paths with an old acquaintance in a strange place and can't for the life of you put a name with the face.

And then, as the sun broke through a low band of clouds before dying in the west, and a single ray bounced off two incisors encased in gold, separated by a gap left by a missing tooth, it hit me: It was my dear friend John. Or more accurately, what was left of him.

So happy was I to see the old rancher, that I kissed him where his lips had once been. Then I wept.

But my tears were quickly replaced by disconcertion and doubt. I knew John had died. I had accompanied him to what was supposed to become his final resting place more than 200 miles from where I now stood. So how did his skull end up back on his own ranch, within walking distance of his home? Where—and how—had he really met his death?

2

I FIRST RAN into John about the same time I started running away from Satan. It happened on an early summer Sunday in the musty basement of a little Baptist church just a few miles from where Buck and I were hunting. The morning was sunny and hot, but I was shivering and shaking and running for my life, fleeing the Devil, Beelzebub, the Evil One himself—visions that had, in the previous hour, been seared into my brain by Miss Lillian, my first-grade Sunday School teacher.

I'd almost made it out of the dank, dark basement and into the brightly lit men's room when I ran into a solid wall of denim and leather, the hard leg of Rancher John. The jeans, starched and creased, looked new, but the boots were well worn and smelled slightly of cow shit.

A big hand the texture of the boot and displaying a heavy ring of turquoise and silver reached down and helped me up.

Sneaking a look upward, I saw what could only be described as the face of God himself, or at least John the Baptist in western wear, shaggy red ringlets around a bald crown, bushy red beard, leathery face with squinty blue eyes and a sunburn line where his Stetson usually sat.

"Damn, son, you okay? You look like you just saw the Lord Jesus himself."

My face turned from pasty white to red. I put my head down and mumbled something about having to pee real bad. But John saw right through my embarrassment. "I just bet you do," he laughed. "Heck, if I'd just sat through an hour of Widow Blackwell's dreadful abominations and lamentations, I'd already have pissed my britches. God Almighty, that woman can go on, pious as one of Ruthie's hot apple pies sitting on the sill: you know it isn't all it's cracked up to be, but you just can't help but believing, so you swallow it down. And then it hits you in the gut, and you want to run as far as you can, as fast as you can."

I looked at him with profound puzzlement.

John sighed and shook his head. "What I'm saying, son, is that Lillian Blackwell's Bible teaching leaves the same bad taste in your mouth and pain in your belly as my Ruthie's pies."

He knelt and placed a just-washed hand on my shoulder. (That night, thinking about it as I lay in bed, I imagined it felt like the hand of the real John the Baptist when he baptized Our Savior in the River Jordan.) He looked me in the eye. "Son, don't you ever be scared of that old Bible-thumping, brimstone-spewing biddy or her gang of decrepit disciples. They're Creekmore's version of the wicked witches of the west, and every bit as mean and ugly. They may not have any flying monkeys, but the words that fly out of their tight-assed smiles are just as nasty."

There was a glint in Rancher John's eyes now, and the line of demarcation on his forehead had vanished. His whole face was glowing red, much like John the Baptist must have looked during his wilderness tour—wild-eyed, his bushy beard showing the remains of his last locust and honey lunch as he gave the good people of Judea a piece of his mind.

Gripping my shoulder hard, he put his face so close to mine that I could smell the remains of countless hand-rolled Prince Albert smokes. "Son," he whispered, "they're nothing but a pious pack of liars. Their souls are drier than the Sawlog in late summer, and their minds are smaller than a newborn's pecker. That Good Book they keep quoting has become their liquor. They've turned The Word into cheap wine, a drink that keeps them fat and happy and believing that they're better than the rest of us because they have this special relationship with Jesus Christ that will make them immortal. Well, it's bullshit, pure bullshit."

He paused. I guess he saw the shocked look on my little round face or my jittery body language that told him I was, indeed, about to pee my pants. He took a breath and grinned. "Sorry for that bit of Bible thumping. Look, it's not that I don't believe in the Almighty—I do. And I sure as hell hope there's something besides maggots and mold in the end. But all that scary stuff is just that—cockamamie crap that helps people like Widow Blackwell feel superior by making little kids like you and big ole ranchers like me feel small and bad. Now go take a whiz before you flood the church."

Lest you think for a minute that the words of Rancher John—words like lamb's blood, immortality, maggots, and wine—would have been incomprehensible to a six-year-old like me, you clearly did not spend any time in the subterranean Sunday School of Creekmore's First Baptist Church in the early fifties. Not only was it damp and smelled of stale church dinners, but through it also floated what I can only describe as the scent of Satan himself, the unnatural stink of hatred and fear which, combined with a small but chronic natural gas leak, seemed unearthly and out of place in my otherwise happy, carefree kid's life.

And it felt that way because by the time I bumped into John, a small group of aging, stern-faced women had, since the day we could walk, bombarded me and dozens of other blameless little ones with angry, malevolent, multi-syllabic words like crucifixion, damnation and fornication.

What I heard that day for the first time that both shocked me and stuck in my mind were words like "bullshit" and "crap" and "pecker," and the idea that there were actually people—grownups—who weren't that keen on the whole Jesus thing, grown men brave enough to voice doubts about God and Widow Blackwell.

I went home that day confused but slightly hopeful and spent a lazy Sunday afternoon watching the St. Louis Cardinals on our neighbor's snowy black and white TV, listening to Dizzy Dean and wondering about the mysteries of faith and how the word "pecker" might have come about.

3

NIGHT HAD FALLEN by the time I pulled into the drive of the small frame house in which I had grown up and then fled from more than forty years earlier, only to rediscover it much later as the ideal refuge from a hectic urban life and the perfect lodge for my fall hunting trips.

Outside, the sky twinkled with the hope of a billion galaxies. But inside a darkness of a different sort filled my mind—a blackness that blotted out that first flicker of joy in finding my friend.

More than a friend. Much more. From that day when I bumped into him in the church men's room until the final journey we'd made together shortly before his death, John Marshall had been my counselor, confessor, life coach, and spiritual guide.

When I was growing up, John and his wife Ruthie were Creekmore's unofficial surrogate parents, offering objective, nonjudgmental advice to me and most of my friends. They were the grown-ups you went to when you wouldn't—or couldn't—talk to your real parents. At one time or another, they had been the voice of adult reason who had kept us from harm's way and our own stupidity.

The last time I had seen John alive, late the previous fall, was when I dropped him off at a hotel near a Native American casino hotel in Oklahoma. I knew he was close to death, that the long trip from his ranch was the last he expected to take, that, as he said, he was "going off to the great hunting ground as the ancients had done," and that he wasn't coming back.

And yet somehow, he had—or at least a part of him. Equally disturbing was not knowing exactly how he had died. While I had not been party to his actual death, I had been involved in the events leading up to it and its cover-up.

Guts and feathers seldom put me in a contemplative mood, but as I dressed the birds in the light of a single seventy-five-watt bulb that hung above the garage, I couldn't help but reflect on the skull sitting on the dash of my pickup and the journey it must have taken from my vibrant friend's final farewell to a calcified artifact that Buck mistook for the mother of all dog bones.

I wondered about John's last moments of consciousness, what he'd been thinking, what he'd been feeling, what had really happened, how a piece of him had wound up in his own pasture, and where the rest of him was.

The bullet hole I half-expected to find wasn't there, which made me feel better. The ending of any life is not without some violence, but it was nice to see that John's final thoughts weren't troubled by a gun at his head, which I knew had been a possibility.

The birds cleaned, I headed for the house. John's skull, I'd decided, would remain in the pickup. Dead pheasants in the fridge were one thing; human remains on the bookshelf another. Sooner or later, I'd have to turn it over to the sheriff and face the shitstorm that was sure to follow. But that could wait. I was cold, tired, and hungry. Besides, I had no clue how I should reintroduce John to those still living.

Buck clearly had other ideas. Instead of squeezing through the back door ahead of me as he usually did, he sat by the truck, yowling softly and staring at me soulfully until I retrieved the skull.

After feeding him his après-hunting dinner of rigatoni, dog chow, and chicken broth, I started a fire, poured a whiskey, and lit the last of several Cubans a fellow Baptist had smuggled back from a Havana "mission trip." Buck, meanwhile, curled up on the rug, chewing contentedly on an old bone—one of many from his collection strewn about the house.

Or so I thought. Perhaps it was the mind-numbing weariness brought on by a day in the field—the evening fog that sneaks up on me more and more these days—or just the warmth of the fire and alcohol. But I had taken several deep draws and an equal number of slow, satisfying sips before it hit me that Buck was sharpening his canines on my old friend's cranium.

I leapt from the chair and grabbed for the skull. Buck, sensing an evening game of chase, side-stepped me and began his teasing, head-shaking dance. I rushed him twice. Both times he nimbly avoided me. Finally, realizing how demented the whole scene would appear if a neighbor stopped by, I retrieved a pheasant wing from the kitchen and proffered a trade. Smelling fresh meat, he quickly agreed, dropping the skull, which bounced oddly on the oak floor like one of those treat-filled dog toys, ringing out a trio of mournful *bonk*s before coming to rest at my feet, smiling up at me.

I picked it up and turned it over in my hand. It was weathered and smooth and very light. Hard to believe this was all that remained of one of the most influential people in my life. A man who had coached me, challenged me, leveled with me, cried with me, and laughed with—and occasionally at—me. A friend and father figure of sorts, who could be brutally honest and straightforward one second and vague and enigmatic the next.

I set the skull on the mantle, went to the kitchen, warmed up some leftover venison chili, opened a bottle of wine, and returned to the fire. Halfway through dinner, Buck wandered over, looked soulfully up at John and once again began to moan softly.

I told him to knock it off, but he gave me his best "up yours, dumbass" look and continued his soliloquy. Clearly, he believed he had something important to share with John. So, I ignored him, returned to the kitchen, scrounged up an apple on the verge of going bad and some well-aged cheese, poured another tumbler of wine, and opened a book of Jim Harrison's poetry.

But Harrison's verse, usually comfort food for the soul, did little to calm or even distract me. My mind and eyes kept going back to the skull above the fire. This was not how it was supposed to end. I'd spent many months coming to terms with John's death and my role in it. Only recently had I begun to get past the lies I'd told and the secrets I'd kept hidden. Only in the past few months had I begun to take responsibility for my involvement and began to see it as the generous, final commitment to an old friend—the last act of affection and love I could offer to a personal hero.

But Buck's discovery that afternoon had carried with it another tidal wave of self-doubt. Once again, I desperately needed to talk about it with someone to rid myself of the guilt that now resurged.

I thought about calling my daughter Lucy in Chicago, but quickly decided against it. I'd never told her the story, and now certainly wasn't the time to bring it up. Since her mother's death four years earlier, she had become my confessor and counselor. She was the reason I'd found myself back in Creekmore the previous fall, involved in the events that led to John's death.

"It's time you and Buck start hunting again," she had told me earlier that year. "A month of walking the prairie kicking up birds will give you that last bit of closure that you're still struggling to find. Mom would have wanted you to go."

Of course, she would have. Throughout our marriage, Anna had been the guiding and grounding force that kept me out of life's rocky shoals and uncharted currents. When I veered off course, which was often, she would gently trim the sails, firmly grab the tiller, and steer me to safe harbor. Her pragmatism countered my irrationality.

I had taken Lucy's advice. The hunting had been exceptionally good for both me and Buck, who also mourned her passing. The wind, the tall grass, the constantly shifting topography calmed me, draining the remaining grief that had still haunted me most days.

But then John had called and told me it was time for his last road trip.

4

"WHAT THE HECK, son. I scare you or something?"

It was John, or at least I thought it was. He looked alive, real. Nothing like those horrible holiday ghosts in the old black and white version of *A Christmas Carol* that played at the local theater when I was little, frightening the hell out of me. Nor did he look angelic, unless God's forces had taken to running around in old maroon-and-white, terrycloth Texas A&M bathrobes and shit-caked cowboy boots.

He bent down and scratched Buck, who, clearly glad to see him, began wagging his tail and sniffing the old rancher's crotch. I didn't want to think what was or wasn't under that bathrobe, but I did, and it must have registered on my face because John gave me a sort of squinty-eyed "what-the-hell" look. It was the same look he used to give us when he and Ruthie taught our church's teen group and one of us proffered something we believed based on our fanatical upbringing, something idiotic to a dry-land farmer and rancher who had worked the earth hard for years and experienced his share of what we so earnestly called *God's plan.*

"Guys, I don't have a lot of time, so listen up." John was clearly speaking to both Buck and me. "First, thanks for finding my remains, or at least part of them—I still wish someone would dig up that antique turquoise ring I was wearing when I made my final exit. It's no big deal, but some of us haven't totally shed our earthly vanities. For example, I still don't like the idea of my bones being used as chew toys for coyotes and dogs. I know we're supposed to recycle, Buck, but Jesus . . ."

Buck hung his head and whimpered.

John reached down and stroked him. "Big dog, little brain. Don't fret, you can chew on me any time you like." And then to me: "I thought this might be a good time—maybe the only time—to answer those questions that have been stuck in your craw all these years."

I stared at him blankly, too stunned by his sudden appearance to speak.

"The questions you used to pester me with every Sunday? Those questions that have kept you from really enjoying life?"

I continued to stare, too shocked to ask him how the heck his skull showed up 250 miles from where he supposedly died.

"Oh, Jesus Christ, you look like you've never seen a ghost. I don't have time to explain everything right now. I've got to get back. Look, I'll try to return when you're more *receptive*, shall we say, to my visitations and I have more time. You'd think I'd have all the time in the world, but it doesn't work that way."

In a flash—and I could have sworn there was a real flash—he was gone.

5

I AWOKE IN A WAVE of confusion and anxiety. I was still in my chair. Buck was curled up on the floor, asleep, as if nothing had happened. Slowly the realization broke that I had been awakened from a weird dream by the early morning sun. Relief. Then my eyes fell on John's skull staring serenely from the mantle, and a second wave washed over me: the reality of the past day, the shock of finding the old rancher's skull, the guilt of knowing that somehow I was partly responsible for how it got there, and the uncertainty of where reality ended and the dream began.

Not that waking to fear and guilt was new. They had been a primary source of dark emotions for as long as I could remember. The first dream I recall—and I can still see it vividly—is of my bed crawling with rattlesnakes. I screamed until my parents ran into my room, picked me up, and started looking for the snakes.

Serpents continued to be a major source of bad juju for years after that, which wasn't surprising given our weekly Sunday School lessons focused more on the satanic side of herpetology than on the saintly side of faith. We had a devilish good time coloring pictures of snakes, making clay snakes—everything but playing with them like our less sophisticated Kentucky cousins. That branch of our family has all but played out, in part I think, because of their persistent and pig-headed belief that the good Lord was a better source of snake protection than a .22 with birdshot and good pair of knee-high leather boots.

Looking back, I realize this preoccupation with snakes was a well-meant but misguided attempt to save our worthless little souls—scaring the holy shit out of us to make room for the Holy Spirit. Unfortunately, the remedy didn't take with me. All I got was the first of many phobias that have taken years and countless hours of counseling to shake.

By the time I was ten and finally coming to terms with the snake thing, another dark obsession—death—had slithered into my already fragile psyche. Its grip tightened when Mom paid a visit to Widow Sherman in her little shack of a home across the street from where we lived, and found her slumped over her stove, face down in a pot of possum stew. Both she and her dinner were quite done.

Widow Sherman always reminded me of the witch in "Hansel and Gretel," and I used to run when I saw her, especially when she tried to lure us into her house with offers of cookies and candy. I know now that she was just a harmless, very lonely woman. But when you're young, the very old sometimes appear alien and scary. And, given that actuarially they are much closer to death than you are, it's easy to think they might be a bit jealous and looking for a way to bring you to Hades as a kind of pet to keep them company.

It wasn't just snakes and decaying, half-boiled women who gave me the creeps back then. Even more threatening was the thought of being vaporized by a warhead launched by some evil Russian general. It was at the height of the Cold War and the reign of those "goddamned communists," as my God-fearing dad called them every night while he washed the dinner dishes.

"They have to be stopped," he'd rant. "And better now than when they're in our backyard—goddamned Red bastards. Why don't we get 'em now? You know why? I'll tell you why: it's the goddamned Democrats. Those pansy-assed liberals have hog-tied one of the greatest generals in modern times. Ike can't do a goddamned thing to fight the goddamned Red Menace (he actually used those words, *Red Menace*) because of the goddamn Democrats in congress."

Then, after the dishes were dried, he'd move to his recliner, switch on the old Zenith console radio, tune in KGNO, and listen to Patsy Cline or two or three innings of the Kansas City A's ghosting in and out of the starry prairie night. Eventually, he would calm down—unless of course the A's were playing those "goddamned New York Yankees."

Many a night I went to sleep to the soft words of Patsy or the quiet patter of the A's announcers. But in the back of my mind, I worried about being burned to a crisp or orphaned by an atomic bomb. In the case of the latter, I kept a survival kit under my bed. In it was my Boy Scout knife, a kid's wallet, some bandages, the Popeye ring my mother gave me, a small cross, and a magnifying glass. Years ago, I lost the ring and broke the glass. But I still always carry a knife and a cross, the latter less a symbol of faith than a tiny talisman to repel all the guilt, angst, and evil shit that surrounds me.

As I sat there staring at the old rancher's skull, now bathed in the soft early-morning light, I realized that I'd need more than a penknife and a lucky charm to get me out of the predicament in which I now found myself.

It was not John's death that troubled me. It was the events that led up to it. It was that final winter evening when I looked into his eyes for the last time, told him goodbye, and then turned and walked away, never looking back. It was not knowing what really happened after I'd gone.

Again, the thought of turning his remains over to the sheriff entered my head. It was the obvious—the right—thing to do. But I knew I couldn't. Not now anyhow. I wasn't ready for the questions and recriminations that this unexpected evidence would certainly trigger. There was sure to be an investigation, starting with the unearthing of his remains, which everyone in town was led to believe lay next to Ruthie's in the family plot. John's daughter, Shelia Mae, would finally learn the truth, as would the rest of the community. And those of us who would be held responsible for his disappearance and death would be hung—if not literally, at least out to dry.

My other thought was simply to return the skull to where I'd found it. It would be much easier. Buck and I would simply "go hunting." I'd slip the skull into my bird vest and, carrying my shotgun, we would return to the same pasture we'd hunted the previous day. Only this time, we'd walk another quarter mile, down to the Sawlog, and place the skull in the crook of one of the old cottonwoods that lined its banks.

6

AFTER THE PREVIOUS DAY'S WEIRDNESS, it was great to get back into the country and make the long walk through the pasture and to the creek. As we made our way, I was both worried and hopeful we'd find some additional pieces of John. But though we made a thorough search of the area, my eyes and Buck's nose turned up nothing but a few cattle bones and a lone coyote skull.

As we neared the creek, however, I started finding artifacts that pointed toward my friend. The first was a half-full bottle of his favorite whiskey. Though caked with mud, the cap was intact, and a taste of the amber liquid proved it still drinkable. I also found an empty faded Oreos box. The combination of the two—John's favorite before-bed snack—was both confirming and confusing.

In our final conversation at the Oklahoma casino right before I left, John had hinted that it was not the last we'd see of him. When I asked him when and where, he just chuckled and told me not to wait up.

"It will not be in this world," he said, eyes twinkling. "Like the ancients of old, I will leave no trace. Dust to dust, if you prefer the Good Book's version."

So, had it all been a ruse? Apparently. It appeared John had purposely put us off his trail. But how did he end up back at the ranch? Where did he really die? And how? His final text message, signaling he had met up with Rev. Shaman Ricky Running Bull and was initiating the final phase of his plan, had come just twenty-four hours after I dropped him off. Still on my phone, it read:

My limit shot,
I hunt no more,
It's time for God
To even the score.
John

At the time I had marveled at his humor, mourned his passing, then texted the others that Operation Duck Duck Goose had been successfully completed. But apparently, it hadn't.

I continued to scour the ground under the trees for evidence. I was about to give up when I spotted something shiny in a pile of dead cottonwood leaves. It was John's old silver and turquoise ring.

According to John, it had been crafted more than a century before by Jimmy Iron Tail, a displaced Kiowa brave who, to keep what little respect and sanity he had left, turned to working with silver and stone.

To John, it was a talisman and something he never removed, even when butchering a hog or birthing a calf. I witnessed the latter late one night as he was washing his hands of blood and afterbirth and asked him about it.

"I don't take it off for anything or anyone. It's a holy relic, right up there with the bones of the saints. The old Indian who made it and gave it to my dad claimed it had special powers to ward off evil shit— sort of like the St. Christopher medals our Catholic brethren wear.

"Now, I know what you're thinking, 'it's just a load of crap.' Well, I used to think so, too. But the older I get the more it reminds me that it's not so much what you get out of life, but what you leave for those who come after. Besides, although Ruthie thinks I'm a heathen for talking such nonsense, I swear it has saved my ass from really bad things on more than one occasion."

I put the ring in my pocket, and then began looking for a final resting place for John's skull. I thought about burying it, but somehow that seemed wrong. As John had explained to me on more than one occasion, he did not want to be buried like some "stinking bag of garbage."

I began scanning the trees, looking for a place where he—I had begun to equate John's skull to his soul—would be secure and unseen.

Suddenly, like spotting a camouflaged Waldo in a sea of greens and browns, it materialized: a platform of branches resting on two large limbs about ten feet up. I tried to climb up, but it was impossible without a ladder.

I don't remember much about the trip to town to retrieve a ladder. I was too distracted, thinking about what I might find atop the platform. Had John died there, high above the banks of the creek? If so, how did he get there from Oklahoma, where he told me he planned to die?

By the time I returned, I had convinced myself that it was nothing more than a simple deer blind, something John had put up years ago. The whiskey and cookies were probably just the remnants of an early morning hunting snack.

But of course, they weren't.

When I climbed to the platform, I found a ripped sleeping bag, John's old Colt revolver, still fully loaded, his cell phone and an old ammo box. Inside was a flashlight, a bottle of what I assumed were pain pills, and a Bible. There was also a rope ladder, clearly John's final stairway to paradise.

I sat there for the next hour trying to untangle the emerging riddle of Rancher John. Was he lying to me from the beginning? Or did something go wrong with his Oklahoma-medicine-man deal? Did he return to the ranch alive, or were his remains somehow secreted back home? If so, by whom, and why had they created such an elaborate setting to indicate suicide?

At some point I must have fallen asleep. It was late afternoon when Buck's barking woke me. I peered down and saw that he had taken my nap as an opportunity to do a little hunting on his own. Laid out carefully on the ground were two squirrels and a rabbit.

I climbed down from the platform, but not before collecting

what was left of John's possessions and replacing them with the skull. I spent the next hour wandering the banks of the creek and nearby pasture, looking for additional remains or other evidence of John's demise. The chilled air and amber colors created the aura of walking through a tumbler of fine scotch, but without the warmth and contentment such a drink delivers. Although Buck flushed two small coveys of quail, I never shouldered my gun.

My mind pin-balled between the practical and philosophical implications of John's death. Why had I gotten involved in his crazy plan? For the first time in years, I had finally achieved a comfortable equilibrium—a cease-fire of sorts between the good and dark angels who dwelt in my head, constantly critiquing and advising me on how I lived my life. True, I'd had my share of fuckups and failures, including a lengthy trail of broken relationships. But my last, with Anna, was strong to the end. And our daughter had morphed into a beautiful, passionate, productive adult. I'd been a good provider—had a couple of successful careers and had managed to land in a tolerably agreeable post-fifty lifestyle.

Now this.

At dusk we started for the pickup. But part way there, I paused and then headed back to the creek. Climbing the platform, I retrieved John's skull. "No way I'm going to leave you out here again, pal," I said, stuffing it into my bird bag. "You're going to be a pain in the ass as long as I hang on to you, but I still have a lot of questions that you need to answer."

7

I WAS EXHAUSTED when we got back to town and opted for an early dinner at Mary's. The place may have lacked the atmosphere of an upscale bistro, but once you got past the cat on the counter, the stale essence of decades-old cigarette smoke and Mary's grease-stained bedroom slippers, it was still a great place for a burger and beer. Also, I had personally witnessed Mary degreasing her grills, traps, and filters at the local carwash, so I could attest to her kitchen's cleanliness.

Inside sat Lucas Johnson, the county sheriff, his cousin WD, the lone deputy, and two of my old high school pals, Norm and Bobby at the large communal table.

Norm had returned home after a little-known but distinguished career in the CIA to take over the family farm. Deciding that cattle and corn were not his calling, he had quickly opted to lease out his land and spend his time painting landscapes and teaching sociology at the regional community college the next county over.

Bobby, after spending an undistinguished but well-publicized decade in the state penitentiary for cultivating pot, also returned home—supposedly to grow legitimate, albeit genetically modified, crops that probably did far more damage to mankind than all the weed in the world. He confined his marijuana production to two small food plots he planted on public hunting land to allegedly attract deer. In his free time, Bobby was a blogger who wrote a wicked "culture" column in the local newspaper, under the pen name Arthur J. Oswald III.

As usual, the conversation—about the sad state of the country—took a sharp turn when the sheriff saw me walk in. "Well now," he began, "if it isn't our wealthy, cultured friend from the big city. What are you in town for, Scooter?"

"No doubt our diversity-loving, liberal-leaning brother has come to save us all from our good Christian ways," WD answered for me.

Norm reached up and gave me a solid handshake. Bobby winked.

"Sheriff Luke," I said, offering a hand, which he ignored, "so glad you're still making the world safe for socialist heathens like me and my friends here. Good to see you too, WD. Where's your gun? Lose it again?"

WD was known for leaving sidearms in bars, restaurants, even at crime scenes. Once a suspect he had been chasing doubled back and found the deputy's 9 mm Glock in a pile of fresh cow manure and returned it. As the arrested man explained it to the county judge, "It was worth getting caught just to make WD take back that disgusting, shit-coated weapon so's he could arrest me. Hell, it was either that or shoot him, and I'd never shoot no one, Judge, even WD."

WD gave me a sullen stare while spitting a stream of chewing tobacco into his coffee mug.

"How's the hunting?" Norm asked, attempting to steer the conversation in more palatable direction. "See many birds?"

"Just enough to keep Buck and me happy. How's the life of an artistic academic?"

Before he could answer, the sheriff interrupted: "Old man Williams said he saw your vehicle parked out at the Marshall ranch. I'm assuming you got permission. You know I'm pretty particular when you out-of-state boys start poking around in our county."

"Course I do, Sheriff," I said, ignoring the barb. "John gave me permission years ago."

"Well, John's dead. Ruthie too." He gave me one of those gotcha looks I'd seen too often in rural law enforcement types, especially elected ones like Luke. I took a deep breath and was thinking about how to respond when Mary, who had changed from bathrobe to bib overalls for the evening crowd, came over to take my order. I paused while she scribbled it down and poured me some coffee, sprinkling it with a bit of ash from her cigarette for extra flavor.

"Well, Luke," I said, my civility about to be hijacked, "never mind that I *still* own property and *still* pay taxes in this county and am not one of your so-called outsiders, before they died John and Ruthie gave me what is known in legal terms as *perpituis permissi huntus*, which is Latin for perpetual permission to hunt."

Lucas and WD stared at me blankly. I thought I'd fooled them until Bobby decided to make a rare move to the right side of the law.

"He's bullshitting you, Sheriff. There is no such thing."

"You should know, Bobby," I said. "You know the laws better than any of us, given the number you've broken over the years."

"I take that as a compliment," he said, laughing.

"Like I knew you would," Norm said, as he and Bobby rose to leave. "Sorry guys, we've got to get back to work. We'll leave the legalities to you to sort out."

He started for the door, and then turned back. "Give me a call when the hunting slows, Scooter," he said, raising his eyebrows and winking. "I'll catch you up on all the local news."

When the two were gone I turned back to the sheriff, who with eyes squinted and arms folded, was clearly spoiling for a verbal smackdown. "Okay, Lucas," I said with as much sincerity and politeness as I could muster, "to whom should I speak to gain continued permission to hunt the Marshall Ranch?"

"Dunno." He stared at me and shrugged. "I guess you need to talk to Shelia Mae."

Shelia Mae Marshall. The name sent chills down my spine and dread through my soul. A name I'd consciously been trying to avoid since discovering her dad's skull.

Shelia Mae, the cartwheeling, barrel-racing she-devil. Shelia Mae was beautiful. She was also a ballbuster. Literally. Our first close encounter came at the end of recess one spring morning in the first grade. The bell rang. I bailed out of the swing I was on and ran toward the school. Shelia Mae was inbound too, but as usual, cartwheeling across the playground. Our trajectories intersected. She caught me mid-stride with one of her Mary-Janes. I rolled, grabbing my crotch and yelping in pain. Our eyes met briefly before she ran off with a bemused look on her face that I've never forgotten.

By fifth grade, Shelia Mae and I had put our differences aside and become pals, and in the eighth grade, we went steady over the summer. But then the realities of adolescence took over. She blossomed into a gorgeous young woman, a champion barrel racer and head cheerleader with a steady boyfriend—one Lucas Johnson—while I morphed into a geeky man-child, B student, and mediocre jock who was too shy to date, but who, unfortunately, continued to harbor a sophomoric crush with accompanying technicolor fantasies.

With the exception of youth camp and other church events, I saw little of her in high school, until once again our paths collided in a near-carnal, life-altering way, this time in view of half the town. Our high school basketball team was losing big to the Prairie City Beavers. I was chasing down a wild pass from Billy Bard, a routine move, given Billy's limited eyesight and coordination. Just off court, Shelia Mae was ending a particularly raucous cheer with another of her famous cartwheels. Again, we met as her legs were coming over the top of the maneuver. Again, she caught me in mid-stride, one foot to my groin, one to my temple. I woke to her frantic voice proclaiming, "Oh shit, I killed Scooter." She was standing astride me with a horrified yet angelic look, and as I peered up at the satin infinity between her well-developed, barrel-racer thighs, I tended to agree that I was no longer of this world.

From that day forward I was forever haunted by what I'd seen. It would take more than my share of failed relationships and many hours of therapy to get to the bottom of the trauma I'd suffered at the sight of that first, beautiful female form. And, despite time and distance, I never quite eradicated the crush I had on her.

8

AFTER A FITFUL NIGHT spent wrestling with dreams of John's wayward spirit, his winsome daughter, and the self-important Sheriff Luke, I decided a hard day of serious hunting was needed to regain my mental equilibrium. To avoid the risk of bumping into additional reminders of John's untimely return, Buck and I headed seventy miles and two counties north to some property that, rumor had it, was awash in birds. We had a good morning, with Buck kicking up enough birds for me to get my limit and still have time for a late lunch before the drive home.

The cafe we stopped at was a step up from Mary's. While Buck dined on his hunting lunch of a Snickers and a Coke—my vet claims it gives him much needed energy—I enjoyed a leisurely meal of pasta carbonara and a couple of glasses of a decent Italian white.

As smoothly as it went down, the lunch brought up several romantic repasts, which led to thoughts of the women I'd shared those meals with, which led to a recollection of my first such meal—burgers and fries at the Dairy Bar with Shelia Mae—which, before I knew it, got me thinking again about my conversation with Sheriff Luke, which quickly darkened and sobered my spirits.

Neither the thought of reaching out to Shelia Mae, hat in hand, to ask for permission to hunt nor the ire of the sheriff if I didn't were options that excited me.

The truth was, except for the random flashbacks and daydreams that occasionally entered my still maturing mind, I knew very little about Shelia Mae the adult. Except for cordial but superficial greetings we exchanged at church on those infrequent times we both happened to be in town for the holidays, we'd seldom spoken since high school.

Like me, she had fled Creekmore at the first opportunity, dumping her college sweetheart husband soon after graduate school—she'd long before dropped Luke—and moving to London to pursue a career in global marketing.

A few years later, I ran across her picture in *People* magazine. Downright gorgeous in some designer number, she was shown at a charity event thrown by an apparent up-and-coming Londoner at his Belgravia home. They were smiling lovingly at each other, and the caption confirmed that, indeed, they were an item.

I felt a pang of jealousy at that moment, made worse by the fact that the years abroad had clearly been good to her, transforming the tomboyish farm girl I knew into a sophisticated, beautiful woman. But I comforted myself by imagining that one day, while turning a passion-induced cartwheel, she'd nail her Prince Charming much as she'd clipped me, and they would not live happily ever after.

My dream apparently came true. Several years later another picture of her appeared, this one in a high-end British shooting magazine. It showed her in a similar pose with what the magazine called her *partner*, Lady Something-Rather, a tall, elegant, athletic-looking woman in her early forties. This time the scene was a charity shoot at some Scottish castle, and both were decked out in the traditional hunting garb of gentlemen and women. To say they pulled off the look well is an understatement. Standing there in their tweeds and Wellingtons, they looked classier than the matched pair of Purdeys casually resting in their arms. The accompanying story noted that the "couple now makes their home in Paris."

I taped both clippings above my workbench, much to the

annoyance of Anna, who never passed up a chance to needle me about my "garage girls," and who, I suspect, was the artist who drew moustaches on both.

It was John's death that finally reconnected us, albeit briefly. I reached out to share what I supposedly knew about his passing and give her my sympathy. The sympathy was sincere—the story of her father's peaceful, heart-attack-induced death in a goose blind following a successful hunt, pure subterfuge, concocted to protect her from the truth and those of us involved from legal trouble.

Our conversation that day was short and one-sided. Her reaction was sad, stoic, mono-syllabic. She thanked me, apologized for not being able to return home for the funeral, offered sympathy for the loss of Anna, said goodbye, and hung up.

Relieved that she had not inquired deeper into the details of John's final moments, I had avoided talking with her since. Lying once was bad enough. Maintaining the charade, I knew, would be untenable. I put her out of my mind as best I could. After all, I kept telling myself, life was too short to cling to a faded old romantic daydream.

Lusting after women, once a serious personal shortcoming, was generally no longer an issue for me, or so I liked to tell myself. Life— marriage, children, divorce, aging, death—had seen fit to take care of that. Also, my relationships with several smart, independent women had dramatically altered my perspective on how the opposite sex should be viewed. Granted, I still could be momentarily distracted by the shape or physical beauty of a woman. But I'd come to accept those feelings as a pleasant if bittersweet side effect of God's wiring of the male of our species—nothing to be ashamed of, but also nothing to boast about either.

Given that mindset, I reflected as Buck and I drove home, and the fact that Shelia Mae was no longer attracted to men, I really had nothing to fear in talking to her. At least in terms of my continued hunting on her family's land. As for an honest conversation about her daddy's death, finding his remains in a pasture, and getting her thoughts on what we should do with them—that was another matter.

That evening, after a second scotch, I emailed the sheriff.

Luke—Am seriously taking your advice about getting permission to hunt the ranch. You have SM's current email? Tks—Scooter

Luke's reply didn't arrive until the next morning: *You've never taken my advice before asshole . . . Why now? You know she's going to tell you to fuck off—L.*

Because it's the right thing to do, Sheriff, I shot back, *and because I respect your office if not you personally.*

Luke responded with three lines of disgusting emojis that I didn't know existed, followed by two lines of exclamation points, and then after a pause, a UK email address.

Composing a brief email to Shelia Mae took most of the afternoon. It had to be something that would (a) not piss her off, and (b) encourage her to pick up the phone and call me. I put off actually writing anything until it was past time for a drink. But knowing that I could not risk even the minimal effect of alcohol on anything I sent, I opened my laptop:

Shelia Mae—I hope you're doing well in Paris. I ran into your old friend, our beloved sheriff, at Mary's the other day and your name came up. That reminded me: now that your dad is gone, I probably need to check with you for permission to hunt your ranch.

Cheers, Scooter

I was into my third scotch when my phone buzzed. It was Shelia Mae emailing me back.

Scooter—What a pleasant surprise! You've been on my mind recently and I've been meaning to call. I assume he told you that I'm back home and out at the ranch. Of course, you can hunt. In fact, I saw someone hunting the pasture the other day and figured it might be you.

Talk soon,
Shel

———————

I got up before dawn the next morning after another sleepless night spent wishing John would pay me a return visit and wondering why no one had bothered to tell me that Shelia Mae was in town.

I also was troubled by Shelia Mae's comment that I had been on her mind. Why? Was it the fact that she had seen me hunting? Or had she discovered something more about her dad—perhaps something that implicated me in his death?

I called Norm, a seasoned professional not only in international intrigue but also in the minutia of local gossip.

"I should have told you," Norm said, "but I assumed you knew. Also, I was afraid we'd be overheard—Mary's is small, but as we know, her diners have big ears. All I know is that she showed up a month or so ago. I've spotted her a couple of times in town. But she seems to be spending most of the time lying low on the ranch."

"And the word on the street?"

"Rumor has it she is back for an extended period. Recuperating from a nasty break-up with her . . . partner. Someone—an unnamed source—told me the sheriff had been out to see her. Some speculation as to whether it was a personal or professional visit. We all know that Luke still has the hots for her."

I laughed. "Surely you jest. Luke's not the brightest bulb in town, but he must realize he doesn't have a chance with a beautiful, sophisticated, cosmopolitan woman who gave him the brushoff three decades ago."

"One would think," Norm said. "But we know Sheriff Lucas has matured at a lot slower pace than the rest of us."

"Yes, and given the welcome he gave me at Mary's, he continues to nurse very old grudges."

"Yeah, he's still pissed that you and Shelia Mae were platonic pals, and that you had the balls to ask her to the prom. And it didn't help that we didn't notify him about John's death."

"It was none of his fucking business," I said. "He was out of town when it happened, and it was not in his jurisdiction."

"You think he's still sniffing around?" Norm asked.

"I don't know. But I wouldn't be surprised if he was. And that's what scares me. Shelia Mae said she'd been thinking about me recently. I can't imagine why she would say that unless Luke has said something to her about John."

"Surely not," Norm protested.

"We can only hope."

I spent the rest of the morning muddling through the best approach to take should Shelia Mae actually call, or should we bump into each other. I implored John to return with a bit of advice about how to handle his daughter. When that didn't work, I got down on my knees and asked for forgiveness for lying to Shelia Mae about her dad's death, adding that I also was sorry for having lusted after her, which immediately triggered another round of heartfelt desire.

Finally, when my fifth cup of coffee failed to fuel any insight beyond the need to relieve myself of the first four, I gave up and dialed the ranch. Shelia Mae picked up on the first ring, greeting me before I had a chance to identify myself.

"Scooter. I knew it had to be you. No one ever calls on the old ranch line anymore. Jesus, it's been ages since we talked. How are you doing?"

Comforted by the fact that she again sounded like the old Shelia Mae and still spoke midwestern English and not some French or *Downton Abbey* dialect, I pushed boldly forward. "Hey, Shelia Mae, great to hear you, too. Didn't know you were back in civilization. How long are you here for?"

"Good question. I came here to clean out the house, collect a few things, and get a handle on the property. But after a couple of weeks, I kind of felt at home again."

"Did your . . . partner come with you . . . you know, Lady What's Her Name?"

There was a sigh. "No. Elizbeth and I broke up. Or rather, I left Elizbeth." Another pause. "Truth be told, Scooter, that's why I'm back at the ranch. I needed some time to lick my wounds and regain my sense of direction. I'm kind of untethered these days—drifting. How about you? It must be hard without Anna. I can't imagine. What a tragedy."

"It hasn't been easy. But life goes on . . . I guess."

"I understand. I feel the same way about Daddy. His death, I'm beginning to realize, was a big factor in Elizbeth and I breaking up." Another pause. "You here for your annual Thanksgiving hunt?"

"Yeah, that was probably me you saw hunting. I apologize for not stopping by the ranch first, to ask permission. Truth is, I thought you were still in Paris."

"Oh, for heaven's sake. Of course, you can still hunt out here. Shoot anything you want but the cattle and horses. That includes coyotes, rattlers, and prairie dogs. The furry fucking little squatters have all but taken over the big pasture.

"Thanks. I thought you'd let me, but—"

"Wait a minute. Did Luke put you up to this? That fucking jerk. He drove all the way out here the other day, supposedly to see if you still had permission to hunt the land now that Daddy's gone. He really came out to rekindle our high-school romance. Seriously. Spoke of his undying love for me. Said I needed a real man like him to save me from my life of depravity and sin. Said that he believed our 'union,' as he called it, had been ordained by God."

"What?"

"I'm not making this up, Scooter. At first, I just stood there laughing. Then I realized he was serious, and before I slammed the door in his face, I told him it would be a cold day in hell before he ever got into my pants and to go fuck himself."

"No wonder he sounded so pissed off when I ran into him at Mary's. Still thinks he's the studly high-school football star."

"A seventeen-year-old masquerading as a cowboy lawman."

We both laughed.

"God, Scooter, it's so good to hear your voice again. I needed a dose of your cynicism and irony this morning."

"Thanks, Shel. I'll take that as a compliment. It's good to hear your voice, too. I'm glad we caught up. To be honest, I still miss your dad a lot. I don't think a day goes by that I don't think about him or your mom."

"I miss them too—more than I thought I would. It's been really hard going through the house sorting out the odds and ends of their lives. I'm constantly running across things that make me laugh and cry at the same moment. And then there are those bits and pieces of their past that just make me wonder."

"Such as?"

"Such as a little red spiral notebook I found in Daddy's bedside table. It looks like a journal of sorts he kept before he died. It's very strange—chock-a-block full of weird stuff about life, death, and what he called 'the next chapter.' He even titled it: *My Death and Resurrection*, By John Willard Marshall."

Oh shit! I panicked. *She knows.*

"Hmm, that doesn't sound like John," I lied. "What did he say?"

"He talked about embracing death like a new friend, about passing to the next life in a 'simple, unstructured, objective fashion.' He wrote about senilicide, the idea of going off alone to die, and about Native American scaffold burials, where the body is placed on a scaffold or in a tree, so that nature can 'take its course.' Knowing Dad, he wasn't trying to be morbid, but it sure felt that way reading it."

"Interesting," I said, dancing cautiously around her comments. "Well, John was a practical, no-drama old rancher. I'm sure he wanted to leave this world with as little fanfare and drama as possible."

"I know. But Scooter, it sounded like he was planning his own death—not his funeral, which I could understand—but his *death*. Tell me again how he died. Please, Scooter. You were there."

I repeated my now oft-told tale of how we had taken John goose hunting on a big lake near the Oklahoma border, smack dab in the middle of the Central Flyway. One of those proverbial waterfowl honey holes. How it was single-digit cold, windy, and snowy, how he was the first to get his limit, how he had napped in the blind as we continued to hunt, and how, when we got ready to leave, we found he had silently slipped away with a look of sheer happiness on his face.

I told her how we had wrapped him in a blanket and old sleeping bag, laid him in the back of Norm's pick-up, driven home, and called Dan Farenbacher at Creekmore's funeral home.

"And then I tracked down your email, Shelia Mae, and told you to call me immediately, which you did. Remember?"

I could hear Shelia Mae's muffled sobs.

"Look, Shel, as I told you then, I'm sorry you lost your dad. He was a great man. I'm sure he was a wonderful father. But he was old and tired, and not well. He told me so himself. Said he didn't think he had much longer. To be honest, that's why we took him goose hunting that morning. He'd told me he thought he'd seen his last hunt—something that he loved dearly. Said he wished he could experience one more dawn in the blind, even if it was the last thing he ever did. So, Norm, Bobby, and I decided to grant him his wish. Little did we know that it would truly be his last. Shel, if you could have seen the look—that smile—on his face, I think you would have agreed that he couldn't have planned it better. That is, of course, if he *had* been planning it, which I'm positive he hadn't. What I think . . ."

Before I could dig my hole of deceit any deeper, Shelia Mae interrupted me. Whether by chance or fearing that I was about to say too much, I don't know. But she suddenly was telling me that of course I was right, that it was the way her father would have wanted to go, that she was being irrational, and that was silly of her to think he'd been planning his own death.

Yes, I reassured her, John undoubtedly had just been in a reflective mood when he had written those journal entries. "Your dad was a life-long intellectual explorer, Shelia Mae. He was an inquisitive individual, continually learning, applying, and teaching others. Heck, I doubt I'd have ever become a hunter if it hadn't been for him. Nor would I know the history of this land."

"You're right, Scooter. Daddy took the road less traveled, that's for sure—a kind of poet philosopher in Levi's."

"Yep," I agreed, "even when it came to his religion, he was a bit of a rebel—a spiritual cynic."

Shelia Mae laughed. "So true. Mom used to say he loved sinners but loathed the self-righteous."

"Amen to that."

I took the silence that followed as a good stopping point, thanked Shelia Mae for the continued hunting rights, and said we should get together while I was in town.

"That would be lovely," she replied, and we said our goodbyes.

9

IT WAS JOHN who gave me a love of birds and bird hunting. John fed birds, rescued birds—including owls, hawks and one bald eagle—and nursed them back to health. A self-taught birder, he never left the house without his battered old binoculars and kept a list in his pickup of all the species he saw.

But for John, the one pastime that trumped watching birds was shooting and eating them. Although the typical rancher who ascribed his health and longevity to a daily diet of well-done beef with the fat left on, John turned into an all but overbearing foodie when it came to preparing and serving game birds, whether it was dove pizza, roasted, three-day-hung pheasant with wild rice, Dutch oven quail with apples and sauerkraut, or simple crockpot goose 'n' taters.

His feathery feasts, as he called them, were exquisite. They always began with a prayer to the "Red God of the Hunt," bypassing his Christian deity as if He were some secondary gamekeeper in the heavenly chain of command.

It was a prayer of thanksgiving, extolling the greatness of nature and all that resided in it, including the succulent game we were about to eat, and a plea for forgiveness for destroying God's exquisite creatures for our pleasure and sustenance.

Despite the question of the correctness of killing, John loved to hunt. He found no pleasure in hunting large animals like deer, but small critters, squirrels, rabbits, and birds—especially birds—were another matter.

His season began late each summer with dove, then moved to quail and pheasant, and finally to waterfowl, ending with goose hunting in the steel-hard cold of winter. Unlike upland birds, which he pursued with joyous abandon, John approached goose hunting with a quiet reverence that bordered on mysticism. Geese, he often observed, were always on a journey, a trek both arduous and exhilarating, much like the lives of those who hunted them.

Sitting with him in the chilled quiet of a winter sunrise felt more like a high holy service than a goose hunt. And when a bird he shot fell from the sky, the blind filled not only with the earthy incense of gun smoke, but also a profound sense of reverence and melancholy.

It was on one of those hunts several seasons before he died, that John first told me that he was considering unloading his ten-gauge goose gun for good. Watching thousands of birds make their twilight return to their nests, he calmly proclaimed that the next season might be his last.

"I have a year or two left, and then I'm finished," he said quietly. "Death is stalking me as I stalk these beautiful creatures."

Only the north wind and the mournful, muted honking of hundreds of geese circling high above made the suffocating silence that followed bearable.

Finally, when it became clear John's statement was indeed his last on the subject, I spoke. "John, you're too good a shot and love hunting too much to give it up. Granted, walking up pheasant and quail may be difficult for man of your age, but as long as you can climb into a blind, you can still go after honkers."

John shook his head. "Nope. The Red God has spoken. It is what it is. I've been blessed with a long life and soon it will be time to move on."

His stubbornness angered me. "Fuck your 'Red God' shit, John.

Yes, you're an old coot, but you don't have to be a morbid old coot. The weather is crappy enough without your 'time to move on' soliloquy. Just stop it and have a good time."

John looked at me and smiled apologetically. "Sorry, Scooter. I didn't mean to upset you. Look, I love you like the son I never had. The last thing I want to do is make you angry."

There were tears in his eyes as he spoke, but before I could respond, he looked skyward, jumped from his seat in the blind and put his call to his lips. "Canadas," he whispered between rifts, "a whole bunch of 'em! Low! Very low!"

10

AS MUCH AS I TRIED, I couldn't stop thinking about my conversation with Shelia Mae. It had been cordial but incomplete. John, except for his remains, was clearly in a good space. And Shelia Mae's questions, I told myself, were the sort of normal concerns voiced by those who unexpectedly lose a loved one. But on my end, too many details concerning his death had been left unsaid—lies of omission driven by fear and guilt.

After an hour of pacing the house, unsuccessfully arguing my innocence, I gave up. If I was going to burn shoe leather, I might as well do it in more pleasant surroundings. I put Buck in the pickup, and we headed out to public hunting land the next county over. It was new territory for both of us, and I figured its unfamiliarity might clear my mind.

We spent the early afternoon wandering around some beautiful, birdy creek bottom and grassland. Technically, I guess you could call it hunting. Buck searched for birds, while I continued to search for answers, peace of mind, and some backbone.

It wasn't the best of excursions for either of us. Buck did his usual journey-dog work, but every time he flushed a bird, I was too distracted to shoot. After the third rooster flew to safety, Buck went from perplexed to pissed. He slowly walked back to me, gave me an angry stare, and then, despite my pleading, loped the half-mile back to the truck.

Clearly these armed, meditative treks were getting old for both of us, as was my obsessive attempt to walk away from my own angsty existence. Buck may have been done for the day, but my mind was still racing. Why did I give in to John's wishes? Why did I go along with his cockamamie plan? Why did I keep lying to Shelia Mae? Why did I suddenly find her voice so . . . sexy?

My life, it seemed, was continually fueled by indecision, inferiority, and uncertainty. I had never lived up to the person I thought I should be. Hadn't since I could remember. It may have started in that demon-filled church basement, but it hadn't stopped there. It had continued at home with well-intended parents who put pride up there with fornication, not only as a sin to be exorcised, but also as a socially repugnant midwestern behavior that was to be avoided at all costs.

They were not alone. Most town folk were quick to own their failures but seldom spoke of their successes. Part of it may have been their religion. But mostly I think it was the experience of living through the Dust Bowl, the Great Depression, and World War II. They understood the importance of putting the group before the individual. They knew that without a strong community and country, they would have been dead long ago or, if still alive, hungry, dirt poor, and probably speaking German.

If there were war heroes in town, which I'm sure there were, they never let on. Humility trumped victory. Even now, old-timers viewed with suspicion people like me who escaped to the city to seek fame and fortune.

Like my parents, I think most really believed in a natural unworthiness of the human condition. Yes, they said, do your best. But always remember, there are folks better than you. Which explains why, at seven, when I told my mother I had a solo in the school musical, she smiled, said I was mistaken, and called the music teacher to double-check; why, when I told my father I was suiting up for the high school varsity basketball team, he had reacted similarly, although in fairness, he had good reason to doubt my athleticism; why, when I was forty he willed my sister the better piece of farmland because, as he told me later, he wasn't sure how I'd "turn out."

The unintended outcome of these best intentions was an ever-anxious man who, despite having a good life, always went to bed wondering what he'd screwed up that day and what he would screw up the next.

So it should have come as no surprise that I spent the rest of a gorgeous late fall afternoon wandering and wondering, dogless and birdless.

It took a cold wind out of the north and a steady drizzle to shake me out of my wretched reverie and end my contemplative "hunt." Since we were just a few miles from Dodge, the only town of any size near Creekmore, I decided to kill the rest of the day man-shopping, which for me meant browsing Wal-Mart and the local farm and hardware stores in search of items I already owned or didn't need. Like hunting, such outings usually took my mind off my angst, at least in the moment.

One hour, a nonstick wok, metric socket set, and Duck Dynasty dog toy later, we drove to a small cafe run by a Vietnamese family that served a cà phê đá that more than made up for the town's lack of a Starbucks. That, and a steamy bowl of noodles with pork, finally put me in a better mood, and I began looking forward to a toasty evening reading by the fire.

But as we left Dodge, the rain turned to sleet driven by a howling north wind, and before we'd completed the twenty-minute drive home, the tempest outside had overtaken my mind, and thoughts of Shelia Mae, John, and unneeded woks and socket sets again put me in a major funk.

11

BY THE TIME I GOT HOME, the sleet had turned to snow. To make matters worse, within thirty minutes Lucy called to tell me O'Hare was iced in and that she would not be coming for Thanksgiving.

I'm not a fan of holidays. Never have been. I can tolerate them when I'm with family or friends, in part because there's always a relative or guest who, even more clinically depressed than me, gives me hope. I guess it's a competitive thing: I may be screwed up, but I'm in better shape than that poor bastard.

But being alone during the holidays and keeping myself company is another story. I can't stand that person who glares back at me from the bathroom mirror every morning. He's a bully. He scares me, and I don't trust him.

Once, he almost killed me. It was during my Miami days. I was on my third wife in twelve years, and stupidly thought this time was different. Megan, recently divorced, was a loving, caring mom of two boys. By day she was a successful corporate attorney, the picture of a perky professional. By night, after the kids were in bed, she was the consummate companion and lover.

That she enjoyed cocaine as much as sex didn't bother me at first. I found it charming in an exotic sort of way. Not that I was much of a drug user myself. Except for smoking a Thai stick one Christmas Eve with Wife Two and waking up naked under the tree Christmas morning, my experience with drugs had been limited to the occasional party toke of local weed.

But being the needy, impressionable dope I'd become, I quickly succumbed to Megan's habit. I knew better but had never felt so . . . happy . . . confident. Apart from one tennis match at an exclusive Miami Beach club after a night of too much blow, when my heart pounded so hard I had trouble seeing the ball, I never suspected drugs were having a negative effect on me.

Had I been thinking clearly, I would have seen that the dark cloud that had followed me since my Sunday School days at Creekmore Baptist Church was slowly morphing into a nasty, menacing squall line in my soul. But I was too busy happily screwing and snorting to look up. And when it finally broke a few months later as a full-blown shit storm, I was an angry, pathetic mess of a man.

Megan, quite appropriately, kicked me out, and I found myself living in a rundown cottage behind a friend's place that his kids had turned into a clubhouse. The first morning there, I discovered as I shaved that I shared The Firebird Club, as a hand-painted sign on the door proclaimed, with the bully in the mirror.

At first, we tried to get along. But it was like trying to rekindle a broken romance: too much hurt and too much hate. Then I went to my ace in the hole: find Megan's replacement. Another bad idea, although one that I had yet to come to terms with. Lucky for me, I was too seriously broken to make even the shallowest connection with another woman.

So, I decided to check out.

Having fallen in love with the ocean, which I'd found as open, fluid, and peaceful as the High Plains, my first attempt was to rent a small sailboat, head the few miles out to the Gulf Stream, and jump overboard. I'd make it look like an accident, my body would never be found, and no one would be the wiser.

I rented a tattered old sloop and sailed east until I reached the vivid blue of the Stream. I dropped the jib, let the main sail flap in the light breeze, and walked to the bow, willing myself to leap into the deep. But after an hour of staring off into the horizon, lacking the courage or insanity needed to walk the plank, I finally accepted defeat.

The sail back, with dolphins and pilot whales dancing across my bow, was oddly exhilarating and validating. Clearly, my plan was not meant to be executed. God—there I went again, giving credit where credit was doubtfully due—had different designs for me. I'd had my Saul-on-the-road-to-Damascus moment. Life was meant to be lived. Things were looking up. I would be okay.

Only I wasn't. Even with the added aid of science—a hefty dose of antidepressants—my holy moment was short-lived. Within a week the euphoria disappeared and the asshole in the mirror was back in control. So, after another week of sleepless nights struggling to keep him at bay, I launched Plan B.

I drove to a popular gun store on Tamiami Trail near the edge of the Everglades. I gave the clerk the standard story I'm sure he'd heard hundreds of times: I was not a gun owner but given the increase in crime—I think I said something about "never knowing when I might come face-to-face with some coke-crazed Cracker or Columbian drug lord"—I was interested in purchasing a handgun.

The clerk showed me several, included a couple of .44 magnum cannons that could take down an angry grizzly. I finally settled on a shiny .32-caliber revolver. My scrambled logic, although I didn't tell the clerk, was that it was simple and small enough that I could handle, yet powerful enough that it would do the job efficiently without being too noisy or making too big a hole in my head. Like I said, I was depressed, and clarity of thought at that moment was not a core competency.

What happened next may simply have been a good salesman attempting to close the deal but looking back I see it as a real *god moment*, albeit a god with a dark sense of humor: the salesman said he thought I'd made a good choice, as it was a stainless-steel weapon that would "last a lifetime."

A lifetime? I looked at him like he was the crazy in the room, giggled hysterically, handed back the gun and ran out of the store.

As I fled, I again was overcome by a fragile sense of calm and confidence. My nemesis in the mirror was still standing, but as long as I could cling to a small slip of faith and my own weird sense of irony, he could never defeat me.

I casually related my botched efforts to my therapist at our next weekly session. She found them neither humorous nor ironic, and immediately called the police, who put me in handcuffs and took me to the psych ward of the city hospital. That the cops got lost on the way to the loony bin and had to turn to me for directions I also found ironically amusing. Ever try to point to street signs and local landmarks in handcuffs? It's hard.

The two weeks I spent in the hospital were among the most relaxing I've ever experienced. I was able to keep my bully at bay while catching up on some reading, including finishing a biography of Hemingway, which as we know, ends badly and probably wasn't the best choice for someone on suicide watch.

I also played Scrabble with the counselors, who were always accusing each other of cheating, which I found far more therapeutic than the endless rounds of group sessions during which we were encouraged to share our sad and pathetic stories. In both cases, I quickly learned that the line between normalcy and madness was indeed fine and fragile.

Although I worked earnestly with the staff and my fellow crazies to face my depression, I often found the other Scooter inside me, the irreverent outside observer. The irony of it all was as helpful as the drugs and counseling they were continually shoving down our throats—like the time I had to break up a fight between two of my Scrabble-playing counselors, or when I had to tell a psychiatrist new to the floor that, no, unfortunately none of my fellow inmates were my patients, rather I was one of them.

It finally got the best of me when we were forced to participate in a talent show for friends and family. Sick is it sounds, I leapt at the opportunity to put my weirdness on display. I asked Angelica, an attractive young woman also suffering from depression, to be my assistant, borrowed a deck of playing cards from the staff, and began planning my act.

The show was about what you'd expect from a bunch of disturbed folks on heavy medication, most held against their will, who have been asked to perform like some wild, doped-up circus chimps. There was a bit of singing, a couple of readings (one from Edgar Allen Poe by a rather morose, schizophrenic young man), and an aborted pole dance by a college student with perky breasts and strategically placed tattoos of Peter Pan and Tinker Bell—at least that is what I think they were; she was tackled and quickly wrapped in a modest straitjacket before she got far into her performance.

The audience was clearly uncomfortable, as were the participants and staff. Only the show's producer, the flakey Dr. Merriweather, an over-accessorized bottle-blonde with a PhD in performance therapy from some small North Florida college, seemed to be enjoying the show.

The longer it went on, the angrier I got. By the time I went on stage, I was locked and loaded. I started off with some really bad jokes, moving quickly from a couple I'd picked up from *Boys Life* when I was nine to some I remembered from a Lenny Bruce recording I'd found in my dad's workshop, to a really good one from George Carlin about a psychologist, a nun, and Ronald McDonald.

At that point, Dr. Merriweather intervened and told me it was time to move on to my magic tricks. The audience, who was clearly enjoying my routine if for no other reason than easing their embarrassment, started muttering, and the father of the young stripper shouted for the good doctor to let me continue. "Hey lady," he yelled, "let the crazy bastard keep going. He may be whacko, but he's really funny."

Alas, from the look on Dr. Merriweather's face, I knew she meant business, so I asked Angelica to bring me the cards, and announced that I was about to do a never-before-seen trick. "And," I said, building suspense, "whoever guesses the right card will get a free weekend pass out of here."

The trick went well. Unfortunately, Billy, my roommate, picked the winning card, the queen of spades. A troubled young man who prayed every night that God would make him a Marine and send him into combat so that he could kill bad people, Billy was none too happy when I told him it was a joke. "Billy, my man," I said, "I was just trying to be, you know, ironic."

"Well, next time," he said, with tears in his eyes, "you need to try harder."

Later that night, Dr. Merriweather came by to tell me I was being discharged the next morning. "Looks like you picked the winning card," she announced with that hard, painted smile she always wore.

"From your performance tonight, we believe you're well enough to go home. Time to pack your bags and take your 'act' to another venue."

She started to leave, then stopped. "Oh, and no more tricks until you're back on the street."

"Got it," I said. "By the way, if you were trying to be ironic just now, well, let's just say you need to try harder."

Her smile vanished, and with a slam of the door, so did she.

Despite Dr. Merriweather, my Madland Tour, as I like to call it, was time well spent. I made friends like Billy and Angelica. I had a lot of time to read and think. I enjoyed the required journaling and even the group sessions, which were as enlightening and entertaining as they were sorrowful and strange. And, I felt very safe, even with Billy asleep in the next bed, who wanted nothing more out of life than to kill bad guys—a noble vocation in its own weird way.

It was the one time in my life when the bully in the mirror pulled his own magic act and vanished.

12

AS THE EVENING and blizzard wore on, I began to seriously wish there was a nearby psych ward I could check into for the night. While I've never again come close to removing myself permanently from this life, the concept has remained in my subconscious like a grimy, wallet-worn get-out-of-jail-free card. Which is why I continue to religiously take my meds and own no handguns.

I sensed the holiday eve was quickly turning into a real Black Dog night when I saw my own yellow dog give me his cocked-head, *what-the-fuck* look. I thought he was sensing my rising panic until I realized my cell phone was ringing and he was really giving me his *why don't you answer it, dumb-ass* stare. The two are very similar.

It was Shelia Mae.

"Scooter, where are you? Lovely weather, isn't it?"

"Yep. Buck and I just got back from Dodge, and from the looks of the highway, it's going to be a very quiet Thanksgiving here at the old home place. Lucy's flight was canceled, and I have a feeling all the roads will be closed by morning.

"I know. My cousin who was coming in from Omaha just called to say she's snowed in. That's why I called. They're saying much of the area may lose power tonight, which will make tomorrow even darker and bleaker than you were anticipating."

That stung. She knew me better than I realized.

"So, I thought maybe you'd like to drive on out to the ranch tonight before it gets too bad. You could spend the night and we could have a nice Thanksgiving here. I have a generator, and if it runs out of fuel, we'll keep the holiday spirit bright with the fireplace and some old kerosene lamps. We certainly won't starve. I brought a couple of cases of vino back from the old country along with some good cheese. Both will go well with the pheasants *you* shot on *my* land, which technically belong to me. I know I said you could hunt out here, but I don't think I said anything about taking any game."

"You assumed I wouldn't or can't hit anything? That I just wander around uselessly holding my gun."

"That," she said in faux British accent, "is what *he* said. Now come on out. We haven't really caught up since high school. It'll be fun. Besides, you can tell me more about Daddy's last days."

Shelia Mae's invitation was tempting—at least the part about catching up on the past.

"I'd love to come out, Shel, but I'm not sure I should. You know what would happen if one of your neighbors so much as saw my truck at the ranch? In an hour the whole county would know."

"First, my nearest neighbor lives two miles away. Second, everyone in the county already has you pegged as an unredeemable heathen. I hate to break it to you, Scooter, but your reputation in Creekmore started going south when you divorced your first wife. It left the tracks when you broke up with Number Two and married Wife Three. And, when she dumped you and you had the gall to try for Number Four, you punched a one-way, non-refundable ticket to hell, although I'm told everyone thought Anna hung the moon, despite her obvious lack of judgment in marrying a loser sinner like you."

I'd always wondered what my hometown reputation really was. I knew it wasn't pristine. That I'd fled Creekmore after high school, returning infrequently to visit, didn't help. Nor did the fact that I'd gone to a school back east, even though *east* was relative. I went to the more liberal of two state universities, staffed, it was said, by radical professors and attended by long-haired hippies, all of whom were no doubt communists. That I was an English major and became a journalist was the icing on the cake.

But I didn't know how widespread the knowledge of my personal life was beyond that. I usually attended church when I returned, had seldom gone to a local bar except for lunch or dinner, and never said squat about my marital bliss or lack thereof.

True, for the first few years after I'd left, I'd periodically bring a new woman "friend" home to visit the family, but we always kept it low-key—no touching in public, no lingering looks into each other's eyes, etc. I knew from growing up in a small town that word gets around. But people are polite in Creekmore, at least to your face, and although I'd had my suspicions, I never really knew.

Now I did. And it hurt. But I had to hand it to the fine townsfolk for their acute judgment and excellent news-gathering skills. I wondered where they had acquired such an objective, balanced approach to reporting, given that most watch Fox News nightly and quote it daily.

"Thanks for sharing, Shelia Mae. I've often wondered what the good citizens of Creekmore thought of me. It stings, but it's not surprising. I would tell you what they think of you, but I don't want to make your cold, bleak evening any worse than it is."

She laughed. "Thank you very much, Scooter. Seriously, I didn't mean to hurt your feelings. I assumed you had a good idea of your rather tarnished image."

"I do," I admitted. "But it doesn't make me feel any better about myself. Knowing and accepting are two different things."

"Tell me about it. In fact, come on out and we can tell each other all about it."

The idea of spending the night at Shelia Mae's was intriguing. I wanted to go. Granted, I would have been happy if I'd been asked to overnight with a serial killer or a two-headed ogre—anyone who could carry on a conversation, cook a decent meal, and keep me company.

But Shelia Mae—now that had possibilities, albeit most of which, when I stopped to considered them, were unrealistic and had near if not fatal downsides.

"Thanks Shel, it's very kind of you to offer. I would love to, really. But I best stay here tonight."

A pause.

"I understand, Scooter. Maybe we can have dinner when the weather clears."

She sounded genuinely disappointed.

I put another log on the fire, poured another scotch, picked up the novel I was reading and spent the next thirty minutes thinking and discussing my life with the two angels who visited during times such as these. Unlike John, they are shapeless voices inside my head. I picture them as good and evil versions of Casper, with whom I discuss ethical dilemmas—like whether I should spend the night with Shelia Mae.

One typically argues why I should do something, while the other, in great and gruesome detail, tells me why I should not. In this case, the dark spirit said I should get in the car and drive out to the ranch. It would be good for me to catch up with an old friend, who would no doubt make me feel better and who, herself, needed cheering up. It also would give me an opportunity to finally tell her what I really knew about John's death, helping heal her grieving soul while cleansing my own dark heart.

Besides, he said, it would be fun.

"No, no, no," cried the good angel, shaking her little head. "Bad idea. Why do you really want to go? You know. You're hurting. She'd comfort you. She might even seduce you. Or you might seduce her. Hey, who knows, she sounds sexy. And it will seem like a good thing in the moment, because your lagging self-worth will spike and you'll feel great, until morning when, after momentarily deciding you want to run away with her and live happily ever after—which you know from experience is a bad idea—you will immediately feel tremendous guilt, as you should, and you'll decide that you're a bad person, which you're not really, and you'll make the decision to put a bullet in your brain or just go off and die, which you won't, because you're a wimp but also because you know it's wrong and would hurt others more than you.

"Besides which," she added, after finally discovering the need for a breath, "as you turn to leave, she's sure to ask you, in a hurt voice, that at least you owe her the truth about her daddy. And then, you'll give in, and she'll never speak to you again, or you'll lie and hate yourself even more."

"Objection!" cried the first angel, ruffling his tiny wings. "Shelia Mae is gay! She's not going to seduce you. Trust me, it will be nothing more than a nice evening with a friend whose dad was like a second father to you. Put your coat on, put Buck in the truck, and go before the roads get impassable."

"You two dumb asses!" retorted the other winged muse. "You both know what will happen. Scooter will try to "convert" her, making a total ass of himself and ruining what, if anything, remains of their so-called friendship. And then—"

"Wait," interrupted the glass-half-full spirit, "if he gets beyond first base, she may change. It's happened. You know it has."

"Bullshit," shouted his adversary, her little halo now a fiery red. "You both are *so* full of bullshit!"

At which point they started calling each other names and disappeared, forgetting about me.

As usual when these things happened, I pondered their advice, considered their points, many of which made sense, and then acted purely out of my short-sighted self-interest and gratification. I picked up the phone and called Shelia Mae, who answered on the first ring.

"Scooter!" she exclaimed before I could identify myself, "I knew you'd change your mind! Lovely! Hurry on over, but be careful, the weather is truly shitty. Bye!"

Shitty was an understatement. Buck and I arrived at the ranch two hours later, after sliding off the road twice, once following a heart-stopping spin-out, and then pulling another motorist out of the ditch.

Although the icy roads required my full attention, I spent much of the drive thinking about the evening to come. With help from my evil angel, who had suddenly returned, I'd conjured up an image of the twenty-year-old woman I once knew, in cutoffs and a T-shirt. Then, acknowledging the thirty-plus years since I'd seen her in person, I began to speculate on what she looked like now.

It was then, as I pondered the impact of aging and gravity on her physique, that I hit an icy patch, spun, and wound up on the wrong side of the road with a car coming toward us. Thankfully, the driver hit the brakes and slid into the ditch, avoiding a collision.

After helping him pull his car out, I continued toward the ranch with renewed focus, which lasted for about three miles, when, picturing a fiftyish Shelia Mae in an elegant French camisole, I almost missed my turn onto the road that led to the ranch.

When we finally arrived, the real Shelia Mae, who had heard our pickup, was waiting on the porch. She was older than I'd imagined but every bit as statuesque and elegant, even in the old pair of Wranglers and ragged camo sweatshirt she was wearing.

Standing barefoot in the snow, she gave me a big hug with one of those Continental double-cheek kissing moves that I instinctively tried to dodge.

"I was getting worried," she said with a smile. "Glad you made it."

The house, a large limestone structure, had changed little over the years. The huge, vaulted living room was still filled with simple but comfortable ranch furniture from the 1800s. At one end a fire burned in the large stone fireplace, watched over by the stern head of Hodgeman Hellboy, the prize bull that started the family's generations-long breeding dynasty.

Lit only by the fire and a several antique kerosene lanterns, Hellboy seemed to come alive. Buck quickly moved between us and the mount, growling protectively.

"Guess I should have left the lights on. But the power's probably going out before morning, so I thought we might as well get in the mood."

"I thought you said you had a generator."

"We do. But I can't find the fuel." She shrugged and smiled. "Don't worry, I have plenty of food and drink to keep us from starving. You want beer, wine, or something hard? I have some really good single malt."

After the treacherous drive, I needed the scotch. But knowing how strong drink can screw with my sensibilities—which were already being threatened—I opted for wine.

Shelia Mae returned from the kitchen with an antique silver platter laden with a bottle of French something that I couldn't pronounce and enough food to feed a harvest crew.

"You must expect this storm to last a while," I offered, piling my plate with an array of strange but delicious looking things. "That or you're expecting a few more guests."

"Nope, just you." She smiled, curling up on the big leather couch in front of the fire. I instinctively moved to a matching wingback, but she motioned me to sit with her. I did, but feeling awkward, moved to the far end and stared silently at the fire.

"Wow," she said, apparently examining my profile, "you've turned into quite the handsome man. Older than I expected, but definitely more good-looking."

"Certainly older," I said, eyes still on the flames. "Not so sure about the handsome part."

Pushing her toes into my thigh, she laughed and then said something—I had no idea what—in French.

I gave her a sideways glance. "Sorry Shelia Mae, me no speaka French. I'm still an unsophisticated country boy."

"Bullshit," she said. "I know more about you than you think. I have my sources. They tell me you're quite the man-about-town. . . or used to be. Rumor has it that you were a spy at one time, had a major coke habit during your Miami days, and spent some time in either the big house or the loony bin as the result. And, as I told you earlier, everyone in town has met at least two of your serial spouses and knows them by name."

"Okay, Shelia Mae." I faced her. "Can we just drop the spouse thing. It's not something I'm proud of. Look, I've been married to four very fine women. Smart, sexy, independent women. All successful. Clearly, I own the three that failed. And those failures still haunt me. I used to think divorce was the sport of poor white trash and the soulless rich, not us normal middle-American god-fearing folk who learned early the importance of keeping our emotions under lock and key. And look at me now. I probably hold the county record for most failed marriages in one lifetime. Honestly, I start feeling guilty every time I come over that last hill and drive into town."

"Don't be too hard on yourself, Scooter. You aren't the only one driving around with a pickup full of emotional shit. I put a cart of gin and tonics away on my flight back just thinking of how people would react when I walked into the grocery store—how they would whisper and shake their heads and thank the lord that I wasn't their sister or daughter. And to be honest, I've pretty much stayed out here at the ranch since I got back. If I need any groceries, I head over to Dodge where people won't recognize me.

We both went silent for a moment, pondering the prickly predicaments in which we'd found ourselves.

She reached over and touched my shoulder. "I'm sorry. I didn't mean to bring back old pain. Believe me, I know how you feel. My life has not turned out like I thought it would either. Coming back here has gotten harder and harder. It was another reason I didn't rush home when Daddy died. I was afraid to face the home folk."

Shit. Now I found myself staring at a stunningly beautiful woman—a lesbian in camo no less—who was the picture of vulnerability. Not the needy sort, mind you, not the weepy, frantic ones you find sitting alone in bars, but a portrait of elegant, measured vulnerability.

I started to reach out to her, but my better angel stopped me, and I simply shook my head. "Shelia Mae, I am so sorry—"

"Scooter, please. Just call me Shel. I dropped the Mae in college and shortened it further when I met Elizbeth. Elizbeth liked short names and short hair."

"Okay Shel. I'm sorry you've had to go through all of that that. I should have known, but I just assumed—"

"No pity. Please. We're responsible for the lives we make. We may not have picked our sexual preferences, but we certainly chose how to operationalize them. I could have chosen to be a quiet, quirky, dike rancher but decided on a flaming Continental lesbian. You could still be married to Wife One, with a boatload of grandkids, and be bored to death. Instead, you kept searching until you found your true soulmate. Despite what other folks may say behind your back, your perseverance paid off. You guys had a good marriage. That she was taken from you suddenly was a tragedy. But it wasn't your fault.

We both grew silent, she, like me, no doubt flipping through the albums of our minds—pausing at moments remembered, happy and sad, ugly and beautiful. I think we both were trying to be objective observers, but, at least for me, it was still a difficult, bittersweet exercise.

Finally, Shelia Mae rose, went to the kitchen, and returned with more wine and food.

"Cheer up, old boy. Tomorrow's Thanksgiving, and I for one am thankful that I get to spend the day with a dear friend. She raised her glass.

"To friends."

"Yes, to friends."

13

I AWOKE DAZED and disoriented. I was in a comfortable bed, with a delightfully warm body next to me and the remnants of an interrupted dream of Wife 2 and Wife 3 still working its way through my booze-obscured brain.

Given the light snoring, I initially thought Number 2 had mysteriously teleported herself to my side. But, as I reached out to stroke her back, I realized, with disappointed relief, it was only Buck. I sat up, banged my head against the bed above me, and realized we were bedded down in the bunkhouse.

How did I get here? I peered out one of the small dusty windows. It was still dark and snowing heavily. Any tracks we might have made had been covered. I found my clothes folded neatly on a chair. On the mantle was a thermos of coffee and a note:

Good morning! Hope you slept well. Breakfast will be ready at 8:30. If you're up early, light a fire and enjoy the coffee.
Shel
PS: Last night was delightful!

Oh shit, I thought, suddenly fully awake. *What had happened? What had I done? What had we done?*

I poured myself a cup of coffee and lit the fire. It was only six-thirty, which meant I had two hours to ponder what delightful thing had transpired the previous night that I did not remember.

Twice, when I was younger, I had been unfaithful. Twice I had listened to that stupid, selfish, son-of-a-bitch that resides in the souls of most males of our species. But two times were enough. The momentary pleasure of such encounters, no matter how great, fades far sooner than the lingering blowback and guilt-fueled side effects.

Now, decades later, I was sitting in the gray dawn, again facing a sorry, self-induced shit storm of the soul. I considered going for a walk but reminded myself that getting lost in a blizzard was no way to reset one's moral compass. I collapsed on an old leather couch, one of the bunkhouse's few amenities, stared into my coffee, and tried to think.

Anna was dead. I was a widower. I had been faithful 'til death did us part. Why all the guilt for something I wasn't sure had happened? Because I still loved Anna? Because I had crossed a line with Shelia Mae? All of the above?

I thought of Anna. What Shelia Mae had said the night before was true, as far as it went. It was a good marriage. But I always felt, especially since Anna's death, that I could have done better—not in terms of choosing a wife, but in being a good husband. I tried. But did I try hard enough? Was I good enough? I travelled extensively for work. The little time I was home I was often absorbed by job-related distractions, or as now, living in my own head.

Self-absorbed as I was, I failed to realize how hard Anna worked. In addition to her own career, she kept hearth and home stable and secure, nurturing Lucy during the early years and wrangling and wrestling her as best she could during a tremulous teenage period when mother and daughter, both armed with wills of hardened steel, clashed on a daily basis.

Yes, it was a good marriage, but it could have been great, had I only spent more time thinking of Anna and less of myself. And now I was doing the same with Shelia Mae—focused on myself and what I wanted, too self-absorbed to even acknowledge her needs and desires, which, despite what I assumed, were probably quite different than mine.

———————

"Nice work, Scooter. Screwing with my screwed-up daughter first chance you get. What the hell were you thinking? Were you planning some sort of missionary conquest?"

It was John, sitting on the upper bunk. I looked up at him incredulously.

"I am not speaking about positions, although you've certainly screwed yourself into a fine one! I'm talking about perspectives."

I was clearly not following his line of interrogation. He shook his head and sighed. "Son, do you really think you can make her like men again?"

I probably shouldn't have laughed, seeing as he had most likely just flown in from a meeting with the Good Lord, but I couldn't help it. From where I sat, I could see up his bath robe, a view that greatly distracted from his angelic holiness.

That pissed him off. His apparition turned from off-white to a righteous red. For a second, I thought he had performed some sort of holy shapeshifting, again channeling the real John the Baptist.

Shaking a bony finger at me, he roared. "You fuck with my daughter, son, and I'll hurt you!"

I started to speak, but he stopped me. "Sorry, Scooter," he said softly, shaking his head. "That was rather unangelic of me. It's just. . . well, even after you're gone you continue to look out for your loved ones, especially your daughters."

I wanted to hug him, but it seemed too weird. "No worries, sir. I understand. What I don't understand is what happened last night. Frankly, I had too much wine and don't recall much of what took place. I don't think I—we—did anything. But I'm not sure."

John sighed. "Scooter, think about it. Does it really matter? It's the intent that counts. Not the act. Remember Jimmy Carter?"

"You mean the president?"

He rolled his eyes. "Do you know another Jimmy Carter? Of course I mean President Carter. Remember what he said about 'lust in his heart?' The press had a field day. Compared it to his story about the rabbit that attacked his canoe. As usual they missed the point. Anyway, *my* point is that a lustful heart can be just as damning as a real roll in the hay. You see what I'm saying?"

"I'm not sure John. Is this a parable? To become an angel do you have to take Parables 101? No offense, but why when you get all holy, do you start talking in riddles? Jesus did the same thing. If he'd just said what he meant, maybe it would have ended better."

Now John laughed.

"Jesus, Scooter! I know Jesus, and—"

"Of course, you do. I assume that's part of the Heaven deal."

"Don't be a smart-ass. I've met him. He's a nice Jewish fella. And a real comedian. What a sense of humor. Has to have since he's still the butt of so many jokes. But you have to hand it to him. He had a hard life. He was a well-meaning but angry young punk who went up against the establishment and paid for it with his life. Don't get me wrong, he had every right to be angry, what with those Roman bastards running the government and a passel of corrupt priests manning the temple.

"The way he tells it, he and his merry band of pranksters— basically a bunch of uneducated blue-collar types, commercial fishermen, construction laborers and the like—started it as a kind of street theater. Figured they could pick up a few extra coins for wine and stuff by putting on little magic shows. It began well, but Jesus, who was a serious smart-ass with a chip on his shoulder, got all holier than thou and began turning it into a political parody, going after the rich and the powerful. I tell you, if he'd been born 2,000 years later, he'd have his own show on Netflix.

"Anyhow, it got out of hand and before he knew it, he had pissed off the power structure, and had attracted a huge following of mainly country folk, who didn't get the irony of what he was saying and instead believed he really was God incarnate.

"God forgave him. They're pals these days. Have been since the day he died. It's The Prodigal Son redux. They both talk a lot of smack. God calls Jesus a messianic wannabe. Jesus gives God a lot of grief about not bringing him back from the dead as He'd reportedly promised. God barks back, 'I don't know who you were listening to or reading, but it sure wasn't me.' And then, he brings up Jesus' miracles, says he's seen better acts in Vegas. Jesus pretends to pout. Says, in his best Marlin Brando impersonation. 'I could have been a contender; I could have been somebody.' Then they both start laughing.

"The irony, of course, is that God could have resurrected Jesus any time He felt like it. But He didn't think it was necessary, thought Jesus' legacy, the impact he'd had on the world as a mere mortal, was more powerful—magical even—than all his so-called miracles put together. But unfortunately, Jesus' followers couldn't let go. They needed something bigger and better than a mere fisherman who spoke truth to power and got his ass kicked in the process. So, they made him larger than life. Sadly, they missed the irony that in giving him superpowers they cheapened the potential of humankind for eons to come."

John paused. "Sorry, Scooter, I didn't mean to go off on a rant. The point I was trying to make was . . . oh yeah, from now on, make sure you keep your pecker in your pants."

"From now on?" I asked. But by then he was gone.

Holy Shit. Had I or had I not spent the night with Shelia Mae?

John's drop-in rant only heightened my anxiety. I understood the part about Jimmy Carter. And I clearly remembered the lust I'd experienced the previous night as Shelia Mae and I sat in front of the fire. But what had happened after that was still lost in the deep purple haze of good French grapes.

And to top it off, once again I had been too distracted to ask John about his death—how and where had he really died.

Although John had not left through the door, the bunkhouse was suddenly very cold. I had less than an hour to figure out what had or had not happened with Shel before I tramped through the snow to the ranch house, where a hearty breakfast and my fate awaited me.

I poured a second cup of coffee, wrapped myself in an ancient buffalo robe and   began sifting through my handful of serious liaisons for any gems of discernment that might help me now. I may have been overdramatizing the situation, but my relationships with women have never lacked histrionics, with me providing nearly all the *Sturm und Drang.*

A bit of context: with a couple of exceptions, I wound up marrying all the women I fell in love with. I've thought a lot about that creepy statistic, searching for some nugget of insight that would give me a sense of peace and my matrimony record an air of respectability.

I loved each of them, or thought I did, and never meant to hurt or mislead them. But sooner than later, in every case, I did just that. And hurting someone who trusts you and sacrifices for you and stakes a major personal investment in you makes you a real piece of shit—and not just in the eyes of the Lord.

Charlene was the first. I met her in college, a farm-fresh country girl. Smart, practical, and confident. We were married at nineteen. It lasted seven years. She followed me when I served in the military, helped put me through college. It was a good marriage, or at least I thought so. Then I started a career and got full of myself.

That's when I met Bianca, a dark-haired Italian American from Chicago. She too, was smart and confident, albeit a bit more emotional—which I found intriguing. Like me, she was focused on a career and a cause. We'd just experienced Vietnam and Watergate, and decided that, together, we would save the world.

There was romance, there was passion, there was goodness and caring, all elements that should have made for a great marriage. But in less time than it takes for the foundation of a strong relationship to cure, I'd messed it up, too. I knew it was over when, during a dinner argument at a little oceanfront restaurant, she angrily started fastballing her seafood platter at me, one sautéed shrimp at a time. I think she realized it too, when I began picking the shrimp off my jacket and eating them.

The food fight was triggered by her discovery that I had become involved with yet another woman, one whom I also probably would have tried to wed had she not been unsure of her sexual preference.

You would think that at that point I would have paused and reflected on what the hell was going on. But that would assume that I was thinking. I was not. Of all the glorious tools God had given me, the brain was not the one I was using.

And so, within two years I married Megan. An Irish American, she, like Bianca, had been educated by nuns and, not surprisingly, was similarly smart and self-assured. Again, I was convinced everything would work out and I would be happy. It didn't and that's when I found myself in the loony bin, where I was served divorce papers.

Why, after such a hurtful albeit fitting ending to yet another epic failure, didn't I run away to the nearest monastery or at least opt for a single if not celibate life, I'll never understand. But three years later

I was again married. Although nun-schooled and self-confident like her predecessors, Anna's Dutch-inherited sense of practicality and directness effectively modulated the passion and drama that had run amok in my previous unions. It explains, I believe, why, unlike the others, our marriage endured and was good until she was taken from me.

Although I would have liked to believe that my long marriage with Anna had finally revealed to me the real meaning of love and vanquished my guilt, neediness, and lack of self-worth, it clearly hadn't. Which was why I now found myself sitting in a freezing old bunkhouse in the middle of a blizzard, drowning in a cold sweat.

14

THE SNOW HAD STOPPED by the time I made the short walk to Shelia Mae's, but the emotional blizzard still raged inside me. I paused before climbing the steps to the imposing old house, wondering what the few remaining Native Americans thought when they passed by it a century earlier, silent as the ghosts they were soon to become.

I wished I was with them and not here, not now.

When I set foot on the massive veranda, the oak doors swung open and a smiling, silk-robed Shelia Mae greeted me with a hug that was thankfully aborted when Buck jumped between us.

"Good morning, guys! Sleep well? God, what a storm."

I shrugged. Buck wagged. Neither of us spoke.

"You clearly haven't had your morning coffee, guys. Come on in the kitchen and make yourselves at home. Breakfast is ready."

It was a huge country breakfast—French American, after a fashion. The chicken-fried steak was smothered in red-eye gravy, the grits and poached eggs sprinkled with caviar. It was the kind of meal—there was also champagne—that usually awakened my limited social graces.

Not today.

"So, what's wrong Scooter? What's with the serious face? What's going on?"

Here we go, I thought. *'What's going on?' Now she's channeling Marcie, my therapist with that opening line. Well, it's not going to work with Shelia Mae. What's going on is none of her business.*

"I'm fine. Not used to the country life, I guess. Had a rough night. Fire died. Nearly froze before I got up and tended it. Then Buck kept pacing and whining. Coyotes probably. Breakfast is wonderful. Life is good."

"Scooter, it doesn't take a shrink to know something is going on. Look, just above your head. There's a little black cloud up there. Oh! Wait! I think I just saw a tiny twister drop into your hair. Talk to me."

Again, just like Marcie. The left-right combination. Like that's going to thaw my soul so you can pour it into one of your crystal flutes and suck it down in a single bitter gulp, leaving my heart like a tiny, rock-hard sliver of ice. Then you'll casually fling glass and heart into the fire, shattering both.

I started to speak, but my anger died as quicky as it flared, rendering me mute. I felt incredibly sad. I took a deep breath. "Ghosts," I said. "It was ghosts not coyotes that kept me awake last night."

"Ghosts?" Shelia Mae was now standing over me, rubbing my shoulders.

"Yeah, I guess your old bunkhouse is haunted."

Now she was facing me, her eyes two feet from mine. "Are you telling me that the spirits of those old ranch hands Stumpy, Frankie, Juan, and Coyote Jim, the ones Grandad used to talk about, paid you a visit last night?"

"Not exactly."

"Then who? Casper?"

I shook my head. "Your dad."

Her eyes widened. "Daddy? You've got to be kidding. He just showed up unannounced in the bunkhouse, in the middle of a blizzard. Draped in a white sheet going *'Ooooow, Ooooow?'*"

"Not exactly."

"Then what exactly? Did you dream about him? We definitely drank a lot of wine and shared a lot of memories last night."

No way out now, I thought. *Might as well show my cards and hope for the best.*

"I don't know how to say this Shel . . . no, it wasn't a dream. Twice now, your dad has visited me. He *appears*—I'm not sure how else to describe it—just as he did when he was alive, only a little paler. He's either wearing an old A&M bathrobe and boots or old jeans, with those stupid Birkenstocks and the sweat-stained Stetson. Still sounds the same though. Smells the same too. You remember. That faint scent of Old Spice and manure?"

Shelia Mae rolled her eyes and laughed. "Well, I guess that's a better fragrance than Decay of Death. Scooter, please tell me this is a joke."

I shook my head. For the next thirty minutes she sat silently as I told her of John's visits. I did not tell her of the events that I believed triggered his appearance, and I was vague and misleading about what he'd told me. Especially during the bunkhouse visit.

"He wanted to know how you were doing," I lied. "Said he would like to see you but had been warned about visiting close family members who were still struggling with their loss. I guess it slows the grieving process."

She looked at me suspiciously.

"No, really. Apparently, the dead have rules of etiquette, too. I mean, you know, I guess when you die, some things change, and some don't. He clearly still has feelings for you, and concerns, Shel. I'm sure he still loves you. I mean—"

Her face flashed with horror and outrage, and a warm, buttered croissant caught me mid-forehead. "Shut the fuck up, Scooter. You're bullshitting me and you know it and it's really pissing me off."

She fled upstairs in tears.

I cleaned the breakfast dishes and again thought long and hard about what I'd gotten myself into. Never mind the other craziness surrounding John's death, now I was telling his grieving daughter that her dead daddy was making surprise appearances.

It was early afternoon when Shelia Mae finally reappeared. She was wearing an old pair of jeans, a ski sweater, boots, and a John Deere gimme cap. She looked contrite—gorgeously contrite. She hugged me.

"I'm sorry, Scooter. I shouldn't have blown up at you. I thought you were teasing me, like you used to when we were kids. It hurt more because it was Daddy. You don't know how lonely I feel lately. Daddy's gone. Elizbeth is gone. My anchor line has parted, my compass is broken. I'm scared.

"I came home to regain my bearings. Until last night, I hadn't found them. Then you came over and something happened. I went to bed for the first time in months feeling connected and cared for and good about myself. And then you waltz in this morning and tell me that while I was having some of the best dreams I've had in years," she smiled, "you and my dad—my *dead* dad—were having a good old time in the bunkhouse."

"No need to apologize, Shel. I know it sounds crazy. I wrote off his first visit as a bad dream. Then, early this morning, he shows up again. Maybe it's the early onset of senility. I don't know. But I agree. It's very weird."

"I'm sure it was just that," she assured me, "a very realistic dream. Everyone has them from time to time. Besides, it has not been that long since Daddy left us. This is the first year the two of you haven't hunted together. And you were hunting that pasture down by the Sawlog the day before he first . . . appeared to you. It makes sense that it brought back old memories that triggered the dreams."

Yeah right, I thought. *Reminiscing about an old friend may bring back good memories. But the sudden appearance of his partial remains in the jaws of your dog tends to elicit a whole new genre of apparitions.*

"Good point, Shel. I'm sure I just got carried away remembering how he liked to hunt birds. Let's just forget it."

"I think about him a lot too, Scooter, more than ever since I found another old notebook of his. She went to one of the massive bookshelves that framed the fireplace, pulled down a small, worn leather journal, and handed it to me.

"Start reading from the page I marked."

Jesus, I thought, *how much of John's final story had he kept in his head, and how much had he put down on paper?*

I slowly opened the notebook. The handwriting was shaky but readable.

April 23—Such a beautiful spring day. The wheat's up and looking better than it has in five years. It rained again last night. One of those "politician storms" as I call them. A lot of bluster at the beginning, thunder and lightning to beat the band—nearly brought me out of bed—and then a slow, steady rain that just as quickly put me back to sleep.

Wonder what rain feels like to a freshly planted seed? Good, I bet. Peaceful and satisfied. At least I hope so.

Guess I'll find out soon enough. My time is coming. Quicker than I'd hoped. But I guess that's how it goes. Doc Snodgrass says I'm doing fine. But I know he's just BS-ing me to make me feel better. Lately there are lumps and bumps where there shouldn't be, pain where there used not to be, and a growing sense that my time's near.

It makes me sad, even on a beautiful spring morning.

May 4—Wheat still looking great. Should be a bumper crop unless we get hail. Blood when I pissed this am. Doesn't hurt, but kind of scary.

June 2—I've been thinking about that old Kiowa who used to occasionally work for Dad, Jimmy Iron Tail. Shortly before he died, he apparently came to talk to Dad. Told him about how some old men in his tribe had gone off to die alone rather than be a burden to their people. Said that as a little boy he remembered his grandfather doing that, and how sad it was to see his "Koh" just walk away and never return.

Jimmy told Dad that old Doc Bolin had told him he had cancer and wasn't long for this world. Worried that he would be a burden on his son and daughter with whom he lived. Said the idea of simply saying goodbye and walking off, much as his grandfather had done, was beginning to sound like a good way to go.

Dad tried to talk him out of it. Told him it was not something most folks, especially White Christians, would understand. Besides creating unnecessary pain and concern for his family, he might trigger a costly manhunt that, whether or not successful, would, knowing the county's Native American-hating sheriff, be blamed on and ultimately paid for by his people.

Jimmy nodded, thanked him for his advice and left. He returned days later and told Dad that while a disappearing act might upset the White folks, his people would look up to him with much respect.

Dad said his exact words were: "Mr. Marshall, I know you mean well, but your religion has always troubled me—ever since those Sisters of Sacred Cross started slapping me with a switch and calling me a little heathen. You created your god in your own likeness—that of a White man—because you think that if your god is special, he must look like you, even though he's invisible.

"That's just wrong, Mr. Marshall. Just look around you. See the creek over there and them giant cottonwoods that border it? Or take those sunflowers in that pasture, that red tail gliding above 'em. If they don't tickle your holy bone, just take a gander at them thunderheads building in the west. That's what God looks like."

Jimmy Iron Tail said his people didn't have to go and make up an imaginary god that looked like them. No sir. All they had to do was look around them. All they had to do to experience their creator was to take care of his creation and draw from it everything they needed for a good life.

Dad said that was the last time he saw Jimmy.

One day in town a few weeks later, shopping with Mom, he bumped into Mr. Farenbacher, the undertaker and proprietor of the mercantile store, who told him that according to pool hall rumor, Jimmy Iron Tail had died, but that no one had brought in his body. Guessed his people took care of it themselves. Dad said Farenbacher seemed more upset by the loss of a small profit than about the passing of one of the last survivors of a vanishing civilization.

A couple of days later, when Dad went to check the mailbox, he found, wrapped in a small rabbit skin, the turquoise and silver ring that Jimmy always wore. The one he claimed had magical powers.

"Wow," I said, closing the book, "this is fascinating. Especially the part about Jimmy Iron Tail. I wonder what really happened to him?"

Shel sighed. "You're missing the point, Scooter. I think Dad was considering following in Jimmy's footsteps, going off and dying alone. Did he ever talk about that with you?"

"Maybe," I lied, "I don't remember. We talked about a lot of things, Shel. Your dad was very interested in what happens when someone dies. He was a very inquisitive man. You know that. And age didn't dampen that curiosity. If anything, it made it stronger. Hell, at one point he got interested in Buddhism and started going out every morning and meditating in the old hayloft. One day he apparently drifted off and almost fell out, which even he admitted would be a dubious way to meet one's maker. Look Shel, your daddy is over there in the Big Pasture, next to your mom, under that beautiful blanket of snow. Why don't we walk over there and visit them? We need some fresh air, and I think you still need some closure."

"Maybe later. But right now, I want you to finish reading this journal. Besides, I'm hungry."

While Shel went to the kitchen, I slowly and with trepidation, continued reading what appeared to be John Marshall's death planner.

June 7—Another half-inch of rain last night. With the wheat this close to cutting it's a mixed blessing. What we need now is about three weeks of sunshine to dry things out, so we'll have a good harvest. Fingers crossed!

Thinking about what would work better: a scaffold or a pyre. Leaning toward some sort of scaffold. Afraid of heights, though— especially after the hayloft incident. But I'd be up in the air away from critters. Besides, a pyre is problematic. It would be a bit sadistic and god-awful painful—not to mention awkward— to light it while you're still alive. I guess I could rig a timer or something. But then there's the fire hazard. Although we've had decent moisture, it would not look good to go out a pyromaniac, especially if you wound up torching several hundred acres of a neighbor's farmland!

June 24—Went online to research scaffolding. Googled "death scaffolds," and the first dozen entries were about people falling off scaffolds and dying. Not what I had in mind. Finally found a Native American site with a lot of good material. Seems most of them were fairly simple. Also, they were designed for after you die. Since I'm planning to spend the last few hours or days alive on mine, I guess I need to modify the design a bit.

July 4—Independence Day! May be my last here on earth. But assuming the Holy Bible is right—admittedly a fragile assumption—every day in Heaven is Independence Day.
Finished wheat harvest on Monday. Overall made seventy bushels to the acre. Best yield I've had in fifty years of dry-land farming. Not that I'm going to rush out and buy that new pickup I've been lusting after at the Ford dealership. Commodity prices suck. (Note to readers of this diary: DO NOT PLAY THE FUTURES MARKET! EVER! I did once and lost my shirt.)

July 16—Scaffold design complete! Very safe if I don't break my neck getting up there. Will be hidden from view. Don't think anyone will find it. Must remember to bring an air mattress and a sleeping bag. Also, mobile phone in case I change my mind at the last minute. And my Kindle. (Note to self: Make sure to download the Bible—NIV translation.)

For the next three months death and dying were not mentioned. Instead, John wrote about the abundance of late summer moisture and how it would help the winter wheat and the sudden jump in cattle prices. He also spoke of the new tricked-out F150 pickup he purchased. And there were lengthy passages, complete with sketches, of a trout fishing trip to New Mexico and Colorado.
Then, shortly after his return, his thoughts of death reemerged.

Oct. 3—Just came back from seeing the specialist in Dodge. Bad news. Cancer has returned with a vengeance. He says I have six months at the outside—could end sooner. I'm scared and sad. Also angry.

The old rancher's tears had wrinkled the page and blurred the ink.

Oct. 5—Went for a walk along the Sawlog yesterday. A beautiful day. Made me realize how good a life I've had. And how I have no reason to be angry or afraid—only sad. But I need to put even that in perspective. It's kind of like my last fishing trip. I was sad when that was over, too, but driving home I started thinking about hunting season and the new adventures that would bring. I need to view death the same way. While I don't believe most of the Biblical bullshit I was taught as a youngster, I do believe in a Creator and an existence beyond death. And I've got to think it will be a great adventure—even if there are no guns, pickups, good whiskey, or dogs. (Scratch that last bit: I have no doubt my dogs will be there to greet me!)

Oct. 7—Another gorgeous fall day. Planned on building the scaffold. But just too tired to work on it. Hope to get started in the next few days.

Oct. 10—Still too exhausted and sick to work on scaffold. Stayed in bed most of the day. Put together the following list of supplies:
Rope ladder
Sleeping bag
Scotch
Pistol (ammo)
Bible (on Kindle)
Phone (charged)
Wallet with ID (no cash or credit cards)
Snacks (M&Ms and Oreos)

Oct. 15—Out of bed and feeling better. Finally started working on scaffold. But have done a lot of thinking and am reconsidering my plan—not what I'm doing but how I pull it off in a dignified way that doesn't piss people off and unduly upset them. Am mostly worried about Shelia Mae. I want her last memories of me to be good ones. She's dealing with too many issues already. I don't need to pile on more.

Oct 17—New plan! Got it from another old Native American. (Ha!) Should have thought of it before. No one will never suspect! Just hope I'm well enough—strong enough—to pull it off. All I need is a little help from my friends—and from Rev. Shaman Running Bull.

Oct. 28—Long conversation with Scooter today. He called to get a pheasant report. Always liked that young man. Prayed that he and Shelia Mae would get together. Never happened. Shelia Mae liked girls. Scooter apparently liked them, too—too much given his rather dismal track record. I sometimes wish God wasn't so goddamn persnickety in how he responds to our prayers.

Nov 5—Spent the last four days in bed. Dragged myself to Dodge to see the doctor this a.m. He told me it was time to get what he calls hospice care. The Sisters of Sacred Heart have this place where they care for you until you pass. I told the doctor I was born a Baptist and would die a Baptist and didn't need a flock of nuns hovering over me, making all nice and sweet and then when I'm delirious and dying, slipping in their last rites. He said not to worry, they might pray for me, but they wouldn't attempt any end-of-life alter calls. I said I'd think about it. I did. For about two seconds.

Nov 6—Cleaned Daddy's old Colt Peacemaker. Hope I don't feel the need to use it. And if I do, I hope those old .45 cartridges work. Gun hasn't been used in fifty years. While I was at it, also polished up my old motorcycle.

Nov. 8—Final arrangements finished. Everything is in place. Hoping to make it till next Saturday and opening day of goose season.

Nov. 9—Hope I'm doing the right thing. Know most people wouldn't approve. But down deep I know it's best for everyone including me. Luckily, I have a few trusted friends left in this world to help me move on to the next.
Note to self: Must remember to burn this diary before I go!

That was the last entry in the diary—an account of his planned death not unlike the one he'd shared with me. Yet it still didn't explain how he, or at least his skull, had made the journey back from Oklahoma.

15

"I TOLD YOU SHEL, it never got that far. Nor would I have let it."

The late afternoon walk I'd suggested to the family plot should have been peaceful. The wind had died, the sun was out, the heavy snowfall sparkled in silence.

But the air was filled with tension and the conversation strained. Shelia Mae spent the entire time grilling me on what I'd known about John's so-called plan, convinced I'd been part of a dreadful plot to help him die.

My strategy, which I'd landed on after I finished the diary, was to admit I'd known all about her dad's detailed plan, which was true—sort of—but how I had convinced him to give it up shortly before the faux fatal goose hunting trip—total bullshit.

"Your dad told me what he was planning when I called him before hunting season, Shel. I argued with him, told him it was a stupid idea that would upset you and a lot of other people. At first, he wouldn't listen. 'Dammit, Scooter,' he lectured me, 'can't a man at least die the way he wants to? I'm not trying to hurt anybody or create a spectacle. I just want to be by myself at the end. I hate big sloppy endings. They're awkward for everyone.'

"I told him he had a point, but that it would be far worse if you found out what he'd really done. I said it was something for which you might never forgive him, something that might haunt you forever.

"I tried, Shel, I really did. Just a few days before the goose hunt, I came out to the ranch one last time to try to change his mind. I told him that he was old, sick, and frightened, which was nothing to be ashamed of, but that he also wasn't thinking clearly. He continued to push back.

"Then, just as I was about to give up, he drained the last of his scotch, slammed his glass on the table, and put his hands in the air. 'Okay,' he said, wearily, 'you win. But on two conditions: first, not a word to Shelia Mae until I'm gone, and second, promise you'll be at my side when death comes for me.'

"I gave him my word, Shel, knowing that, given death's capriciousness, I might not be at his side when he showed up. Since then, I've often wondered if your dad willed himself to die in that blind, surrounded by friends."

Despite my artful, albeit cowardly obfuscating, Shel wasn't buying it.

"I don't know, Scooter. That goose-hunting story sounds too nice and neat. If Daddy was so sick and staying in bed most of the time, why would he suddenly decide to do one final hunt? Sounds like he could hardly walk let alone climb into a goose pit and put a twelve-gauge to his shoulder."

"You're right. He was not in good shape, and we probably shouldn't have taken him. But he was set on going. And the closer we got to the lake, the more his health seemed to improve. Hell, he was the first to get his limit. But then he got quiet, said he was tired and went to sleep."

We made our way to the tiny hilltop cemetery, bordered by four strands of barbed wire fixed to ancient limestone posts. Ice-covered fall floral arrangements poked out of the snow next to Ruthie and John's gravestones. We stood there in silence, our breath forming miniature clouds in the crystal, late afternoon air.

Suddenly, Shelia Mae straightened and angrily stepped to John's grave. "Goddam you, Daddy!" she screamed, standing over the dirt under which John was supposedly buried. "You selfish old bastard. If you're really down there—and I'm not convinced you are—then fucking listen to me! What were you thinking? Why didn't you call me? Why didn't you talk to me? Why didn't you tell me you were dying? Why did you sit there alone, dreaming up all that silly garbage about going off and dying, when we could have spent the little time you had left together? All I ever wanted to do was make you happy. But I couldn't. What did I do to wound you so badly that you would rather die alone than with me at your side?"

She dropped to her knees, sobbing. I knelt beside her and put my arms around her. Slowly she relaxed. But the tears continued to flow.

"I feel so . . . wretched," she said softly. "If I hadn't been so pig-headed, so selfish, so . . . ashamed." She shook her head. "I didn't have to run away to London. I should have stayed here—dealt with my demons like an adult. It would have been hurtful and hard, but I think that maybe over time Daddy would have made peace with who I am. I can't blame him for refusing to accept my sexuality—for believing that my attraction to women was a sin against God. He was from a different time. A different place. Different values."

She rubbed tears off her cheeks with the backs of her hands. "Admit it, Scooter, life fucking sucks and then you die. It's time we both grew up and got over it."

I didn't try to reason with her. As miserable as I was at relationships, one thing I'd learned was to avoid manly problem-solving. So, I did the next best thing: I knelt there in awkward silence, stared the ground, then finally handed her a handkerchief.

She dabbed at her eyes, slowly stood, and then after a moment, looked me in the eye. "Jesus, Scooter. You're such a wuss. Relax. It's okay. I'm okay." Her smile returned. "We can't live in the past—you and me. Frankly I'm glad you suggested coming up here. I've been avoiding it since coming home. I needed this . . . I needed to get this out. I needed to yell and scream at him. I also needed to tell him I loved him. Besides, it's beautiful up here. Peaceful. Mom and Dad couldn't have picked a better resting place."

She took my hand. "Let's go home and have some wine."

16

IF SOMEONE HAD WITNESSED our walk back to the house and described it as peaceful, they would have been half right. Shelia Mae was laughing and talking, and clearly felt better. But only because she had latched onto a myth that I had concocted—a myth initially created to help grant a dying man his final wish and protect his daughter from the truth.

But myths, based as they are on fragile patchworks of fact, fiction, and our personal perspectives, have a way of rewriting themselves with the emergence of new evidence. Such as when the remains of a man who was said to have died peacefully while hunting are found in a pasture more than two hundred miles from where you thought he really died. And then that man's diary turns up with yet a third, unfinished version of what actually transpired.

The myth I had created had morphed in ways even I no longer fully understood. Yet I continued to cling to the only element of the story that I knew for certain was a lie—John's death in the goose blind.

I had to embrace that lie, I told myself, to protect Shelia Mae from the truth. But selfishly I was trying to protect myself, not only from losing my rekindled relationship with her, fragile as it was, but also from potential legal problems, perhaps even criminal charges, if the whole truth came out.

Shit, I thought. *Shit, shit, shit.*

Back at the ranch house I began collecting my things and told Shel I was returning to town before it got dark and the roads froze over. "No, Scooter," she said emphatically, "you're staying here. You have to. I need you. I may not look it, but I'm a bit fragile right now, and when I'm fragile, I'm easily frightened."

"Why don't I just leave Buck here and come back in the morning? He's a good watchdog. He'll protect you."

"No," she insisted. "I'm not scared of anything out there. I'm scared of this—" She hugged herself tightly.

I wanted to tell her that was exactly the reason I had to leave. Fear. Fear of what was inside me and how it might destroy the bond that I believed was growing between us. I wanted to tell her that I had to leave because, inside, I was a selfish, thoughtless man who continued to lie to her about her father's death, not only because I might hurt her, but also because it would destroy any chances— unrealistic as they were—that she might one day fall in love with me.

I wanted to tell her, but I didn't. Instead, while she opened a bottle of wine and set out a good Spanish cheese and some jamón ibérico she'd smuggled into to the US, I lit the kerosene lamps, built a fire, and collapsed into the big armchair next to it.

Shelia Mae brought in the wine, curled up on the couch, and patting the cushion next to her, motioned me to sit with her.

"In a minute," I stalled, perceiving it more a provocation than invitation. "Kind of tired from all the exercise and emotion of this afternoon. Besides, this chair is very comfortable."

She smiled. "That's what Daddy always said. It was where he sat every evening. I used to sit on his lap." She stopped and studied me. For a minute I feared she was considering trying out mine. "Sorry I got so worked up this afternoon. I said some things I wish I hadn't."

"I'm sure your dad didn't mind."

"It wasn't the things I said to Daddy. It's what I said to you—about life sucking and then us dying. Truth is, I want to have a long, happy

life, not just the occasional random moments of bliss. I don't want
to be constantly thinking that I'm damaged goods, a bad person, an
evil freak of nature."

"Jesus, Shel, you're no freak, and you're certainly not evil."

She gave a cynical laugh. "Please don't bring that sonofabitch
into the conversation."

"Who?"

"Jesus, for God's sake. I've been struggling with Him since I was
five."

For the next hour we talked about growing up in the same small
church, being fed the same fundamentalist, nationalistic brand of
religion, one bereft of genuine love and faith, and based instead on
harsh rules. We recalled the stories and doctrines that were passed
down to us by a generation of earnest, caring, gentle folk, who,
having lived through two world wars, the Great Depression, and the
dark days of the Dust Bowl, had a rather bleak and unforgiving view
of our creator.

The stories we shared were similar: Singing "Jesus Loves Me,"
and then being bombarded by detailed stories of ancient tribes with
weird names who spent their lives killing each other over whose god
was better; tales of an angry, vengeful god who had his son murdered,
and how the son magically came back to life, which was all good
because, somehow, if he hadn't, all us despicable, worthless sinners
would be headed straight to hell in a handbasket.

At some point, over a third bottle of wine, we pondered what a
handbasket was and why the hell it was the preferred transportation
for getting us there.

We talked about going to Sunday evening church and belting
out songs like "He Ransomed Me," "Nothing But the Blood," "There
is Power in the Blood," (not just any old blood, mind you but "the
precious blood of the lamb"), "Saved by the Blood," and "Alas! And
Did My Savior Bleed?" with those memorable lines:

Alas! And did My Savior bleed? And did my Sovereign die?
Would He devote that sacred head for such a worm as I?

"Talk about feeling like a worm," Shelia Mae said, "I remember
singing one of those bloody songs the Sunday after I got my first
period. I lay in bed that night sick to my stomach and scared—
wondering what I had done to deserve such disgusting wrath from a

god who supposedly loved me. Later, when I got the courage, I asked Mom. You know her, she just smiled and told me to never confuse physiology and philosophy. 'Religion has a purpose, Shelia Mae,' she told me in her soft, sweet voice. 'Just like your period. I learned long ago not to put too much faith into a book clearly written by a bunch of old men. Think about it. All that anger and killing. All that blood and gore. No woman in her right mind would ever write stuff like that.'"

"You were lucky," I said. "At least your parents were more enlightened than mine. I always envied you."

"I used to believe that too, Scooter. Until I told them I was gay. Mom was great. She just hugged me and cried, and told me how proud she was of me, and what a fine catch I'd make for the right woman. Daddy, on the other hand, never could fully cross the line. Oh, he tried. After his initial anger and denial, we had many conversations. But he never could get there. And as hard as I tried, I could never make peace with him. Until today."

"I'm sure he understands," I said, finally moving to the couch and sitting close to her.

"Then why don't you ask him? You, whom he still seems to visit on a regular basis. Maybe you can get him to appear this evening. Why don't we a have a séance? The mood seems perfect—a big fire, lamps burning."

I thought she was kidding. "Oh yeah, just like that. I don't suppose you have an old Ouija Board lying around."

"I'm serious, Scooter. Make him appear. I really want to talk to him."

I tried to explain that I didn't have any say about when or where John appeared. "He just kind of shows up when he has something he wants to tell me. He tends to come at odd hours—when I'm sleeping or very early in the morning."

"Perfect. Then let's go upstairs and go to bed." She rose unsteadily, grabbed the wine, and made for the stairs. "Put out the lamps, bank the fire, and come on up. I'll be waiting. Really looking forward to seeing my dead daddy!"

Shit.

I dealt with the lanterns and fire but very slowly. I needed time to think. Had I just been propositioned? If so, was it the wine talking, or did she really want me? Or was it her dad she really wanted, and I was merely the medium? Was it spiritual or sexual?

Damnit, John, I need your holy help. Now. I assume you've been watching this evening's entertainment."

Nothing.

So, what am I supposed to do now? I have no intention of going to bed with your daughter. You know that. Can you at least send me a sign?"

Nothing

Just go upstairs and talk to her. Tell her that it's okay and that you love her. Please!

Finally, a voice.

"Scooter, what the heck are you doing? Get up here!"

And so, I went.

17

SHELIA MAE WAS SITTING IN BED. As I walked in, she hugged her knees to her chest and smiled. In the light of the single candle she had lit, I could not tell what, if anything, she was wearing. But the sight of her long, tanned legs was enough to weaken my knees and resolve.

For the second time that day, she motioned me to come over and sit beside her. Instead, I mumbled something about needing to wash my hands, and made for the bathroom.

"You're stalling, Scooter. Come on out," Shelia Mae demanded over the sound of the running faucet. "Be the man I think you are." When I didn't respond, her tone changed.

"Scooter, please. I'm not going to rape you. I just want . . . I need . . . I need you to hold me."

And for the next two hours, that's what I did. I held her and listened as she poured out her soul. She returned to the subject of her youth. She talked about the beauty of growing up in a small town—the freedom and safety she felt as a child. But she also spoke of feeling different, of at some point, seeing herself as an outsider, looked down upon by the community, especially the church.

"Don't laugh," she whispered, "but most days when I look in the mirror, I still see a shy second-grader, a bad little girl who is on her way to Hell despite her efforts to be good. I can't help it."

I held her tightly, saying nothing but remembering similar thoughts as a child, and wondering how many other young souls like ours had been permanently damaged by well-meaning adults who were desperately trying to save them.

Finally, she fell asleep. I continued to lie next to her, holding her until her breathing and body relaxed. I thought about driving back to town but found myself emotionally exhausted. That tingling horniness I'd felt earlier had long passed, replaced by a sense of sadness and loss. So, I went downstairs and fell asleep on the couch.

Soon, I was visited by a series of troubling, at times terrifying, dreams. It was as if I were being made to watch some dark cable mashup of *Pilgrim's Progress* meets *Dante's Inferno* and *Lolita*. The only spirit that was obvious in his absence was John's. Where, I wondered, is a good ghost when you need him?

The next thing I knew, Shel was shaking me and trying to calm me. "Sorry to wake you, but you were yelling and moaning, and I thought you were going to roll off the couch and hit your head on the coffee table. You okay?"

"Uh huh," I replied hoarsely, my fists clenched, my heart pounding. "I'm fine. Just having a weird dream. What time is it?"

"Ten-thirty. I guess we slept in a bit. Come in the kitchen and I'll make coffee and breakfast."

We ate in silence. After helping clear the table, I told Shel that Buck and I were heading back to town. She walked me to the car and thanked me for coming out.

"Sorry if I made you uncomfortable last night, but I needed you here more than you'll ever know. Please, don't be a stranger. *Mi casa es su casa.*

"I won't," I said. "Truth be told, I'm glad I came. I needed you too."

I realized when I hit the highway that I still was in no condition to drive. The sun was bright, and the snow beginning to melt. But between the wine and the dreams, I was struggling with a nightmarish hangover. Neither my head nor my stomach was holding up well, though the pain I felt was more emotional than physical.

I slowly made my way home, then spent thirty minutes clearing wet snow from the drive and walks before I could get in. The physical labor helped, and by the time I'd finished, I was beginning to feel like myself again.

Buck could clearly sense the change, rushing inside when I opened the door and bringing me his shock collar.

"Wonderful idea," I told him. "You're absolutely right. We need a good walk in the fresh air."

I grabbed a gun and some shells, threw on boots and a hunting jacket, and we headed out. We drove north and west, as far as we could go from Shelia Mae's place and still be in the county. I found a patch of public land with a small creek, and we set off.

Bird hunting in the snow is more tracking than hunting. Buck used his nose like a furry heat-seeking snowplow, searching for telltale scent. In the first hour he flushed two rabbits and a small coyote, each bursting from its hiding spot in an explosion of snow and ice.

On his fourth point, he finally hit pay dirt. An old rooster lumbered skyward like a small B-52. I dropped him before he could light his afterburners and escape. Unlike the day we found John, Buck's retrieve was flawless.

We got two more before dusk came and a full moon rose in the eastern sky. But neither Buck nor I felt like going home. We each had our reasons. Buck's was a simple need to keep following his nose—to chase the mysterious, ever-changing scent of the wilderness. But while he was charging toward one beckoning fragrance or another, I found myself fleeing a covey of apparitions that had been chasing me since I had left Shelia Mae's.

Like a squadron of ghostly nighthawks, they pursued me, each making a swooping, dark thought-triggering pass, only to disappear and be replaced by one of their equally spectral wingmen. They strafed me with images of Shelia Mae crying, of her screaming at her father's grave, of her beckoning me to her bed, until finally, the pain I felt for my role in John's death caught me, scattering the other dark images swirling through me.

We followed a deer trail that stretched across the plains, occasionally dipping into small ravines. The wind had died, and a starry silence enveloped us—the only sounds the crunching of my boots in the snow, the far-away cries of coyotes, and a lone jet high overhead.

Slowly, the dark thoughts faded, and a wave of peace washed over me. Normalcy returned with the stirrings of a few rational thoughts. The first was that I had to deal with the John problem. We had to gather what we could of his remains and give them—him—a proper burial. We—I—had to come clean with Shelia Mae, even if she never spoke to me again.

But that was just the start. I had begun to realize that I must also come to terms with the damage I'd done to the other women I'd loved. Finally, I had to make peace with my faith, and in doing so find some spiritual solace that I'd long been missing.

By the time we got back to the pickup, I felt almost giddy, despite the dark bank of clouds that had scudded in from the Northwest, switching off the night sky star by star. As we slowly had made our way back to the pickup, a plan began to take shape in the form of a few cerebral bullet points that I had to put in motion if I was ever to eliminate the creep who continued to stare back at me from the mirror each morning.

18

MARY'S CAFE WAS PACKED when I went in for breakfast the next morning.

"Hey, Scooter, where the hell have you been? Every time I drove by on patrol the past two nights the house was dark. No lights, no pickup, no barking. We was starting to get worried. Thought you must have headed back to Texas. But that seemed unlikely given the storm. Where were you anyway?"

It was WD, speaking loudly enough for the whole town to hear.

"I was home for the most part, WD. Just Buck and me. Daughter couldn't make it for Thanksgiving because of the storm. Pickup was in the garage, where I usually keep it during weather."

"Yeah right." WD had a way of smirking that made the gentlest of folks want to haul back and pop him in the mouth. But given that he'd just filled his rather crooked smile with a big bite of Mary's Terminator omelet, I demurred, choosing instead to sit at the back corner table with Norm, Bobby, and Roy Ray Simpson, who ran a local welding service and raced late model stock cars on area dirt tracks.

My snub was too subtle for WD. "You weren't per chance banging one of your old high school sweethearts, were you?" he shouted across the room.

I ignored him, greeting my three friends and asking Mary for coffee and the usual.

"Why doesn't WD like you?" Roy Ray asked.

"Don't really know, Roy Ray. Maybe it was something I said . . . back in fifth grade."

"Well, whatever it was, he clearly holds a grudge. Been going around all weekend talking about you having a thing for Shelia Mae. Said you've always had a hard-on for her, and now that you're both in town, the two of you are probably, you know . . ."

"No, I don't know. Besides, Shelia Mae? Really?"

"Norm says it's EES," Roy Ray continued. "You know, that Erotic/ Exotic Syndrome. According to Norm, when two people are kind of odd, they're often attracted to each other's weirdness in a sexual sort of way. Right, Norm? And since you and Shelia Mae are both peculiar, you may be, you know, getting it on."

"Okay, so we know Shelia Mae is gay. Is that what you mean about her being weird?"

"Yeah, kinda."

"And me? What's weird about me?"

"Well, you know, you're kind of different. I remember as a kid you didn't play football, and you had a little red scooter instead of a car like all the other guys. And you wrote poetry and wanted to be a fashionable writer. What the hell was that all about anyway?"

"Fashion writer, Roy Ray. I wanted to go to New York and Paris and cover high fashion."

"Oh, well, that's even weirder. Geez."

"What I think Roy Ray is trying to say," Norm broke in, "is that you fell a bit outside of the *normative curve* in terms of small-town boys growing up in rural America in the mid to late twentieth century. You had a somewhat different perspective on life. You were kind of quiet and intellectual-like. You were never . . ." He paused, looking for just the right word. "You were never a rough-n-tumble youngster like the rest of us."

"Thank you, professor. Sounds like you found the perfect thesis subject should you decide to get your PhD: *When Farm Boys Turn Fruity.*"

Norm laughed. "Fair enough. But you know what I mean. You were the shy, nice kid who always made good grades, went to church three time a week, and didn't swear, talk dirty or pick on the truly weird kids like the rest of us did. And then you went off to college, grew your hair long, flunked out, had to join up to avoid the draft, became some sort of spy—at least that's what people said—got married, got divorced, got married again, moved back East, got divorced, remarried and divorced yet another time. I wouldn't call that normal."

"No," I said. "Not when you put it like that. But that doesn't mean I've turned into some sort of pervert who goes around chasing gay women. Truth is, I'm considering swearing off all women. Period."

"You're going to become one of those celebrity people?" Roy Ray looked horrified.

"No, RR, not unless I decide to stay in Creekmore. I'm thinking about becoming *celibate.* You know, like Father Tim."

Whether Roy Ray thought I was renouncing sex or suddenly turning Catholic, I wasn't sure. But from the look on his face, I knew I'd said too much and that he was very close to sharing the news with the entire breakfast crowd.

"That's between us guys, RR, please. It's not something I'm especially proud of. It's not that I'm gay. Okay? I just don't think I'm ready for the varsity team when it comes to relationships with women, given that my record is on par with that of our high school basketball team. Remember? We didn't win a single game our junior year. And how many of us went on to play college ball? That's right. Sometimes, you just have to walk away from things you aren't good at, even if you enjoy them—or think you do."

Before Roy Ray could respond to this mysterious new metaphor, Bobby jumped to my rescue. "Gee Scooter, I'm really sorry to hear that. I hope—I think we all hope—that any vow of celibacy you take will be temporary—a sexual leave of absence."

RR nodded solemnly. "That would be horrible, right up there with finding out you have cancer. My Daddy always said—"

"Actually, Scooter," Bobby interrupted again, "it's pretty brave of you to share that with us."

"But kind of weird, too," Roy Ray added. "I had an aunt—she's dead now—who was a nun. She was really goofy, too. That celebrity stuff must make you that way. Daddy used say it was unnatural, no matter what the Pope says."

"I knew your aunt," Norm chimed in. "Sister Mary Margaret. She used to come to teach Bible School every summer, remember? She was kind of strange. But in a good way. Remember how she always played softball with us? She was a great ball player, especially for a girl. I remember one time she slid into home plate in her habit . . . But I digress. What Bobby was trying to say, is that Scooter has stood up like a man and not only is facing his demons but has shared some personal knowledge that most people would be afraid to disclose. We need to respect that and keep it amongst ourselves. Okay? Just the three of us. Don't go around blabbing it to Mickey or the guys at the shop or down at the pool hall. Okay?"

"No sir," Roy Ray shook his head. "My lips are sealed. Besides, it's unspeakably weird."

With that he called for his tab and went back to work.

A deep silence fell on the table, as it often did following any conversation involving RR.

"That man is perhaps the best welder in the state." It was Norm who finally spoke. "An artist when it comes to sticking metal together. But his God-given talents don't extend to connecting verbs and nouns."

"I agree," Bobby said. "But Scooter *is* a bit weird. When was the last time someone walked into Mary's, sat down for breakfast, and announced that he was taking a vow of celibacy?"

"Father Timothy eats here regularly," Norm countered.

"Priests don't count. Besides, we've all heard the stories about the good father's so-called mission trips to Santa Fe."

"Bobby, I won't sit here and listen to any more blasphemy," Norm said, slamming his coffee mug on the table. Raised a good Catholic by his single mom, he'd turned agnostic and occasionally downright atheistic after joining the CIA. But he still had a soft spot for the church, especially priests, whom he saw not only as important father figures in shaping his life, but also good informants when he'd worked in Latin America.

"Father Tim is as straight and pure a holy man as there is. Those are lies spread by a certain woman—a certain *married* woman—whose advances the good father spurned."

"We talking about the Father Tim?" Mary, house-slippered as usual, had returned with coffee. "God, what a charming hunk of a man. Why he ever chose to be married to the Church when he could have had any woman in this state is beyond me. Just going to confession gives me goose bumps."

"Thank you, Mary, for that fascinating word picture," Norm said. "You can forget bringing me those pancakes. I just lost my appetite."

"I would tell you to go to hell, Norm, but since you never come to mass anymore, I guess that would be redundant."

"Got me there, Mary. Guess you'll just have to spend more time with Father Tim so you can save my sorry soul. Otherwise, you'll miss me when you get to Heaven."

"Ain't that the truth." She gave him a greasy pat on the shoulder and walked back to the kitchen.

We all laughed. But our brief religious repartee had given me an idea. John and Father Tim had been the best of friends. A bit of an odd couple, to be sure, in a town in which Catholics and Protestants looked at each other with a degree of suspicion. But not that odd, given the only real difference among us came on Sundays when we all went our separate ways to worship the same God. The rest of the week we all were part of one small, homogenous tribe.

In Creekmore, religion was never just a battle between Rome and the rest of us. There were at least five Protestant churches of various denominations, each with a handful of worshipers, each of which, in theory, believed it was on the one true path to salvation.

In practice, most of us could not have cared less about who was right, at least amongst the Protestant churches. The Catholics were another matter, especially with their bingo playing and drinking. That said, every church had its cadre of zealots, made up of their own versions of Widow Blackwell, who wore their brand of faith with a pride that could only end in an ugly fall and who scorned all comers who weren't of "their kind."

I always found it strange that the holy men who headed these local bastions of exclusivity were far more friendly and forgiving of one another than their followers. They met at Mary's for coffee, played golf together and if the rumors were correct, occasionally, with the exception of the Baptist minister, shared a six-pack or bottle of good wine.

Sadly, the only time they officially came together was for Creekmore's Good Friday service. Why they chose that particularly dreary celebration of death and suffering instead of Easter or Christmas, I never understood.

What should have been a contemplative, soul-filling two hours usually turned into a competitive preach-off. The Protestant ministers all tried to out-gun their fellow revs, apparently scoring points on the strength and tenor of their voice, number of references to the Last Supper and wicked Judas, and the detail of gore and agony in which they described the crucifixion.

Brother Earl, our own preacher back then, always walked away with the Freddy Kruger Award for his horrific, anatomically correct depiction of what happens to the human body when it's nailed to a piece of timber. His ghoulish rendition, designed to bring worshipers rushing to alter, more often than not sent them running for the exits.

Which was why, I guess, Father Timothy, with his kind words of love and hope, delivered with an Irish brogue that he picked up one summer in the UK—he was from Iowa—was always the designated closer.

My opinion of Catholics in general and Father Tim in particular, mellowed at one such service—I was probably about twelve—when I saw him roll his eyes and stifle a laugh at Earl's antics. But it was another five years before our friendship really started.

It happened on New Year's Eve after a cigar and beer event several of my more heathen high school friends had planned was broken up by an alert parent. With nowhere to go, we crashed the Catholic youth party. Father Tim welcomed us like the slightly drunk prodigal sons we were, and we rang in the new year playing poker with him using communion wafers as chips. He assured us it was okay, as they had not been consecrated and had long passed their use-by date.

The Blessed Father, as Maria Mulvane, our daily mass-attending neighbor used to call Tim, grew up in a small farming community much like Creekmore. Like me, he was considered a bit of an oddball. In the long talks we began to have, we found that the two of us had been wimpy bookworms who spent hours at the local library feeding our imaginations and daydreams.

It wasn't that we weren't part of the gang. As with all boys, we liked baseball, pranks, and wandering along the creek poking dead things with sticks. We held our own. Still, we were the wise but introverted followers who never led but were respected for the advice we gave those who did. Such as when I told Bobby and Norm it was probably not a good idea to put an M-80 in the tailpipe of the high school principal's new Rambler station wagon. Although they didn't take my advice at the time, they were quick to acknowledge it after spending several weekends picking up trash along the highway as punishment.

Eventually my status grew to that of a sage, and years later both would still reach out for my counsel. Norm once phoned me from an undisclosed location in the Middle East—it may have been Afghanistan, he would never tell me—to seek my advice on accepting a child bride from a local chieftain.

Father Tim was the first holy man I'd come across who didn't use God's word as a theological cudgel. When I told him I was sure I was going to Hell because I couldn't buy into the whole Jesus thing, he just shook his head.

"My son," he smiled, kindly mocking me as he frequently did, "give God a little more credit for his creation and man a little less for his intellect. Don't believe everything you see, hear, or read of a religious nature. God gave you a mind for a reason—*to* reason. Ninety percent of religion is *bovis stercus*—that's Latin for bullshit."

"But—"

"But I'm a priest? Yes. And a damn good one, I think. But that doesn't make me holy or blessed or special. Not in the least. It's not that I'm a poser. I give people hope. I counsel them. I add meaning to the daily tribulations we all must deal with. But I don't for a nanosecond believe all the *equus stercus*—horseshit—my religion teaches. If I did, we sure as hell would never have turned the body of Christ into poker chips. Seriously, Scooter, none of us have all the answers, nor are we meant to. Faith can be a liberating force. But it can also be an existential ball and chain that can destroy the best of us."

"But——"

Tim threw up his hands. "Scooter, shut the heck up and listen. Three things: One—use your head, but don't overthink it. Two—faith is what is it. It is not knowledge. Okay? And three—: Hell is not a physical place. It's where we find it. Where we make it. And in your case and probably mine, it's in our fucking heads. Why? Because we think too much."

Tim's words were and continue to be comforting, at least in the moments when I remember them, which I found myself doing as I finished chowing down Mary's greasy omelet. And at that moment I had a minor epiphany: if I were to escape the intellectual hell I found myself in, I needed to have a serious talk with Norm and Bobby about what *we* should do with John's skull.

19

TWO NIGHTS LATER, when the road was finally passable, Buck and I drove out to Norm's place, a contemporary stone and glass cabin of sorts on a bluff several miles west of town. Although you can see the lights of Creekmore in the distance, it feels remote, naked, with nothing around it for miles but rolling prairie.

As I pulled into his driveway and my headlights flashed on several shot-up silhouette targets in the distance, I was reminded of why Norm picked the location. "I know it sounds silly," he once told me, "but I continue to believe there may be people out to get me, and it's comforting to think that I'll see them before they see me. I guess it's a spook thing."

Spy thing or not, I brought along a wedge of truffle-laced Spanish cheese, a pot of wild hog stew, a couple of good reds, a pan of brownies, a tub of vanilla ice cream, scotch, three nice cigars, and John's skull, the latter wrapped in newspapers and stuffed in a grocery bag. The dinner was my idea, designed to mellow Norm and Bobby before I dropped the skull-shaped bombshell.

I didn't broach the subject until after dinner, having closely watched over the serving of both the stew and the booze, ensuring that my friends were satiated, yet marginally sober. After we were comfortably seated in the cozy firelit living room I began. "Nights like these remind me of John."

"Interesting," Bobby pondered.

"Very," Norm chimed in. "I thought you were going to say nights like these remind you of John's beautiful daughter."

They laughed.

So much for a subtle approach. "Guys, please. *We* have a bit of a problem."

"Are we speaking of you and John or you and Shelia Mae?"

More laughter.

"Stop it, guys! I'm serious."

Buck, sensing my anger, growled and gave them his *don't-move-you-stupid-bastards* stare. Then he turned, walked into the kitchen and, after some serious paper-rattling, returned and solemnly dropped John's skull in my hand.

I placed it on the coffee table, facing Norm and Bobby. Both recoiled.

"Know who this is, guys?"

"Oh shit," Bobby muttered. "Please don't tell me——"

"That's right. Say hello to our friend—or what's left of him. Buck found it while we were hunting."

"Where?" Norm demanded.

"On his ranch. Not far from the creek."

"How did he get there? I mean . . . You took him to Oklahoma, right? And left him there?

"I certainly thought so. But apparently, Ricky Running Bull and the Oklahoma trip was a ruse to put us off his trail. Turns out he built a platform in a grove of cottonwoods down by the creek. About ten feet off the ground. I went back and searched the area the day after I found the skull and discovered it.

"Any other remains?" Bobby asked.

"Not of him. Did find his sleeping bag, a bottle of scotch, and his old Colt."

"Did he——"

"No, Bobby, I don't think so. There's no bullet hole in the skull, and John butchered enough hogs and cattle to know that a body shot was both risky and horribly painful. Besides, the Colt still had six rounds in it."

Norm and Bobby looked on in shocked silence at the ghastly enigma grinning back at them.

"I also found this," I said, showing them John's turquoise ring.

At that point, Bobby started to lose it. "Oh shit," he mumbled. "Oh shit, oh shit, oh shit. What are you going to do? Have you told anyone else?"

"Just you two. And I don't know what, if anything, *we* are going to do. Look guys, we're all in this together. We all went along with John's plan. We fell for his con. We fabricated his death in the goose blind.

"But let's not get hysterical. Trust me, John's in a very good place. And whether he died in Oklahoma or at his ranch, he left this world on his own terms, never dreaming that anyone would discover his remains. The last thing he'd want us to do is dress up in ashes and sackcloth, start beating our breasts, and——"

"Getting all panicky," Norm interrupted. He clearly had his secret agent face on, and behind it you could see the gears engaging. "We all need to take a deep breath, relax, and think this through. What are your thoughts, Scooter? Finding John's skull must have given you a serious head trip, so to speak."

"Yeah," Bobby agreed, "and it certainly explains you acting weird and going dark over the holiday."

"Sorry, guys. I should have clued you in earlier, but I was freaked out about it. Still am. And I'm torn up about what we should do."

"Have you discussed this with anyone?" Norm was in full interrogation mode. "Your exes? Your daughter? Your shrink? Shelia Mae?"

"No. It's been sitting on the mantle at the house since I found it. But having John staring at you is weird, especially during a Dallas Cowboys game or a bad zombie movie. Buck thinks it's a great chew toy, but I'm not sure John approves—would approve."

Bobby and Norm gave each other a quick look.

"What I mean is, would you want someone's dog chewing on your remains?"

"No, but I could see it as a kitschy little piece for your mantle," observed Bobby, who had finally regained his composure. "You could put some of those little lights in his sockets or a candle on top like you see in those old horror movies. Or, you could cut a little hole in the top of his head and drop in a cup for salsa, you know, like during the game when we're always eating chips. It would make him feel like he was doing something useful."

Before I could respond, Buck, wanting to get in on the fun, grabbed the skull and began running around the room hoping someone would chase him. When no one did, he dropped it on the floor. Again, the mournful *bonk, bonk, bonk* as it bounced a few times.

"Oh, Jesus! Everyone, stop!" Now Norm was starting to unravel. "Scooter, please get Buck away from John's . . . head. Both of you! Just . . . please . . . this is a serious problem. Like it or not, we're all co-conspirators."

For the next five minutes, the four of us stared at John's remains in silence. If Luke and WD had wandered in at that moment, which was a clear possibility, they probably would have arrested us for witchcraft.

It was Bobby who finally spoke. "I think there are several options. One, we can take it back to where Buck found it. Two, once Shelia Mae returns to Paris, we can secretly bury it—really bury it this time—next to Ruthie in the family plot. Three, we could keep it as a talisman of sorts. Rotate it among the three of us. Seriously, John was a special man. We all know that, or we wouldn't have done what we did in the first place."

"Or," I said, "we could take it to the authorities, fess up to the error of our ways, promise never to do it again, and take whatever punishment the judge and jury decide to give us."

"But we didn't *kill* him," Bobby protested.

"No, we didn't Bobby. At least not directly. But at this point, we can't prove it. And if anyone learned of our involvement in . . ." I stumbled around looking for right word, "in his passing, we could be brought up on some rather serious charges."

"Like what?"

"Lying to the authorities at minimum. Or worse."

"But we didn't actually *kill* him." Bobby was adamant.

"Bobby, I never spent a day in law school. But I could certainly make the case that we contributed to his death."

"But there's no *body*. Just . . . this!"

"And what, someone will ask, did we do with his body?" I was getting angry.

"Hold on, guys," Norm broke in. "I think we're taking the wrong approach. If they suspect foul play, I'll be the prime suspect. After all," he looked down at his hands, "I have experience in these matters. That said, I don't think telling the truth will benefit anyone at this point. There are times when myth trumps reality. I think this is one of those times. At this point, everyone believes John died peacefully in the goose blind. A fine ending to a final hunt. Hell, we have his last goose."

That we did. Even as we spoke, the Big Canada, wings spread in all its glory, flew over the bar at Mary's, looking down majestically at the handful of late evening diners who were washing down the last of their chicken-fried steaks with one final beer.

"Why change a perfectly good narrative," Norm continued. "No one really cares at this point, except for Shelia Mae. And no matter what was said in the restaurant about her and you, Scooter, I don't think that's a conversation you really want to start."

Leave it to Norm to cut through the crap and get to the nut of the issue. I stared at the fire and said nothing. But I knew he was right. I was beginning to really enjoy Shelia Mae's company. She made me feel good about myself, something that drugs alone, even legit ones, didn't often achieve. It was a foreign feeling, not one I could easily embrace or trust. Yet there were moments with her when life seemed okay. Telling her the truth now would destroy our growing bond. And yet, how could we remain close if I continued deceive her?

"And therein lies the dilemma, guys," I said. "I don't want to go to jail. But I cannot go on lying to Shelia Mae. So, what do we do?"

What we did was pour another round of drinks and stare silently into the fire. Finally, I got up, put on my coat, and picked up John's skull. "Just think about it, guys—that's all. And for God's sake, don't share any of this with anybody. Please."

With that the three of us—Buck, John's skull, and I—left.

20

EVEN WITH BUCK asleep beside me, the old creek road felt dark and foreboding as I drove back to town. All I could think about was Shelia Mae, what she might be doing, and what she would do if the truth came out.

"*When*, Scooter, not *if*."

Startled, I swerved, just missing a bridge abutment on the narrow, winding road. I slammed the brakes and turned to see where the voice was coming from, if indeed it was outside of my head.

It was John, reclining in the back seat as if he'd settled in for a long ride. "Sorry to intrude. Must be kind of spooky to be visited by a ghost on a night like this. But you should have been paying more attention to your driving instead of daydreaming about my daughter."

He flashed that wry smile that I'd often seen when, as kids, he'd caught us doing something stupid.

"Jesus, John! Don't scare me like that. I almost drove into the creek. You could have killed us."

"Again, will you please stop with that Jesus stuff. And who's *us*?

Remember, I'm dead. Seriously, I'm concerned about where you're headed. This plan you're hatching—I'm worried it's going to break bad."

"John," I sighed, "what did you expect, dying like you did and swearing us to secrecy? You're in this as deep as we are, so please cut your holier-than-thou crap. You may claim Heaven as your mailing address, but that doesn't make you a holy ghost."

"Don't get all pissy on me, Scooter," John shot back. "I know I put you guys in a tight spot. I'm sorry. I shouldn't have. But I was thinking like a dumb mortal. That was then; this is now."

Then, in a much softer voice: "I need your help, Scooter. I know you used to look up to me. But I'm no god, wasn't then, and am sure not now. Just a little mass of imperfect humanity trying to earn my wings."

I started to speak, but he stopped me.

"No Scooter, we don't actually have wings. It's just a figure of speech. Old myths die hard, even in eternity."

"John, I understand why you chose to die the way you did, and I have an idea why you lied to us about where you wanted to die. What I don't understand is why you can't just magically—miraculously is probably more accurate—deal with it yourself. You clearly have some powers that we lack. So why don't you use them? Why don't you just zip on over to the ranch and be done with it? Shelia Mae is probably still up. She may freak out a little when she first sees you, but I'm sure you can help her through that. She's got a cellar full of good wine. Just have her open a bottle and the two of you can spend the night talking. She misses you, John."

It may have been a reflection in the review mirror, but I swear he began to tear up. "Shit, Scooter," he said sadly, "I can't. Not right now."

"Why the hell not? You're dead for Chrissake! You have an eternity to think about it, but Shel doesn't. She's struggling with all sorts of pain and hurt and guilt—time she could better spend loving life, starting with herself."

"I know, Scooter, but it's not that simple. I have to finish dealing with my own issues first. Don't get me wrong. I'm working on them every day—every hour. I'm working on them as we speak. But I haven't yet reached post-limbo liberation so that I can, to use a worn-weary Bible-thumpers' euphemism, 'soar on the wings of eagles.'"

He laughed bitterly.

"Huh? You're in paradise, or so you've led me to believe. I thought limbo was fake news, a human construct created by your papist pals who prayerfully figured they could increase their cash flow through well-meaning but gullible folks like yours truly who would do anything to ensure their loved ones ended up at a proper heavenly uptown address within walking distance of the Big Guy's estate."

Glancing at the mirror, I saw him shrug, which really angered me. I hit the brakes, pulled off the road and turned and faced the specter in the back seat. "Listen, you saintly sonofabitch, I'm getting tired of these little chats we've been having. If you think you're doing me a favor, you're wrong.

"Just look at me. Since I found your stinking skull, I've been a nervous, guilt-ridden wreck. Your holier-than-thou little homilies and not-so-subtle warnings to stay away from your little girl are getting old. And now you tell me that you still have some 'work to do.' Well Saint John, first you got some explaining to do. Who the hell are you, really? And where the hell did you come from?"

John placed his head in his hands. "Dear God, I've made a mess of things," he whispered. "When will I ever learn? When?"

With that he straightened up and gave me a sad smile. "You're right, Scooter. I have a lot of explaining to do. Like why my skull turned up at the ranch when you left me to die in Oklahoma. It was because I wanted to die on the land that I loved and knew that you wouldn't put up with that. So, to legitimize it and throw you off my trail I concocted the tale about the Oklahoma shaman."

"So how did you get back to the ranch?"

"Hitched a ride with another Indian—that one was real. Crazy story. I'll tell you about it later. Right now, I've got to run. Look, I'm sorry about tonight. Dropping in on you as I've been doing to give you fatherly advice is clearly not the best approach. I think we need a fresh start. Go on home, get some sleep, relax, have some fun. Next time, we'll find a place to chat that is more convenient for both of us."

With that he disappeared.

I sat there in the dark silence. Memories, questions, and doubts circled around me like a flock of angry birds. With Buck curled up next to me, snoring peacefully I replayed my conversation with John—fast-forwarding it to certain points and then rewinding and starting over.

The next thing I remembered, Buck was on my lap growling and lunging at the truck window, and an official sounding voice was asking if I was all right.

I turned and saw a vision far more disconcerting than that of John. Pressed against the window was the face of a Glock-armed figure in black, bathed in flashing crimson and blue light. I screamed and jumped, banging my head and sending Buck scrambling into the back seat.

"It's me, Scooter. Luke. You okay?"

"I was until you put your trusty cannon in my face, Sheriff. I'm fine. I guess I fell asleep."

"Kind of a funny place to take nap, isn't it? You been drinking?

"Not for a couple of hours. Seriously Luke, I'm fine. I was driving back from Norm's place. Got a little dizzy. Pulled off the road until it passed. Next thing I know Buck's barking his head off and you are pounding on the window."

"Norm's huh? As you don't smell boozy, am I to assume it might have been a little too much of Bobby's award-winning weed that caused the temporary loss of consciousness? I've heard tell it's powerful stuff—or was until we burned off his crop after the fair."

Earlier that summer, as a joke, Bobby had entered his marijuana plants and some brownies laced with his crop in the county fair. He gave the plants some Latin sounding name, but the local agriculture agent who was judging the gardening entries immediately saw through the ruse. Being a friend of Bobby's, he simply threw them in the trash.

The three women judging the baking entries took a different approach. After becoming aware that they had been standing in front of the pie and cake entries for forty-five minutes, debating the merits of chocolate vs. banana cream fillings, Maggie Finkelstein, who had majored in home economics and minored in pot and boys while attending a nearby state college, started giggling hysterically. "Girls," she said, "we're stoned silly."

Her fellow judges, choir-singing Methodists, were horrified and began to panic. Maggie, sensing a scandal in the making, quickly shushed her friends and hustled them out to the cattle barn. Only after herding them to a remote pen where her daughter's soon-to-be champion bull was located, did she speak.

"Remember Bobby's brownies," she whispered. "I think that sonofabitch laced them with some of his marijuana. So now that you two have partaken of his forbidden fruit, what do you think?"

"I know pot is supposedly a sin," giggled the soprano. "But frankly, I don't give a shit. I feel better than I have in months."

"Amen to that," replied the alto. "You know how people talk about God suddenly coming into them and how wonderful it is? Well, I don't know how anyone could feel any happier than I do right now, and I sure as hell don't think it's the Holy Spirit."

"Yeah," agreed the soprano, "happier and hungrier."

With that, the women went back to judging, but not before they had pocketed the rest of Bobby's entry and left the grand champion ribbon on the empty plate.

Unfortunately, WD overheard the ag man retelling the story at Mary's one morning, and before the day was out, Bobby's crop—what was left of it—had been destroyed. Bobby had wisely planted it on public land, so no one could prove it was his, and the investigation, like so many in the county, was soon dropped.

21

AFTER FINALLY CONVINCING Luke that I was neither drunk nor stoned, but probably suffering from some bad food or a stomach bug, I drove home and went to bed. Still troubled by John's visit and the new realization that the sheriff had probably been tailing me all evening, I laid awake for what seemed like hours before falling asleep.

I awoke to bright sunlight and a ringing phone.

It was Dan Farenbacher, a good friend and the local mortician. A champion of positive thinking, "Digger"—no one remembered who first called him that, but the nickname immediately stuck—always had a calming word or a heartfelt compliment, whether for a grieving widow or a bicycle-pedaling Mormon missionary. But today he sounded hysterical.

"We need to talk, Scooter."

"What about?"

"Just come over to the funeral home as soon as you can. Come in through the back so no one will see you. I'll be in the casket showroom in the basement." He hung up.

Sensing Dan's secrecy, I walked, taking a circuitous route—a technique Norm taught me one night when we were drinking. Although Creekmore was no Prague or Moscow, I made more than the requisite number of twists and turns to throw off anyone who might be following me. The longer route also gave me time to think through Digger's panicky summons.

No matter what theories I came up with, only one rang true: it must involve John's death. Outside of Norm, Bobby, and me, Digger was the only person who knew what really happened—or supposedly happened—to the old rancher. Perhaps John had paid him a heavenly visit as he'd done me. After picturing John popping out of one of the display caskets and scaring poor Digger silly, I quickly moved to the next theory: Shelia Mae had run into Digger in town and, quite naturally, inquired about her father's death and burial.

This was not an unusual question. Digger was known in the western half of the state for his post-death cosmetology. If potential customers had a say in the matter, they gave him the honor of dressing them for their final journey. He had an almost mystic touch when it came to making the dead appear as if they were simply taking an afternoon nap on the couch back home. The clothes, hair, skin tone, and makeup were always just right.

A cousin of mine who worked for Digger one summer while in high school told me the mortician's secret was a small leather notebook with the names of everyone in the county over fifty, and notes about their appearance and what they wore. I'm sure it was simply a professional practice, but after I heard that story, I could never view Dan with the innocence I once had, and I always wondered whether my name was in his notebook, and if so, how he planned to prep me for eternity.

I was speculating on an appropriate outfit as I turned up the alley that ran past the mortuary and glimpsed Sheriff Luke's cruiser speed by on the adjoining street.

Shit.

I sprinted the half-block to the Farenbacher Funeral Home, a large Victorian house, and found Dan in the basement looking gloomier than the roomful of caskets that surrounded him.

He gave me a wan smile, shook my hand, and motioned me to a chair in his office.

"It's been a while, Scooter. I don't think I've talked with you since we held Anna's graveside service and burial here in your family plot. How are you doing?"

"It's been hard. I've reached the point of accepting her death but not her absence. Being a widower is a bitch."

"I'm sure it's hard," he said. "Death is never easy on those still living. Anna was such a beautiful person—and I don't mean just physically, although she was that, too." He paused as if wanting to continue, but unsure if he should. "I felt fortunate to be a part of her service here, Scooter, but I have to admit—and I hope you won't take it the wrong way—when I saw her lying in that casket, I was a bit jealous that I never got to, you know, prepare that lovely—"

"Digger!"

"I don't mean it that way," he said, raising his hands. "What I meant was, I wish I could have made her up—her face, just that beautiful face—for eternity."

"I understand," I said. "I miss that face every day. And just so you know, I miss that body, too."

"I shouldn't have said that," he said, shaking his head. "It wasn't only way beyond the boundaries of good taste but also broke every line of the Undertaker's Code of Ethics." He sighed. "I guess everyone knows I'm a frustrated makeup artist at heart. And given the age of most of my clients, I get very few opportunities to really display my talents."

"So, I've heard. And I've often wondered what you've got written down about me in your little black book."

He looked at me in horror. "How do you know about my book?"

"Your reputation precedes you, Digger. Everyone in five counties knows about your dark artistry."

"Jesus! I didn't know. But I got to tell you, it's a great tool in a small town like this. Do you know—for god's sake you can't repeat this—more than a few vain folks, including several guys you know, have confided to me about how they want to appear in death. And the women: down to the shade of lipstick and eyeliner they want. Seriously."

We both started laughing.

"Someday when we have a bit more time, I'll show you the book. Truth is, I haven't decided on your final look. I'm debating between total asshole and evil clown."

"Either is fine," I said. "Just leave a copy of your notes in my *mystery drawer.*"

"Oh I doubt your daughter will spring for those frills," Digger said, shaking his head. "No matter, I'll just put them in a plastic sandwich bag and drop it in the coffin before I close it."

The mystery drawer was an inside joke. When my mom died, my sister and I, knowing her sometimes pretentious taste and harsh tongue, opted for an expensive cherrywood casket with, as Dan proudly pointed out, a hidden drawer where one could leave notes and mementos.

At the church prior to her funeral, John, a pallbearer, motioned me aside and asked where the drawer was located. "We've all but turned the casket upside down," he said. "But we can't find it." I just shook my head and told him it was a secret and to stop banging on Mom's casket, lest he want her spirit to pay him an angry visit.

"Ah, the infamous mystery drawer," Digger said, his voice now turning serious. "Speaking of which, there's a new mystery making the rounds involving John himself. That's why I asked you to stop by. Seems people are beginning to ask some questions about his death and burial."

"So I've suspected. What have you heard? Did Shelia Mae approach you or was it the damn sheriff?"

"Both, actually, but in separate conversations."

"Say more."

"Earlier this month, Shelia Mae asked to sit down with me. She said she wanted to find out more about her dad's death, since she was unable to come home for the burial. I repeated what I'd told her after he died—the story we'd agreed on. But she wanted to know more details, like how he looked when you brought him in and what kind of urn he was buried in. I tried to be as vague as possible. But I'm not sure she was satisfied with my answers.

"Then last week, the sheriff and that idiot cousin of his dropped by. They said there was a rumor going around—a couple, actually. The first was that John was still alive. According to the story they'd heard—from whom they wouldn't tell me—he moved to Oklahoma and was living with a distant cousin.

"They said the rumor was that John had gotten sideways with some Mexicans who were tied to one of the cartels, or maybe some locals cooking meth. Said he reportedly caught them down by the creek one night and ran them off, but not before confiscating all their product. Apparently, whomever it was threatened revenge, so John up and left town in the middle of the night, after getting us to help him fake his death."

"And the other rumor? I asked.

"The other story they'd heard was that John had died, but not as you guys—"

"*We* guys," I interrupted.

Dan let out a sign. "As *we* had reported. Said they'd heard it wasn't of natural causes, that it might have been foul play or perhaps an accident—you know, maybe someone's gun accidentally went off in the blind. Those things do happen occasionally."

"So, what did you tell them?"

"Exactly what we'd discussed. You guys found John dead in the blind and brought him straight here. I, as acting coroner, examined the body, saw there were no obvious injuries, certainly not a gunshot wound, and pronounced him deceased from natural causes. Luke asked me why I hadn't called in the state police, being that he and WD were in Kansas City at a Chiefs' game. I told them it wasn't necessary—that I'd seen enough dead folks to know the difference between natural causes and blunt trauma or bullet wounds.

"I told them that I called Shelia Mae in Paris, and that she was adamant there would be no autopsy and asked me to take care of all the arrangements, including cremation and burial in the family plot. She'd told me she had been ill, was too weak to travel, and would plan a memorial service when she returned home.

"I told Luke that you, Norm, and Bobby were really shaken up by John's death, but that it was clear he'd been in bad health for some time and just picked an inopportune moment to pass."

"Inopportune for us, maybe," I said, "but it would have been perfect as far as John was concerned."

"I agree, Scooter, but I don't think those two bastards bought my story. Before they left, Luke told me they were going to continue their investigation, and to keep my mouth shut about our conversation."

Shit. Just as I thought. I understood Shelia Mae talking with Dan. But what had the sheriff heard that would pique his suspicion? And what, if anything, had he said to Shel?

"Tell me this, Digger, while it sounds like you stuck to our story, did you possibly say or do anything that might have led them to think you weren't telling the whole truth?"

He thought for a moment. "I don't think it was anything I said. But you know me. I'm the nice guy who likes to help people—make them feel they're in control. I probably came off as defensive. I was nervous—sweating like crazy. Always do around those two. Ever since elementary school. They're bullies. They scare me."

"Yes, they are, my friend. Always have been. And good folks like you are easy marks."

"I know," Dan sighed. "I'm too timid to look them in the eye and tell them they need to fuck off." His eyes flashed. "But just you wait. Sooner or later, they're going to be lying in the next room, just like everyone else. And then, I can bully them back if I choose, extract my pound of flesh. No one sees the east end of a casket, Scooter. How I prepare 'em below the waist is my business."

Dan immediately put his hand up and shook his head. "Sorry. I may be a bit weird, Scooter, but not sick. Admittedly, working on certain folk can lead to some fine fantasizing—cadaver dreams and very warped wishes. But believe me, they go no further."

I shook my head and we both laughed.

"Well, we can't wait for our local crime-fighting duo to die before we deal with them," I said. "If they poke their noses too far into the John Marshall affair, we could be in real trouble."

"I know," Dan said. "We must stop them. But how?"

"For starters, we—you, me, Norm, and Bobby—have to make sure our stories of John's death are aligned. Until we can all talk, don't say a word of this to anyone. No emails, messaging, nothing. Anything we say about this needs to be face-to-face. I need to do some serious thinking. In the meantime, Digger, don't worry yourself silly about this. Stay cool. Just keep fantasizing about your tales from the crypt."

I got up, gave him a big hug, and started to leave. But before going up the stairs, I turned back and smiled. "Pleasant dreams, my friend. Pleasant dreams."

22

ALTHOUGH I LEFT THE FUNERAL HOME more anxious than ever, my conversation with Digger and his recollections of Anna had provided a fragile thread of hope: if John could return from the dead to give me divine insight, why couldn't my late wife?

As soon as I arrived home I jumped in the pickup and drove to the small hilltop cemetery that overlooked Creekmore. Built shortly after the founding of the town in 1860s, it is a history in grass and stone, a place of peaceful familiarity.

I had come here often, even before Anna's death, to walk and reflect among people I had known personally as well as those I'd met through the stories of others. Wandering through this silent subdivision that was home to everyone from city founders to veterans of wars going back more than a century, to homesteaders and freed slaves was great for one's soul and sensibilities. Accompanied by a good cigar and red Solo cup of scotch, an evening stroll to visit family and friends out here put life in perspective far faster and less costly than fifty minutes of professional therapy.

But today I went directly to Anna's grave, next to my parents, and knelt before it.

Hey Anna. It's me. Scooter.

I hope you're doing okay. Lucy and I are fine. We . . . I miss you. A lot. I could really use your advice right now. I don't know how much you've heard—or seen. I don't know how it works up there, or wherever you are. But I've gotten myself into a bit of a pickle.

If you've bumped into John, you know the whole story about how he died, my involvement in his death, and what has happened since. About that I can honestly say I did the right thing . . . at least I think I did. You know my cowardly conscience. But, yes, I think I did what I should have to help him.

His daughter is another story. I don't know if you ever met Shelia Mae. She was that friend of mine growing up who moved to Paris. The one in the picture above my workbench. The one you . . . disfigured? Well, if John hasn't already told you, she's back in Creekmore, and we've reconnected.

No, it's nothing like that. Well, I guess it could become like that. But I never cheated on you when you were alive, and I'm not sure I could now. Oh hell, what am I saying. She's gay.

But I really like her as a friend. And you know about my past relationships with women who were "just friends," especially when I got lonely and needy, which I still am most of the time. Nothing's going to happen like that now. At least I don't think so.

Anyhow, that's not the issue. The problem is this: she doesn't know the real story behind John's death. And John swore me to secrecy. Part of me knows I should tell her. But another part of me is afraid to because I don't want to lose her friendship.

I'm a basket case over this, and I could use your advice—that pragmatic voice that I too often ignored when you were here. I know, because John has visited me more than once, that people can communicate from the grave. Yes, that sounds weird and gross, but anyhow . . . if you could somehow stop by and visit, even for a couple of minutes, it sure would be nice.

That said, I understand you had enough of my weirdness long before you died and are probably ecstatic not to have to deal with it anymore. But, well . . . I miss you. And I still love you.

I sat there, staring at her tombstone for probably an hour, hoping that she would appear. When the noon whistle sounded and she hadn't, I decided she was a no-show, and drove to Mary's for a burger.

23

I WAS HOPING Norm or Bobby would also show up for lunch, so I could fill them in on my conversation with Digger. Luckily, my hunch was right. By the time I got there they were already seated and ordering. But sitting in the next booth was Luke and his cousin. I greeted the lawmen with all the faux friendliness I could muster and sat down with my with partners in crime.

Before either could speak, I gave them a stern stare and put a finger to my lips. I pulled out my phone and began tapping furiously. Finished, I looked up at them, winked and smiled.

"My daughter just sent me some great pictures of the twins," I said, handing them my phone and giving them an icy stare. "Just look at these cuties."

Sheriff asking questions about John's death. Grilled Dan. Thinks he's alive or was victim of foul play. We must s talk—privately. I HAVE A PLAN!

"Damn cute little bastards," said Norm.

"Yeah" chimed Bobby. "I bet they're a handful, running around like two-year-olds do, getting into things they shouldn't. I bet their mom spends all day running around keeping them from poking their little fingers in wall sockets and—"

"Wonderful pictures," Norm said, grabbing the phone from Bobby and handing it back to me. "You must be very proud."

"I am," I said. "Very proud."

At that point Mary sidled over, aimed a few disparaging comments—excerpts from her standard repertoire—at Norm and Bobby, welcomed me warmly, and took my order. When she left, we stared blankly at each other until I typed a second message.

Ask me about hunting and tell me you'd like to go out with me this afternoon, given the beautiful fall weather.

"Hey," said Bobby, reading the message, "what a fucking gorgeous day. You going hunting this afternoon?"

From there, the conversation flowed naturally, with me telling them that I was indeed going hunting, and asking if they would like to come along, and them replying that, yes, they would love to.

After several minute of mindless banter comparing our shooting prowess, Norm abruptly changed the subject and lowered his voice. "Have you seen Shelia Mae lately?" he asked. "Understand she may not be going back to Paris. Has she said anything to you about that?"

"Only that she's tired of Paris and is thinking about making a change. And she really misses the ranch."

"Must, if she's willing to give up the Louvre for the local historical museum," Bobby said.

"Well," I said, "sometimes you have to go home again, even if you think you can't. I certainly have been in her position. Still am. Love the city. Need its noise and hubbub to drown out the noise and hubbub in my head. At the same time, it's easy to OD on urban life—the speed and seeming superficiality it offers. It's then, when I begin to lose focus on the things that matter, that I have to come back here, if even for just a few days."

What I didn't say was that, try as I might, when I did come home, I could never keep the ghosts—both the virtuous and the vile—from tagging along. My marriages and other mistakes, the regrets and guilt, were all there, piled in the backseat of my brain wherever I went. Even now, what I really wanted was a solitary hunt with Buck.

But I couldn't go back on the plan I'd hatched. We had to throw the law off our trail.

As we left Mary's, I asked the sheriff and his cousin if they wanted to join us, knowing they would decline. "We need some blockers who are good shots, and far as I know, you two are the best around," I said, with all the sincerity I could muster.

WD lunged for the bait. "Sure, Scooter, we'd love to go. It'll be fun. We can give you some shooting tips, too."

"Easy partner," the sheriff cut in, "you have a stack of reports due today, and I have some stolen livestock to chase down. Besides, these fellas might embarrass us. They're better than they let on. Have fun boys. Bring us home some bacon."

24

WITHIN AN HOUR, we were jammed in Bobby's pickup tearing across the county, trying to find a long-forgotten honey hole in the next county over that we'd once hunted years ago, while at the same time making sure we weren't being followed.

It took us another hour to finally find it, but it gave me time to brief the guys on what I'd learned from Dan.

"So, what do you think sparked Luke's interest?" Norm asked.

"I don't know. I know he was pissed at Dan for signing the death certificate instead of first calling in the state police or waiting until he got back from the Chiefs game."

"Yeah," said Norm, "and he was suspicious from the get-go about how we handled things—going straight to Digger, not requesting emergency assistance, driving John back here ourselves laid out in one of our camo-colored coffin-blinds instead of calling a local mortuary for transportation."

"But Dan is the acting coroner," Bobby said. "He had every right to sign the death certificate."

"Not when the person is still alive," I reminded him. "Let's face it, Luke isn't a fan of ours, hasn't been since we were little kids. And for good reason. Remember when we were in Cub Scouts, Bobby? The pinewood derby in the church basement?"

"Yeah, I won."

"Do you remember how you won?"

"By super-gluing the wheels on Luke's car?"

"Exactly. And Norm, what about the high school prom in the gym, when Luke so carefully crafted that river out of plastic irrigation liner?"

"I remember it really set off our "Return to Shangri-La" theme, it and the paper lanterns."

"But then, Luke's river leaked and flooded the gym, ruining the basketball court. Remember? And why did the stream run dry? Because you and Bobby cut holes it in."

"Okay, okay," Norm said. "You made your point. But that finger you've been waving has your own shit on it, too. Your relationship with Luke has always been sketchy at best. Especially in high school."

"He was a jock and I wasn't. Jocks pushed wimps like me around. It's the natural order of things. And it's also natural for wimps to surreptitiously seek occasional revenge.

"Like gluing Luke's football cleats to his locker before the homecoming game?" Bobby asked. "And squeezing jalapeño juice in his jock strap? Remember? He could hardly stand still long enough to be crowned homecoming king."

"Yes," said Norm, "and remember who was queen?"

How could I forget. Luke and Shelia Mae started going steady the night of their coronation. It had been a long time since I'd thought of that horrible October evening. Not only was I a wimp, I was also a geek, especially when it came to girls. Unlike many of my friends who had steady girlfriends to take to the homecoming dance, I'd never had a date.

Norm and Bobby tried—sincerely, I think—to help me find someone. But I turned down every girl they suggested, even a couple of cuties who, looking back, would probably have loved to go out with me. The problem wasn't them. It was me. Fearing rejection, I couldn't work up the nerve to ask them.

Which is what I got when I finally screwed my courage to ask

Shelia Mae, who unbeknown to me, had started dating Luke. Her sweet rebuff stung, but not as bad as the one I got from him after school the next day.

So, after sabotaging his football gear, I spent the night of the homecoming dance at the local hangout on Main Street playing pinball by myself. I knew even then how pathetic I looked, awkwardly dancing with the noisy machine, shoving, twisting, and performing other strange gyrations in an attempt to shape the ball's trajectory down the incline. But it was far better than sitting in a loud, dark gym, watching Shelia Mae and Luke make out.

"Scooter?" It was Bobby, jerking me out of my reverie. We were parked at the entrance to the abandoned farmstead we were going to hunt. How long we'd been there I didn't know, but from the concerned looks, I assumed my mind had temporarily left the premises.

"Jesus," Norm said, "snap out of it. It's clear, from your sudden onset of melancholy, that we have more than one loose head to worry about. We can't deal with the first—John's—until you get yours screwed on straight."

"Yeah," said Bobby, "it's also clear you still have a thing for Shelia Mae, which is messing with your loopy logic in dealing with this whole issue of John. On top of that, I have a hunch her old high school boyfriend has similar feelings for his homecoming queen and would like nothing more than to expose you as the creep he thinks you are."

"Thanks, guys," I said, getting out of the truck to open the fence. "I think you've just solved our problem. Let's bury John's skull in Luke's backyard. Better yet, let's put it in the trunk of his cruiser. Just picture the look on his face when hears it rolling around and goes back to investigate?"

A smile began to play on Norm's face. "Scooter, as crazy as that sounds, you may be onto something."

For the next hour we walked the tall grass and deep draws, discussing how to sneak John's skull into the trunk of the cruiser and other farfetched options for dealing with the brewing crisis. Buck worked hard, flushing three large quail coveys and the occasional pheasant—none of which we shot, consumed as we were with the problem at hand.

"We're not teenagers, and this is no prank," I finally said, stopping at a deep ravine. "John is dead. We didn't kill him, but we helped him plan his death—or thought we did—including faking it to cover up what really happened. And we lied about it. Then, a year later, Buck finds John's skull spitting distance from his own house, a couple of hundred miles from where I left him, and where he supposedly died. Then Shelia Mae flies in from Paris and begins asking questions.

"Truth is, we should never have honored the old man's final request given how weird it was. But we did, and now we have to own up to it."

"Honorable as that sounds, Scooter, it's a machoistic, narcissistic bullshit plan," Norm said. "Think about it. We do that and everyone suffers. We'll get arrested. Shelia Mae will be heartbroken and spend the rest of her life blaming herself. And all of us will be run out of Creekmore.

"Norm's right," Bobby said. "What's done is done. Trying to undo it now will only create a shitload of trauma and trouble for everyone involved. Besides, as we've all agreed, it was what John wanted. At least for him we did the honorable thing."

"I hear what you're saying, guys, but I personally feel responsible for the whole affair. It's just another Scooter fuck-up to add to an already long list."

Norm walked over and put his hand on my shoulder. "Don't do this. First of all, you did not fuck up anything. Second, and please don't get mad at me for saying this, I think this whole *affair*, as you're calling it goes beyond John's death. Am I right?"

I stepped back and gave him a hard look.

"What are you saying, Norm?"

"I'm worried that your concern for Shelia Mae goes way beyond any guilt she may be carrying because she was not with her dad at the end."

Norm's comment, truthful as it was, stung. I said nothing.

"I think," he continued, "that deep down—subliminally—you have reconnected with Shelia Mae in an . . ." he paused, searching for the right word, "in an emotional way. Perhaps the fear of losing that newfound connection is distorting your thinking. Maybe—"

"Shut up, Norm. You too, Bobby. What the hell do you know about my so-called emotions anyway? Come on, Buck, let's go home. We're done hunting."

I turned and headed toward the truck. But, once again, Buck was nowhere in sight. I called for him, hit the beeper on his collar, but there was no sign nor sound of him.

Shit. Even my best friend has turned against me.

We walked through the deep, brush-filled draw we'd been hunting, searching and calling until almost sundown, before heading back to the truck.

"I'll come back tomorrow, guys, no use looking any more tonight. Let's go home." I stormed off, pissed and depressed. The disappearance of a bird dog—even a mediocre one—is heartbreaking. Coupled with Norm's accusations of my involvement with Shel, it yanked me back into a black mood. By the time I could make out the truck in the distance, I was on the verge of going ballistic.

Then, suddenly, a wet, furry snout bumped my hand and brought me out of my darkness. Buck, apparently fed up with our bickering and bad shooting, had at some point simply strolled back to the truck to wait for our return. Tail wagging, it was clear he was as happy to see us as we were to see him.

"Good dog," said Bobby, patting his head. "At least this time you didn't bring a zombie back with you."

25

ON THE DRIVE HOME, we stopped for dinner in what in its prime had been a vibrant German Catholic farming community. A small bar, covered with Coors and Budweiser signs welcoming hunters, stood a few feet from the highway, which also served as the town's main street. Across the street, an imposing gothic church of native limestone stood guard over the dying village.

The silence that enveloped us as we got out of the truck was suddenly shattered by a cattle-filled semi that roared out of the darkness and just as quickly disappeared down the two-lane asphalt ribbon and into the night.

The bar's interior, like the exterior, was sparse and worn, but the atmosphere was warm and welcoming. The barkeep, a thirty-something woman also sparse and worn but in an attractive way, smiled and offered a friendly greeting. So did the two patrons sitting at the bar. One, in faded jeans, a torn Carhart jacket, and a gimme cap from a local feedlot, was clearly a farmer and rancher. The other, a young African American in a clerical collar, we took for the local priest.

Both turned their attention to us and began launching the usual questions: where were we from? How was the hunting? Could they buy us a beer? While Lu Ann, the bartender, prepared our burgers and fries, Father Mark and Farmer Frank served us beer and joined us at our table.

"Creekmore, eh?" Frank asked. "You know the sheriff there? He's my nephew."

"Know him well," Bobby said. "Went to school with him. We used to pal around when we were younger. Did some stupid things as kids together. But he turned out to be a good friend and a fine man."

"Yeah," said Norm. "A good lawman, too. Decent and fair."

Frank shot them a questioning look. "Hmm. Either he has a twin, or we must be talking about two different people. The one I know is a pompous dick."

"Well," Norm started, leaning in and smiling, "Sheriff Luke can be a bit—"

"A bit of a stickler for going by the book," I interrupted, stomping the heel of my boot on Norm's toe. "We certainly get what you're saying."

"I believe he's a good man who, unfortunately, has a bone up his butt," Father Mark said. "I met him once while I was down visiting Father Timothy. Within seconds of being introduced, he started teasing the two of us about being 'pervert priests.' It was all I could do not to replace that bone with the crucifix I was wearing."

He chugged the rest of his beer, then slowly put done the mug, looked toward the ceiling, and asked God for forgiveness.

"Father," Norm said, "forgive *me*, but are you really a priest?"

The young priest laughed. "Yes, my son, I am, although admittedly, I don't always act like one, especially in the local tavern."

"Well," I said, "I can certainly see why you are friends with Father Tim."

He laughed. "Yes. He and I go way back. Obviously you know him."

"Yes," I said. "Tim's a friend and trusted advisor."

"You one of us?" Father Mark asked.

"No. A fallen Baptist."

"Southern or Northern?"

"Northern on the outside, but with a strong post-Civil War Southern flavor inside."

"Sort of a Christian Oreo," Norm added.

"Should I leave now?" Mark asked with a straight face.

"If that's your parish," Norm said, pointing his thumb at the church across the highway, "then you've clearly learned to deal with pesky White Protestants like Scooter."

"It's been a heavy cross to carry," Mark said. "But the Lord has given me strength."

"The Lord and a few outspoken parishioners," Frank piped in. "Hell, the first Easter the good father officiated I was scared to come to church. Afraid someone might have nailed him to the cross."

"Frank!" It was Lu Ann, who was shaking her head as she pulled our fries out of the hot grease. "Don't say things like that. People will think we're all ignorant rednecks."

"Well," Frank said, "some of us, present company excluded, still are."

"As the Holy Book says," intoned Mark, "blessed are the fearful, the stupid, and the bigoted, for they shall be cut from my will."

"Amen," Norm said. "I don't recognize that particular version, Father, but I'd love to get a signed copy."

Amid laughter, Lu Ann brought out our burgers and joined us at the table, at which point the mood quickly morphed into that of a family dinner. We talked about our kids, our communities, falling crop prices, the rural drug crisis. Shortly before we left, Frank, who was a fourth-generation farmer and rancher and far more well-read and cultured than I assumed given my urban bias, raised a question.

"Did any of you boys know an old rancher down your way by the name of John Marshall? He was a good friend of mine who died about a year ago."

A chill shot through me. It was not that Frank knew John. People are sparsely planted across the Great Plains, but their roots go wide and deep. It was the questioning tone of his voice.

"Oh yeah," Norm quickly chimed in, knowing how thin the ice on which we were standing was and worried that I might unintentionally break through. "Everyone knew John. A wonderful man. Wonderful family. It was a big loss."

"Do you know *how* he died?" Frank asked. "I'd heard he had a heart attack hunting geese. But just last week, at our family's Thanksgiving dinner, Luke said something about possible foul play."

Norm shook his head. "That's an old rumor. Not sure where it started or why the sheriff continues to spread it. Hell, for all I know he started it. But it's not true. Not a word of it. We—the three of us—know, because we were with John when he passed. Sitting in a goose blind about three hours south of here when he went. Nodded off and never woke up. He'd been sick, had cancer I suspect and a weak heart, and wanted to go on what he said would be his last hunt. Very sad."

"Sad," Frank said, "but not a bad way to go either."

"No," agreed Bobby. "And frankly we were glad we were there with him."

"Well," Frank said, "I appreciate you sharing that with me. It makes me feel a lot better. I didn't think anyone had a reason or the guile to do anything bad to John. I just wish my nephew would grow up, do his job, and quit pretending he's some hot-shot TV detective."

"Don't be too hard on Luke," Norm said, trying to end the conversation on a positive note. "Being sheriff in a small berg like Creekmore is a tough job. Long periods of boredom with nothing to do but round up stray cattle and drive drunks home, and then rare moments of tragedy, like having to tell some young mom with two kids that her worthless high school sweetheart hubby is brain-dead from a meth overdose."

On that happy note, we said our goodbyes, paid our tab, and headed home.

We were halfway to Creekmore before anyone spoke. It was Bobby. "Guys, I've been thinking about our earlier conversation. We do have a problem with the John thing. And it goes beyond any relationship Scooter might have with his daughter. Look, we all have a soft spot in our hearts for Shelia Mae. She was one of our gang. She is all that remains of the Marshall family. And her life has not been a bed of roses. Exciting, yeah, and exotic, but also—at least in the eyes of the folks back home—weird and embarrassing.

"We have to make sure she isn't caught in the middle of this and attacked and smeared more than she already has been. She's a victim here. We have to protect her. And to do that we have to come clean. We hold the truth. We lied, faked a death, and broke a law or two in the process. And the man we did that for isn't likely to come back from the grave and testify in our behalf."

If only they knew, I thought, *and if only he would.*

"To make matters worse," Bobby continued, "the sheriff, no matter what you think of him, is like a dog with a bone. If we don't fess up, he's going to pursue this with everything in his power until he finds out what really happened, and that includes harassing and humiliating Shelia Mae."

We must have driven another thirty miles before anyone spoke. In addition to what Bobby had said, I was thinking about the evening we'd just shared with Lu Ann, Frank, and Father Mark. There was something in that small roadside tavern besides greasy burgers, cold beer, and the decades' old aroma of tobacco and booze. There was a sense of family and friendship, humility and hope, struggle and survival. We'd all left with a little less cynicism in our hearts, a little more tolerance in our thoughts, and a little more faith in our souls— not the framed-up faith of our particular brand of god, but faith in plain people like ourselves.

"What are you thinking, Scooter?" Norm asked. "You've been awfully quiet ever since we left the tavern."

"That life is strange. Good, for the most part, but weird as hell."

"And . . .?"

"And I don't know where to go with that. Or maybe I should say, I don't know where the heck it's taking me."

Bobby and Norm both nodded their heads.

"Ain't it the truth," Bobby said.

"Amen, brother," Norm replied.

26

I SLEPT SOUNDLY that night and woke with a clear head, the first in many days. Rather than question my sunny mood, I plunged into creating a plan of how we should move forward in methodical, practical fashion, to address the *John problem*, as we had begun to call it.

On an old chalkboard I found in the basement, I began diagraming a strategy for addressing several aspects of the problem, including:

John's plan: His Death—Cover-up—His Skull—Investigation—Shelia Mae

I started to add John's posthumous visits to the list but decided against it. As realistic as his appearances were, I continued to question his spectral legitimacy. Then, I listed the names of all the people involved, starting with John and including everyone from the phony shaman, to Shelia Mae, to the sheriff.

I spent the morning charting what each knew, their role, if any, in his death, who else they might have talked to, and how they would respond if questioned and the truth came out. I had just begun listing potential strategies—from lying, to hiring a good lawyer, to publicly laying out the entire story—when the phone rang.

It was Father Tim. "Scooter, how are you, my friend? I heard you were in town and have been meaning to drop by. Hear you had dinner last night with a padre compadre of mine."

"A what? Who?"

"Father Mark. He called me this morning and said you and he had shared a burger and beer at his parish tavern. That must have been a bit of a culture shock for an urban cowboy like yourself."

"Uh, yeah." I suddenly felt slightly untethered. Why was Tim calling me? Certainly not merely to chat about his friend. "Seems like a really nice guy, though if he hadn't been wearing his collar, I wouldn't have known he was a holy man. A real potty mouth. You might suggest he start swearing in Latin so as not to offend his flock."

Tim laughed. "Yes, Mark does put on a foul face, especially with the unwashed who might be offended by a more pious tone. Hey, do you have time to talk?"

"Sure, what's up?"

Tim paused. "I'd like to sit down with you and chat. You know, an informal ministerial visit of sorts. We haven't really talked in a long time. Not since John's death. I thought we could catch up on the past year. I might even be able to provide you a bit of moral support—that is, if you still need some."

Moral support? What had Father Mark told him? What does he know?

"Sure. Want me to come over to the church?"

"No!"

"You want to come over here?"

"How about we drive to Dodge for dinner tonight? I'll pick you up at seven."

I forgot my strategy planning and spent the rest of the afternoon thinking about why the good father was so adamant about meeting with me. We'd been friends a long time, but there was an urgent tone to his sudden invitation that troubled me.

Promptly at seven, an old, battered pickup pulled up in front of the house. It clearly wasn't Father Tim's official nondescript, tan Ford sedan, so I ignored it. Then my phone rang.

"It's me," Tim whispered. "I'm out front. You ready?"

I walked out. The car was idling, but the headlights were off. When I opened the door, a stranger greeted me—someone with Father Tim's voice but decked out in full country western garb—boots, shirt, jacket, even a bolo tie with a silver clasp and a cowboy hat.

"What the hell is all this?"

"Just get in and close the door."

I did as I was told, and Tim slowly pulled away, driving several blocks before, after a careful scan in the rearview mirror, turning on the headlights."

"Hey bro," he said, grinning and gripping my hand, "it's been a while. I've missed you. How are you doing?"

"What's with the old clunker and country look?" I asked, baffled by the bizarre disguise. "Are you running from the law?"

"In a way, that's exactly what I'm doing, Scooter," he said, scanning the mirror again before pulling onto the highway and suddenly putting the pedal to the floor.

"Father, do you have a problem?"

"No, my son, *we* have a problem. There's a rumor going around that you and your local buddies may be in trouble with the law. And after a call from Brother Mark this morning, I'm worried that it might be true, and that you might be the ringleader."

I said nothing.

"Don't play dumb, Scooter. You know the rumor. You heard it last night from a rancher friend of John Marshall—Frank, I think his name was. Mark said it sounded like something only a small town could brew up, probably after watching too many dark crime shows. But while your pals were quick to laugh it off, you sat there with a troubled look and said nothing. That made him think there actually might be something to it. Which is why he called me, and why I reached out to you."

For the next thirty minutes I lied through my teeth. In a calm, sincere voice, I told him the now often repeated tale of Death in the Goose Blind. It wasn't easy. I gripped the handle above the door tightly as I recalled the story, sweating more with each little lie. But given it was dark, and Tim was keeping his eyes on the road, I was confident he believed me.

We stopped at a small cantina in Little Mexico, the city's Latino neighborhood. The only Anglos, we went to a small corner table by the bar. In flawless Spanish, learned during a stint in Latin America, Tim ordered for both of us.

When the waitress left, he smiled and shook his head. "Your story makes perfect sense Scooter, and I'd like to believe you. "But I'm not sure I do."

Shit.

The sin of lying was one of the first rules of the faith that Widow Blackwell and her squad of fearsome fanatics, wielding their big black Bibles as emotional cudgels, beat into us as little children. True, their pedagogy sucked. But, leaving sin and Hell out of the equation, honesty is a fundamentally sound concept.

Still, being called out by a holy man for lying prompted an amygdala-sparking reaction. "You asshole," I began, before my neocortex wrestled back control. "You pious . . . you . . . Father, that hurt. I'm not sure what to say."

Tim reached over and put his hand on mine. "Scooter, you're a good person. A good friend. But you're a very bad liar." He laughed. "I can read you like an open book. Tell me what happened to John. I won't tell a soul. It's just you confessing to the parish priest in one of the best Mexican restaurants outside Mexico."

I jerked my hand back, glared, and took a deep breath.

"Sorry," he said, "'confessing' was a bad choice of words. Knowing you, I seriously doubt you murdered John, hacked him to pieces, and hid them in your freezer."

"Not exactly," I said, after a pause, "although I do have his skull on my mantle."

For the next two hours over a wonderful dinner and a pitcher of margaritas, I told Tim the truth. I told him about helping John carry out what I thought was his own plan for dying. I told him about the story we concocted and how we pulled it off. I told him about finding John's skull. Over flan and Mexican coffee, I told him of my conversations with and concern for Shelia Mae, omitting the more personal parts. Finally, I told him of Luke's growing interest in the subject.

When I'd finished, Tim smiled and shook his head. "You, Norm,

Bobby, and Digger are amazing. John was so lucky to have had you as friends. What the three of you did was downright noble. Not exactly normal, but noble nonetheless."

"Tell that to the sheriff."

"Ah, Luke. I like to think his motives are pure, but sometimes I wonder."

"Pure or not—and I'm not so sure they are—he's going to cause a lot of hurt if he blows this open."

"Agreed. But how are we going to stop him?"

"We? Father, you need to stay as far away from this as you can."

"Unfortunately, Scooter, the sheriff already paid me a visit. Grilled me at length. And I know for a fact that he's also talked to our good friend, Brother Leon."

Shit.

Brother Leon was the current pastor of the First Baptist Church of Creekmore, which, considering the aging membership, was soon likely to also find itself the town's last Baptist church. A retired car salesman, Leon was a sincere, well-meaning man of faith who tended to his flock as if they were his own children. Sadly, his faith was of the tribal variety—distrusting of other tribes and those of us who had fled his to find our own.

An outsider, Leon had been called to our little church by a handful of elderly deacons, all men, who had run off the church's first woman pastor after she had the balls to tell them that God was most likely both male and female, and that the female part most likely was highly pissed at them for their continued belief that the church was better off in the hands of men.

Brother Leon saw his calling as a chance to save a community of believers that had been drifting slowly toward the shoals of Hell. His brand of nationalistic, hellfire homiletics linking conservative Christian values with those of the far right and claiming both were ordained got mixed reviews: a few Methodists decided to become Baptists, and an equal number of Baptists found a new home a couple of blocks over, in the Methodist church.

Despite Leon's preaching, for a long time we continued attending church when we were in town, even though more than once Anna had to hold me down to keep me from rising and launching into an angry rebuke of every evil, stupid thing he said. Yet as much as

I would have liked to quit coming, I couldn't bring myself to walk out on the dwindling but committed faithful that still came together every Sunday—many from that community of saints who first shaped my spiritual, cultural, and world views.

True, there were those, like Widow Blackwell, who fostered in me feelings of guilt and unworthiness that decades and thousands of dollars in counseling fees and failed to erase. But there also were the ones like John and Ruthie, who gave me a sense of worth and purpose and who instilled in me the freedom to shape my own faith, not one dictated by fables and fear and the need to control others. And no matter how they came at their faith, or what they thought of me now, they earnestly cared and meant well.

Then, on a Sunday when I counted less than thirty congregants, average age pushing eighty, and over half using walkers, wheelchairs, or canes, I began to think it was time to move on. Brother Leon's sermon, a lengthy rant about gays, heathen city folk, and godless socialists, sealed the deal. I wanted to storm the pulpit and point out that Christ himself was a socialist, but thought better of it, and when the alter call came, I quietly walked out.

One morning a few days later, I happened to run into Leon as I left the post office. "Brother Scooter," he said, giving me a full-on bear hug, "great to see you in church. I trust you found my message yesterday helpful in your struggle with the darker angels, who, I'm sure, assault you daily."

I pulled away and stared hard at him, all the while trying to restrain Buck, who was not a happy dog.

"What the hell are you talking about?"

He looked at me with confusion and fear in his eyes. But a deep, cleansing breath or a quick prayer—I couldn't tell which—seemed to restore his confidence. Standing as tall as he could, he grabbed both my hands tightly and smiled.

"My friend, although you've yet to realize it, you are one of Creekmore's most . . ." here he faltered, "most legendary sons, the proverbial prodigal son, who as a young man turned your back on your home, family, and faith, and ran to the city where, you thought, you could live a depraved and debauched life of wicked pleasure. Am I not correct?"

Stunned, I again pulled back. "Buck," I said, kneeling and trying to calm my now growling partner, "guess we really are back in Kansas after all."

"What did you say?" Leon asked, clearly missing the context of my comment.

"I was talking to my dog. What I told him was to bite you in the crotch should you ever touch me again without my permission."

Confusion returned to the reverend's face.

"What I'm telling you," I said, "is that in the future, you should keep your vile preaching to yourself, that you should never ever give me more than a polite handshake, and that you should go back to the parsonage and take a good look in the mirror at your sorry, misguided soul."

With that, Buck and I walked off, leaving Brother Leon and two townspeople who had overheard the conversation staring and speechless.

It was not one of my better moments of grace. My verbal smackdown felt good for about thirty seconds before regret set in. Brother Leon was a good man. All he wanted was to save me from myself and protect his flock from rabid wolves like me. He wasn't like some folks I knew, who used their faith as a personal club, belittling and condemning others—pissing on those around them so that they alone, or so they liked to think, could bask in the golden grace of their personal "savior."

I knew I should go back and apologize. But I didn't. Nor had I ever returned to church.

Now, I wished I had. I didn't think Leon had any firsthand knowledge of John's death. Nor would he consciously throw me under the bus, even if he did. But the sheriff was just smart and sneaky enough to get a statement from him, which if edited or taken out of context, could be used against me.

"So," I asked Father Tim, "what do we do now?"

"Maybe it would be best if you went back to Texas and let things die down a bit. You know, out of sight, out of mind."

"I could," I said. "But that might look suspicious, and I'm not sure it would end the investigation, not as long as Shelia Mae continues to hang around—unless we convince her to return to Paris, which, from what she says, is not happening any time soon."

"Probably not," he agreed. "But there is one other possibility.

What if you just told her the truth? Leveled with her. Don't you think she'd understand? Face it, Scooter, you're in possession of property that belongs to her. At some point, you have to return John's skull."

I looked at him blankly. *Why*, I thought, *doesn't he and everyone else get it? Why can't they understand my dilemma?*

"Scooter, he continued, this time with his hand on my shoulder in full-on priestly mode, "you just told me you are in possession of the last remaining piece of John's earthly life, a holy relic of sorts. You can't just leave it your mantelpiece or give it to Buck to chew on."

"If it matters, he already has."

"I figured as much," he said, shaking his head. "But seriously, we have to find a proper eternal resting place for it. And only Shelia Mae can rightly make that decision."

He's right, I thought. *But I'm not ready to tell her the truth—no more than she is ready to hear it.*

27

ON THE DRIVE HOME we continued to ponder the mystery of how John got from Oklahoma back to the ranch. We speculated on Ricky Running Bull and whether he was real or simply a mythical decoy John created to throw us off his trail. We discussed the odds of Buck retrieving a human skull while looking for a dead bird. We reviewed what I'd discovered along the creek, and what it said— or didn't—about John's apparent death on his own ranch. But we avoided discussing the implications of the discoveries.

We could just see the lights of Creekmore on the horizon when I sensed we'd picked up an unwanted hitchhiker. I would like to say it was John, flying in for a counseling session with me and Father Tim. But no. Curled up next to Buck was Winston Churchill's infamous Black Dog—depression's doppelganger.

He got out with me when Tim dropped us off, and although Buck growled and tried to chase him off, he slipped inside before I could shut the door.

I poured a rather large scotch, neat and considered leaving one for the Black Dog or John, should he drop by, thinking it might mellow either of them, minimizing their unsetting natures.

John never showed. But Black Dog brought his usual bag of seriously bizarre nightmares, ending any thought of a good night's sleep. I was up at four that morning and spent the next three hours staring at the skull above the dark fireplace.

So, John, what the fuck am I supposed to do now? What spiritual elixir would you recommend, given your lofty perspective? Now's not the time to get all tight-lipped or, in your case, lockjawed. Speak up, man. Tell me what I should do. Should I drive out to your lovely daughter's and tell her the whole story? Or maybe just sneak over, put your damn skull on the front porch, ring the doorbell and run like hell? You got me into this mess. Show me a little mercy and get me the fuck out. Please.

Silence. And the realization that I was pleading with a forlorn, faceless *objet 'de art,* begging this utterly inanimate relic to find its voice and tell me what to do. Suddenly, I jumped up, grabbed the skull, and flung it across the room. Then I fell back into the chair and wept.

Minutes later, I heard the now familiar *bonk.* In front of me sat Buck, who had recovered the skull and placed it at my feet. I gave him a hug and put the skull, no worse for wear, back on the mantle.

Although I felt better, I worried that if I didn't act quickly, the emotional undertow I was in might blossom into a full-blown tsunami, the likes of which I hadn't experienced since my stint at the funny farm years earlier. But as anyone caught in the tide of depression knows, extricating oneself often defies logic, which is in short supply at such times. It's much easier to simply wallow in self-pity and despair. Which probably explains why, at that point, I went back to bed and stayed there the rest of the day.

––––––––––––

The sun was setting when I finally rose. I felt much better, but knew I needed some human interaction to pull me back to shore. My first thought was to call Shelia Mae. But I realized the folly of such a move almost as soon as her image flashed in my mind. Instead, I called Norm and suggested we get together for dinner.

"Why don't you come out to my place," Norm said. "I'll ask Bobby to come over and . . ." here he paused, "how about you bring Father Tim along?"

"Why?"

"I think you know why," Norm said flatly. "Understand the two of you went to dinner and confession last night."

"I thought confession was between the sinner, the priest, and God."

"Not in Creekmore."

Shit, I wondered, *who is spreading these Troubled Tales of Scooter? Who else has heard them? Has anyone not?*

28

DINNER WAS NOT the social distraction I'd hoped for. The venison stew was exquisite, as was the Spanish red we washed it down with. But the conversation quickly turned into an intervention, of which I was the honoree.

Norm and Bobby already had discussed *the problem* and had devised a plan of their own: I should put the skull back where I'd found it. Then, I should meet Shelia Mae at a neutral, but public site, preferably at church or Mary's, and politely announce in a voice that could be overheard by parishioners or diners that I had to get back to Dallas on business. After which, I should leave town.

"It needs to be a warm, friendly parting," Norm said, "casual, relaxed, but not too warm. Nothing that hints of intimacy––"

"Or of guilt or intrigue," added Bobby.

"How about I just walk up and bitch-slap her in front of the entire Creekmore First Baptist congregation next Sabbath morning?" I said. "Or publicly out her in a full-page ad in the *Creekmore Clarion*? What you're asking me to do is hide the evidence, renounce a friendship, and then just walk out, leaving the wreckage of my misdeeds behind. Sounds kind of cowardly, don't you think?

"It's a plan that protects everyone," Norm said. "Besides, you need to walk away from the Shelia Mae thing and—"

"Protects, but also deceives," Tim said. "And in the process, provides no real closure for Shelia Mae—or us, for that matter. I agree that Scooter should head back to Dallas until this thing dies down. But before leaving, he needs to tell Shelia Mae the truth."

For the next hour, the three argued, intensely debating the issues and alternatives I had been batting around since the day I discovered John's skull. The only thing we all seemed to agree on was that I needed to get out of town, the sooner the better.

At some point, I couldn't take it any longer. I shook my head, tried to smile, and got up to leave. "Thanks for all the unsolicited advice, guys. Seriously, you've offered up some good options to think about. I'll sleep on it. Okay?" I turned and walked out. Sensing they'd crossed that very fine line between advising and annoying, they didn't stop me.

I was back on the old creek road, roaring through the turns as if it were Les Mans, having one of those angry I-should-have-said conversations with myself, when I saw the flashing red and blue lights. I pulled over. This time both the sheriff and WD got out of their cruiser and slowly approached my pickup, hands on their weapons.

"Sorry, guys. Was I speeding?"

"You sure are spending a lot of time racing up and down this road," Luke said, ignoring my question. "You doing some after-hours hunting? No? Maybe scoring a little dope, or hurrying to a late-night tryst with that girlfriend of yours?"

"Yeah," WD chimed in, "you wouldn't be the first hippy or meth-head we've busted out here. It's where all you druggies come." He paused. "Though this would be our first tryst bust, right Sheriff? I don't think much of that has come into the county yet."

"Shut up, WD," Luke snapped, shaking his head. "I'm talking about hooking up, you idiot. Getting it on. Sex. From what I know about Scooter, that's his drug of choice."

"Oh," said WD, the dim light behind his eyes suddenly switching on, "you mean Shelia Mae."

The mention of Luke's high-school sweetheart clearly stung him. "For the last time, WD, shut the fuck up. Please, just go back to the cruiser. I'll take it from here."

WD walked away and Luke leaned in. "We just happened to be out this way checking on some stray cattle. We were heading back to town when you blew past us. You been drinking with your pals again?"

"Just a couple of shots," I said, leaning out and blowing in his face. "Honestly, I was just enjoying the evening, admittedly letting off a little steam. Coming from the city, it's rare to have a road of your own. To be honest, Luke, I was reliving a bit of our youth. Remember how we used to time ourselves from the three-mile corner to the highway?"

Luke stared back down the winding country road, momentarily lost in thought. Turning back, he flashed a rare smile. "Oh god, do I remember. Those were fun times. You have a good night, Scooter. But slow down. Our reflexes aren't what they once were."

He tipped his hat and walked back to his car.

As I drove on, I thought about what he had said. Those *were* fun times—fun and simpler. Back then, we had a long future ahead of us, and a very short past to ponder. Now, with our futures quickly fading, our pasts—for better or worse—often dominated our thinking. We turned to it for solace and stability, but often found ourselves stuck in its swamps of regret.

Anna's death had left me in an existential no-man's land, with a past too dark to revisit, a future too forlorn to face, and no fellow traveler to join me in either place. I'd never played the role of recluse well. Sure, I loved the occasional solo hunting or fishing trip. But after a few days, the freedom and independence I felt always gave in to loneliness. And with it came that bastard in the mirror. The only way I could escape him, or so I believed, was to find someone who would love and, although I hated to admit it, protect me.

Yet as Norm had rudely but accurately pointed out, with one exception those relationships had ended badly. Why? Because in truth, romance, intimacy, and sex, like most pleasures of the flesh—everything from buying more shit to eating good food and drinking expensive wine—provide temporary pleasure and meaning, but never vanquish the ghosts who haunt our souls.

So why was I pissed at my friends for suggesting that it wasn't just the sudden appearance of John's skull that had turned John's death into yet another life crisis, but also my misguided infatuation with his daughter? Why did I continue to avoid the truth? The issue was neither Shel nor the skull. It was my own, extremely fucked-up mind. And the only permanent fix I could think of, at least at this point, was the one I had contemplated that dark, sunny day in a tiny sloop on the edge of the Gulf Stream.

Well, screw that, I wasn't going anywhere except back to the house for another drink and an equally good night's sleep.

29

I AWOKE RESTED but hung over. The clear, objective mind I'd hoped for was nowhere in sight. I drank three cups of coffee and went back to bed, sleeping it off until the early afternoon. By then, the symptoms of the previous night's drinking had disappeared, replaced by an emotional hangover triggered by the evening's discussion.

After another cup of coffee, I dialed Shelia Mae, then immediately hung up, chiding myself for being weak and needy. I briefly reconsidered packing up and returning to Texas, but trashed that idea as being rash and stupid. I paced. I brooded. I dreamed up a number of other, equally idiotic scenarios for dealing with Shel and her dad's death.

By late afternoon, with a half-baked plan spinning in my head, I put Buck in the pickup and headed for the Marshall ranch. No one answered the door at the big house, and, feeling fortunate that I had averted disaster, I turned to leave. But before I got to the truck Shelia Mae can running out to greet me.

"Scooter," she smiled, throwing her arms around me, "you're

back! I'm so glad you came by. I thought you were upset with me or something. Come on in. I was just out riding. What a beautiful day."

And what a beautiful woman, I thought, *in those tight western jeans, that silk shirt with the turquoise buttons, the fancy boots.*

Shit.

We went inside. She brought out wine, stoked the fire, and sat next to me on the big leather couch. She gave me a hug and a friendly kiss on the cheek.

"I missed you," she said, now serious, the smile gone. "It pisses me off, but I missed you a lot."

"The feeling's mutual," I admitted. "I've had a hard couple of days and thought seeing you might help."

"I've been having a few of those myself," she said. "After Thanksgiving—after you left—I called Paris. I'm not sure why. I guess because I felt good about myself for the first time in months and wanted to share that happiness with someone close."

"And?"

"And when it's over, sometimes all you can do is walk away from the wreckage and resist looking back. Fuck the hope, fuck the dreams, fuck the shoulda-woulda-couldas."

I reached out and hugged her, not in the way I wanted to, but as a father or friend might, struggling to keep my passion locked in a cold shower of pragmatism.

We spent the entire evening staring into the fire, taking turns playing the role of therapist. We talked about our lives, our loves, our dreams, our regrets—those details that, repeated in the clear light of morning, sound like the banal, boring narrative of a poorly written romance novel.

We talked about losing our virginity, our faith, our idealism, our youth. We talked about coming home again and the clash of contentment and estrangement one faces.

We tasted several good French wines. We got very drunk. We went to bed.

I got up early the next morning while Shelia Mae was still sleeping. I left a note saying that I'd promised to take a friend hunting, but that I'd had a wonderful time and would call her later. I kissed her on the forehead and left, having never mentioned her father's death or the real reason for my visit.

A thaw had crept in during the night, accompanied by a subtle southern breeze and a predictably exquisite High Plains sunrise that as always gave me a sense of renewed hope and happiness.

As I drove back to town, I pondered the previous night's conversation: the discoveries we'd uncovered about each other's pasts since we left Creekmore, how the lessons learned—both the successes and abject flops—had shaped the arcs of our lives in the world, and how, in many ways, eerily similar our lives had been.

Then, I arrived home, and my new-found optimism died.

The back door, which I always kept locked, even though such behavior was frowned upon by most town folk, stood wide open. A bad feeling came over me. Break-ins were rare in Creekmore—too many honest people and a scarcity of bad actors. I considered calling the sheriff, but remembering John's skull on the mantle, decided against it.

Armed with a pocket-knife and Buck beside me, I cautiously entered the house.

I called out. No one answered. I turned on the lights. The house had been ransacked—drawers opened, books and papers strewn about. I went from room to room, checking closets and looking for anything that might be missing.

At first nothing appeared to have been taken Then I noticed that one of my guns—an old .22-caliber pump-action Remington my grandfather had given me—was missing from the gun rack. Oddly, the thieves had ignored several guns of more value, including a restored Parker twelve-gauge.

I kept walking from room to room, looking for clues and other missing items. Nothing. I sat down in front of the fireplace to think. Never in my life had I been burglarized. Who could have done it? Why? What were they after besides a battered old rifle of little but sentimental value?

Reluctantly, after regaining a crumb of composure, I dialed the sheriff's office. And that's when it hit me: John's skull was no longer smiling at me from its home on the mantle.

"Shit!"

30

"WHO ARE YOU calling a shit?" It was WD. "This is the sheriff's office. To whom am I speaking, and why are you calling me a shit?"

"Sorry, WD. It's Scooter."

"So? Why did you call me a shit?"

"I didn't. I was expressing surprise. I just got home and discovered the house has been burglarized."

"Where were you when it happened?"

"Out."

"Out where?"

"None of your fucking business. The issue at hand is a burglary, not my whereabouts. You sound like my parents."

"What'd they take?" WD asked, ignoring my barb and sounding more curious than official.

"As far as I can tell, just an old .22 my granddad gave me years ago."

"Hmm. You sure there wasn't anything else?"

"Not that I know of," I lied.

"Well, Scooter, you may be in luck. We just happened to recover some stolen property last night that includes a rifle like the one you described. Why don't you come down to the courthouse and see if it is yours? We've got some other stolen stuff too, so you may want to make another sweep of your place to see if anything else is missing. Seems kind of weird that they'd just take an old rifle."

I took my time getting to the sheriff's office. Something didn't smell right, and I didn't know whether it was just WD, who never met my smell test, or something else. Was I being set up, or was it just my usual, low-grade paranoia?

The sheriff was there to greet me when I finally arrived. WD was nowhere in sight.

"Understand someone broke into your house last night, while you were out catting about," Luke smirked. "Hope you were having a good time."

"Yep, someone broke in," I said, ignoring his taunt. "And I understand you may have recovered something they took."

"Maybe. We got a call about a couple of suspicious looking Mexicans down by the rodeo grounds this morning. They ran when we came up on them. Got away, but dropped their loot, including this here gun." He pointed to a table where my .22 lay. "Is that yours?"

"It is. Can I take it home?"

"Technically I should keep it ninety days as evidence. But I guess you can."

"Do I need to file a statement?" I asked. "I assume you also want to come by the house and look around?"

Luke gave me a surprised look. "Oh, yeah. I guess we should. Might find some prints and stuff. I'll send WD over this afternoon when he gets back from the doctor's. Getting some stitches. Cut himself sharpening his knife." He laughed. "Better, I guess, than if he'd been loading his gun."

I picked up the worn rifle and started to leave. But Luke stopped me. "Don't you want to know what else they got? I believe it might be something of yours you haven't missed yet."

He grinned and, reaching into a desk drawer, pulled out a large plastic bag containing John's skull. "This belong to you?"

Be cool, I told myself. *Don't get all pissy or defensive.*

"It does indeed," I replied, in as steady a voice as I could muster.

"I found it several years ago, while hunting quail in west Texas. I took it to the local sheriff, who kept it for a couple of years and then, when he retired, sent it back to me with a note saying it was probably the remains of some poor soul who'd lost his way on a cattle drive or buffalo hunt. Said it was technically mine, that and I could do with it what I pleased. I've kept it on the mantle as kind of a tragic good-luck piece."

Luke looked at me skeptically and shook his head. "Scooter, I don't know if this is just another of your strange peculiarities, or if you're bullshitting me, but we'll soon find out. I've already looked up the names of all the dentists in a four-county area in case we can track down dental records that match."

"Good luck with that," I said with forced distain.

"We'll see," he said. "Meantime, I'm keeping it. Let me know if anything else comes up missing."

"Will do," I said, walking out.

Shit.

It was all I could do to keep from sprinting back to the house. Latino burglars, my ass. My home had just been ransacked by two malicious, uniformed White farts in what was clearly an illegal search and seizure. Yet, if Luke got lucky and identified whose plastic wrapped skull was resting in his desk drawer, I was dead meat.

After snapping photos of the mess they'd made in the house, I began packing. Maybe the guys were right. Maybe I needed to get out of Dodge until things cooled off. And maybe, I suddenly realized, I should truly assume the persona and mindset of some random bad ass on the lam.

After one last sweep to make sure nothing else had been taken, I called Norm and Bobby, and invited them to join me for a quick lunch at Mary's.

In the corner booth, the only seating out of earshot of other diners, and over jalapeño poppers and beer, I updated them on the latest crime report. I told them I was taking them up on their suggestion and heading back to Dallas.

"What do you think the dimwitted duo thought they would find?" Bobby asked. "It's not as if we'd hidden John's body in your basement."

"I haven't the foggiest," I said. "My guess is that it was a fishing expedition. And, unless someone spilled the beans, I don't think they've made the connection between John and the skull."

"So, whose skull do they think it is?"

"Don't know that either," I said. "I told them I'd found it while hunting quail in west Texas years ago."

"Well, that's sort of true," Norm laughed.

"Yeah," I said, "but the sheriff didn't buy it. As we speak, he's faxing dentists in the area to see if they might have any records that might match. That's why I'm heading south."

"What if they try to extradite you?" Norm said.

"They'd have to have evidence of a crime," I said. "Which at this point they don't."

"Not yet," Norm said. "But what if they try to exhume John's body?"

"Then we're all done for," I said, "including Dan, who will probably lose his license and go to jail with the rest of us."

We finished the poppers in silence.

"Maybe," I finally spoke, "I should do as Father Tim suggested, and just tell the truth."

The booth erupted in angry protests that drew the attention of the other diners.

"Shut the fuck up and listen," Norm commanded, in a whisper only a CIA-trained agent could produce. "Look, Scooter, Luke's out for you. He's going to do everything he can to bust you. But Bobby, Dan, and I can't let you take the rap alone. We were all in on this. If you go down, we go down. Agreed?"

Bobby and I nodded, tentatively.

"So," Norm continued, "here's the plan: Scooter, go ahead and disappear for a week or two. Not back to Texas, but somewhere as far off the grid as you can find. But make it clear that you had to leave for business, and that you're coming back. Turn your phone off. Get a couple of those cheapos that you can toss in the creek or down a storm drain. While you're gone, find a good attorney. And remember, if nothing else you have the sheriff by the balls for an illegal search and seizure. Bobby, you and I are going dark."

"We're White guys."

"We're going to do some *covert* work to see what we can find out about Luke and WD and their so-called investigation. I'll also ask

Father Tim to do a bit of sleuthing. It's amazing what a local padre can learn from an innocent question, a flash of his crucifix, and a swish of his robes.

"Any questions? Okay then, let's go."

"Hold on a minute, Norm," I said. "Just what are you two going to be doing in the 'dark'?"

"Spycraft. Secret stuff. But not to worry, we're not going to eliminate anyone—just yet."

"Well, aren't you special," I sniped. "Does this mission of ours have a code name? Maybe *Bobby and Norm's Excellent Adventure*?"

"Too long," Norm replied.

"How about *Resurrection One*?" Bobby suggested.

"Very Catholic, but I'll bless it," Norm said. "Now, let's go."

When I got back to the house, I called Shelia Mae and told her I had to go away on business but would return in a couple of weeks. I said I was leaving early the next morning.

"I wish I could come with you," she said. "I'll miss your visits, infrequent as they've been. I've found the solitude I was looking for when I returned tinged with a bit of emptiness when you're not around."

"I know the feeling," I said. "But I'll keep in touch. And I'm not going to be gone that long."

We said our goodbyes and I started packing. But then it struck me that I didn't know where I was going. I needed to get as far away as I could, but not too far in case I needed to return quickly.

New Mexico. It had birds to hunt, trout to catch, good food, and beautiful vistas. It also had plenty of places to camp and was still just warm enough to make sleeping in a tent enjoyable.

Before I could get all my gear together, the phone rang. It was Shelia Mae.

"Scooter, I know you're getting ready to leave, but before you take off, why don't you come out and spend the night? Please."

I knew I shouldn't. It was a bad idea. But the more I thought about it, the more I reconsidered. Why not spent the night? Why not, despite Norm's and Bobby's counsel, get everything off my chest— get right with Shelia Mae, God, and myself. Then I could leave town with a much lighter load of guilt than I was now lugging around.

Sure, telling Shel the truth would be like removing a fishhook that you've buried deep in your thumb. Sooner or later, you have to push it on through until you expose the barb, snip that sucker off, and then work the shank back out through the wound. It hurts like hell until you splash on a bit of alcohol and drink the rest. But a minute later, you're casting again.

True, Shelia Mae would probably never speak to me again. And I could never return to Creekmore. But that was better than being arrested by the sheriff and facing a trial in which all my linen along with Shel's would be aired, not to mention the shit that would rain down on Norm, Bobby, and Digger.

I spent the next two hours packing. Camping gear, guns, flyrods. I loaded up enough equipment and supplies for a month's stay in a style somewhere between spartan and luxurious.

All the while I kept working on my Shelia Mae script. It did not come easy. At times it felt as if I were squeezing a narrative from the remnants of a used-up toothpaste tube of events, thoughts, decisions, and actions that had culminated in John's death and the discovery of his skull.

The first draft was still rough in my head when I headed out to the ranch. Before leaving, I posted "No Trespassing" signs on the front and back doors, along with hand-written notes: *Luke, WD: This means you! I know my fucking rights!* On the way out of town, I drove by Mary's to confirm the sheriff and his cousin were taking their usual evening respite and not staking out me or Shelia Mae.

When I arrived at the ranch, I put the pickup in the barn, closed the door, and walked with Buck to the house.

"Why all the secrecy, Scooter?" Shelia Mae had been watching me from the front porch.

"In case anyone comes sniffing around."

"Like?"

"Your old boyfriend."

She gave me a dubious look as we went inside, and I began unwinding the events of the day. I started with my discovery of the break-in and ransacking of my house, and then told her about my conversation with the sheriff, who said it was the work of two burglars. I did not mention the skull.

"But why would they trash the house and only take an old rifle?" she asked.

"Because it was a setup. There were no burglars, and if there had been, they would have been locals looking for drugs or money to buy them. Hell, sometimes I think a third of the county is either selling or using."

"Then who?"

"Luke and his cousin."

"But why?" She shook her head in disbelief.

"Because they believe I had something to do with your dad's death.

Silence and suspicion consumed the space between us, but despite my urge to retreat, I knew I had to plunge ahead. "Shel, I have to ask you: have you been talking with Luke about your dad since you came home?"

"We had dinner a couple of nights after you first came out to the ranch. He'd called to apologize for his earlier behavior. Said he just wanted to be friends. Asked me if we could have dinner and talk about old times. I invited him out to the ranch. I should have known better.

"I could tell he'd already had a few when he arrived. But he was a real gentleman. Not at all like the old Luke. I opened a bottle of wine. He said he was technically on duty and couldn't drink but urged me to go ahead. So, I did.

"It was a big mistake. I was already in a bad place. Elizbeth had called earlier that day and we'd had words. I felt shitty and I thought the wine would cheer me up. It didn't. I just got maudlin and sloppy—a little drunk.

"At some point we started talking about Dad. I told him about the guilt I felt over his death and not coming home. I told him I never got to say goodbye and often wondered what his last days were like and what he looked like lying there in Digger's parlor."

She paused, as if considering whether to continue.

"Unfortunately, I talked about you, too. A lot. About how sweet you'd been during that time. You being with him when he died, the conversations you'd had with him, how reassuring and kind you were. I babbled on and on.

"By the time I'd opened a second bottle of wine, I was telling him how I'd just seen you, and how well age and time had treated you." She shook her head, laughing. "My exact words were how hot you are for an older man, and how if I weren't a dyke, I might fuck you senseless. As I said, Scooter, I was shit-faced at that point."

"And what did he say?" I asked, certain I already knew the answer. Another pause.

"*Il est devenu fou*—he went crazy. Told me you were an asshole. Started yelling at me. Told me never to mention your name while he was around. Stormed into the kitchen and brought out a bottle of bourbon. Started drinking. Had two or three before he calmed down."

"His shift must have ended," I said.

Shelia Mae gave me a withering look. "It didn't stop there. He again started telling me how much he still loved me and how we should get back together. I laughed, reminding him that I was gay. He got all churchy-preachy on me. Told me my *gayness* was an *acquired perversion*, and that I could and should change. 'You've been living a sinful, godless life in a godless country for too long, Shelia Mae. It's time you repented, accepted Jesus, and went straight.'

"At that point I lost it. I told him God loves my kind more than dumbass Christian do-gooders like him. Then we both told each other to go to hell. By then he was too drunk to drive home. I told him to call his cousin to come and pick him up. He refused. So, I found him an old sleeping bag and told him he could sleep it off in the barn."

"And did he?"

She looked out the window to avoid my gaze.

"Sort of. Sometime before dawn he returned to the house, which of course I never lock. He came upstairs and tried to get into bed with me. He picked up right where he'd left off, telling me how lonely he was and how much he loved me. He tried to hug me, but I rolled out of bed and grabbed the Glock I keep in the nightstand. I pointed it at his groin and told him to get the fuck out and never come back. He mumbled something about being sorry and left. I have no idea how he got home, and frankly I don't care. I haven't seen him since."

"Jesus, Shelia Mae. Have you told anyone else about this?"

"Who would I tell? And what good would it do? Why would anyone take the word of a known pervert over that of an elected official? Besides, I felt I'd been complicit—inviting him over, getting drunk, spilling my guts, telling him he could spend the night in the barn."

I reached out to her, squeezed her hand tightly. "But you didn't invite him to get into bed with you, Shel. What he did was vile, and you know it."

"What can I say?" She shrugged and smiled wanly. "I should have known better. All men think with their dicks."

Now I was the one avoiding eye contact. Much as I would have liked to argue that she was over-generalizing, I couldn't. I'd always told myself that I wasn't that kind of guy. But who was I kidding? How many purely platonic relationships had I been in with women? A few may have started out that way, but sooner or later the friendship, the companionship, good as it was, wasn't enough. I always wanted—needed—more.

"I didn't mean to hurt your feelings, Scooter. You're different."

"Not so much, Shel, not so much." I shook my head.

She reached over and gave me a hug. I was scared to reciprocate, suggesting instead that I fix us dinner. I put together a peasant's pasta with broccoli, garlic, Italian sausage, and a little olive oil, while Shelia Mae sat watching, slowly sipping her wine.

"So," she said, finally breaking the silence, "what are you going to do about Luke's so-called investigation? It sounds to me like he has—or thinks he has—evidence that there is more to Dad's death and your involvement in it than you've told me. Is there more to the story than what you've shared with me? Or is he just being a jealous, juvenile prick?"

Her question caught me off balance. She still harbored doubt, suspicion. For whatever reasons, my story had not been convincing.

I sighed, initially out of frustration, and then to stall as I considered how to respond. "You know as much as I know, Shel. I'd like to think it's just Luke being Luke. But after he broke into my house, I'm not so sure. He obviously still has the hots for you, and I have a feeling your rebuff of him at gunpoint may have pushed him over the edge, and he's decided to take it out on me."

"Are you going to confront him?"

"I don't want to," I lied, "but eventually I may have to, if not about how he's treating me, at least about how he treated you."

"Don't, Scooter. Please. Let's both be adults here and just walk away from his sophomoric behavior."

I laughed. "Good point. This does have all the makings of a bad high school drama."

Neither of us brought up the sheriff or John's death the rest of the evening. Instead, over dinner and for the next three hours, we returned to the past, continuing to catch each other up on the long gap in our friendship—our journeys from childhood to where we now found ourselves.

I talked about Lucy, and how proud I was of her. I talked about my career. How it had shifted as old dreams died and new ones emerged. I talked, with some reluctance, about my marriages, the love I sought, the pain I caused.

"You were such a straight, buttoned-down kid," Shelia Mae said, shaking her head in disbelief. "What led you to a life of serial marriage?"

"I think it goes back to the statement you made earlier—the one about all men thinking with their dicks. I never learned the difference between love and lust—between physical and emotional attraction. I loved the lust but had trouble with the love. I don't know how to do that very well, you know, really love somebody.

"Down deep, I'm a needy jerk with low self-esteem who's always living in his own, troubled head. So, I always turn to women for that emotional fix—that confidence and sense of worth I can't give myself.

"Lasting relationships require more than getting your own needs met. You have to be an equal partner in the equation. You've got to give as good as you get—emotionally as well as physically. I didn't . . . still don't. I was incapable of real love, instead judging everything—including my self-worth—by the quality and frequency of sex. When that subsided—when the mundane reality of daily life kicked in, which it always does—the emotional high faded, and I reverted to my annoying pain-in-the-ass mode, and one of us, usually me, would walk away."

"I'm confused," Shelia Mae said. "I understand the love and lust part, and the emotional need, but why, with your abysmal matrimonial batting average, did you continue going back for more? Why didn't you just skip the official part, fuck them until the relationship fizzled, and walk away?"

"Good question. It was hell."

"Clearly," she said. "I understand that. So why did you keep doing it?"

"Like I said, it was Hell. Actual Hell. I was afraid of burning in Hell."

"You're saying the fear of burning in Hell forced you to marry, again and again? How did you come up with that sick theory?"

"I didn't," I said. "It was your mom's theory."

Indeed, it was Ruthie who finally helped me understand my unholy conundrum. It was one of the last conversations we had before she died. I'd gone out to the ranch, as I often did when in town, to see how she and John were doing and to catch up on the local gossip.

Somehow, we'd gotten into a discussion of faith and marriage. Well into her eighties, draped in an old housecoat, her trusty walker at her side, she had, in five minutes, provided more insight than twenty years of professional therapy.

"You were raised believing in the holy sanctity of marriage," she told me. "But you took it to an unnatural extreme. You figured that once you had sexual relations with a woman, marriage had to follow. Otherwise, you'd be doomed to eternal damnation."

I was speechless, though I shouldn't have been. If her husband was a modern-day John the Baptist, then Ruthie was a twenty-first century Mary Magdalene, an assertive, plain-spoken, thoughtful woman who spoke truth to power, or in my case, to an emotionally near-sighted idiot.

Shelia Mae shook her head and laughed. "That was Mom, a guided missile when it came to matters of the heart. As much as my gayness troubled Daddy, she confronted it head-on. I'll always remember one of the first things she said when I came out: 'Too bad Maudie's not here to help. She would have been so proud.

"Turns out my late Aunt Maude, a Christian vaudevillian and elementary school teacher, well-loved by generations of children and their parents, was also queer. It was never discussed. I always assumed her tray table and seatback were not locked in the upright position, but never knew the details.

"She traveled with Wilhelmina, a *close woman friend*. She and Willy traveled the country visiting local schools and churches doing puppet shows for children. She also was a ventriloquist. Her dummy, Winston, was a rather obnoxious little guy. In her shows, she and Winston would talk about God and Jesus, Winston played the goofy smartass, whom Miss Maude would sweetly but firmly put in his place. When she died, her beloved Winston was buried with her."

She laughed again. But this time it was mixed with tears. "Sometimes I think we all should have secret lives. Coming out isn't all that it's cracked up to be. Take Mom and Dad. Mom never blinked twice when I told her. Dad was still struggling with it when he died. He couldn't understand why I didn't stay with Robert—Lord Fancy Pants, he called him. 'Fancy Pants loves you,' he told me, shortly after we split up. 'I see it in how he looks at you. That kind of love is a rare thing. How can you leave someone who loves you like he does? How can you hurt someone like that?'

"He was right. Robert did love me. And I clearly hurt him. Only after I'd been through a couple of relationships with women did I discover that the ability to love is not related to gender—that love like Robert's is indeed rare."

I wanted to say something or put my arm around her. Instead, we both sat in silence, reflecting on our own and the other's story. Finally, she suggested a walk. The night was cold and clear, the moon full—just the sort of night, Shel said, to visit her parent's graves. I agreed, reluctantly, fearing it would trigger more questions, more emotions.

We walked slowly, silently up the hill, serenaded by the snow crunching beneath our feet and coyotes calling in the distance. Ahead, the two gravestones shone in the moonlight, marking the end of far more than the short trail to the family burial ground.

We climbed the three small limestone steps and, still in our own thoughts, looked down at the graves. Shelia Mae began crying softly and shaking—from the cold or grief I couldn't tell. Sensing I was a guilty intruder in a deeply personal moment, I stepped back, my shoulders hunched, my hands deep in my coat pockets.

"It's okay Scooter," she said softly. "It's okay if you stand close to me. I would like that. Please?"

There was desperation in her voice. I put my arm around her.

Held her close. She gripped me as if she feared falling into an unseen third grave next to her parents—a hole infinitely deep and dark. We stood there for what seemed like eternity, the only sounds her sobs of anguish and the equally haunting yelps of distant coyotes.

After several minutes, I felt her relax her hold on me. "I needed that," she announced, smiling, tears gone. "And I needed you too, Scooter. Thanks."

We walked back holding hands but saying nothing. Back at the house, she again asked me to lie in bed with her. I complied, holding her lightly until her breathing slowed and her body relaxed. Then silently Buck and I made our way to the bunkhouse.

31

SOMETIME AFTER MIDNIGHT, Buck nudged me and, in the low guttural sounds he uses for words, warned me there was trouble afoot.

I assumed it was just a mamma coyote doing some grocery shopping for her family. I peered out the window. Nothing. But as I turned to go back to bed, I caught the brief reflection of moonlight on a barn window.

Half asleep, it didn't hit me until I was crawling under the covers that there was no window on that side of the barn. Taking a closer look, I saw the reflection came from the windshield of a car with the suspicious outline of a police cruiser.

I pulled on my boots, grabbed my headlamp and the battered old pump-action Winchester that hung over the fireplace. With Buck following closely, I slipped out the door. It wasn't until I'd circled around the bunkhouse and was sneaking up behind the car that I realized I was still in my boxers and T-shirt.

As I moved closer, I could smell cigarette smoke and hear the low voices of Luke and WD. I made my way to the open driver's window, pressed the barrel of the unloaded twelve-gauge against the sheriff's neck, and cocked the gun.

"Don't move, or I'll blow your brains out."

Although I realized how hackneyed and silly it sounded, my whispered demand, combined with the all too familiar sound of the gun's action sliding back and forth, was enough to scare both men silly.

I turned on my headlamp and peered into the car.

"WD, get out with your hands in the air and walk slowly around the car until I can see you. If you do anything stupid, I'll take out your cousin."

He did as he was told, and I ordered him to lie face down in the snow. "Move a muscle and Buck here will rip your head off."

Buck growled appropriately.

"Now it's your turn, Sheriff."

When both men were out, I made them drop their weapons and strip down to their underwear and boots. As we all stood there shivering in the cold, I made them put on their badges and hats. Then, using Luke's phone, I took a picture of them standing by their cruiser with the barn in the background and emailed it to myself.

"What the fuck were you thinking?" I demanded, keeping my voice low as to not wake Shelia Mae. "Since when did you start breaking into the homes of law-abiding citizens? Since when did you start staking out innocent single women?"

Neither spoke.

"Here's the deal: I never want to see either of you out here again. Do you understand?"

Sullenly, they both nodded.

"If you ever are, or if you ever again come into either of our homes uninvited, I will personally take both of you down. Understood?"

Again, nods.

"And, Luke, give up your hard-on for Shelia Mae. Just walk away, man. What you did the other night was stupid and inexcusable. I'm sorry things didn't work out between you two. But that was more than thirty years ago. We've all moved on," I lied. "You need to do the same. Seriously, let it go—both your desire for her and your jealously of me. You'll be a better man. Shit, you'll be happier and feel a hell of a lot better about yourself. Okay?"

WD started to say something, but Luke, continuing to glare at me, stopped him.

"Now, both of you get the hell out of here. Go home and get a good night's sleep. I'll drop off your clothes and guns in the morning. Meantime, if you do any more stupid things, I'll go public with that cute picture of you. Understand?"

Again, they nodded, then got in the cruiser and quietly drove off.

As I watched them go, I realized I too, had to get the hell out. I gathered their guns, put their clothes in a garbage bag, returned to the bunkhouse and packed. Before leaving, I wrote a note to Shelia Mae.

Shel—

I had an unfortunate run-in with the sheriff and WD last night. The good news is that they won't be bothering you anymore. The bad news is that I need to get out of town quicker than I'd planned.

Sorry for the hasty retreat. Last night was special. Seriously.

Don't worry, I'll be back soon.

Love, Scooter

PS—phone me when you get this!

Buck and I took a back road into town and parked behind First Baptist, which I knew would be unlocked. As Brother Leon always said, "Our search for the lost sheep don't stop at sundown. Our doors are open twenty-four seven for drunks, whores, and anyone else who needs refuge from Satan or bad weather."

It also was good refuge, I'd learned as a teenager, for necking and underage drinking.

I walked down the aisle, carefully laid the confiscated weapons on the communion table, and dropped the garbage bag with the lawmen's clothes in the baptistry, where it floated briefly before sinking. As I watched it settle on the bottom, I offered a silent prayer, asking the Almighty for forgiveness and to please watch over Shelia Mae.

"Also," I suggested, "calm the hearts of my fellow brethren, Luke and WD, and while you're at it, knock a little sense into them."

As Buck and I headed out of town, I called Maddy, the sheriff's dispatcher, and told her where her boss and the deputy could find their gear. "Oh God," she laughed, "I just have one question, Scooter: why didn't you put Dumb and Dumber in the bag too? You missed a big opportunity."

The long drive southwest toward New Mexico gave me a lot of time to think. I kept replaying the last twenty-four hours: the alleged break-in, my evening with Shelia Mae, and my early-morning confrontation with Luke and WD.

I decided I had every right to be pissed off about their illegal search of my home. I also believed I acted appropriately in calling Luke out for his inappropriate if not illegal behavior toward Shelia Mae. As for disarming the lawmen, making them strip, and then dumping their clothes in the holy water of the baptistry—that was a stickier issue. Frankly, it made me feel better and I couldn't think of anything in the Bible that would qualify it as a sin, but as for its legality, I wasn't sure.

That left my relationship with Shel. Why had I still not come clean with her about her dad's death? Why did I continue worrying how she would take it? Why did I care about her so much in the first place? More importantly, why did I assume she cared about me in the same way?

As the stars began to fade, so did my confidence in what I was doing. A road trip was one thing. A full retreat from one's past, another. And that's what this whole adventure was beginning to feel like.

"Kind of early for such dark thoughts, my friend."

At first, I assumed it was my evil twin. Just like the bastard to show up at a time like this. But then Buck, tail wagging, jumped in the back seat, and, looking in the mirror, I saw John, twinkling eyes and familiar grin.

This time, his sudden appearance didn't startle me, and I smiled back.

"Good to see you, my friend," I said. "How's the afterlife been treating you?"

"Okay," he said. "Never a dull moment—but never a bad one either. Life is good."

"They have those T-shirts in Heaven, too?"

He laughed. "By the way, Anna sends her love. She said it was great hearing from you, despite your "woe-is-me schtick," which is still annoying. She said to tell you that she wishes she could visit you but has to finish dealing with some of her own issues first. It's the same reason I can't talk to Shelia Mae."

"That's too bad," I said, somewhat disappointed. "But I'm glad you decided to join us. "I have a lot of things on my mind and could use your advice."

"Tell me about it. From what I've been seeing, your recent wheels-off behavior has landed you in one heck of a swamp—a muck of moral, spiritual, and ethical if not legal tribulations. You're spinning your wheels so much I'm afraid they're going to come off. I have to admit though, there are parts that have been fun to watch, like your little showdown with Luke and WD. How did you come up with that one? Everyone who saw it was impressed."

"Everyone?"

"It's one of Heaven's perks. An endless variety of shows and no monthly fees. Everything but fantasy and superheroes—those genres become so passé when you're dead."

"Are you serious?"

"Totally. It's a much better benefit than those alleged gold-paved streets we read about growing up. What a load of Biblical bull crap. It's a standing joke. First thing everyone asks is, 'where are the gold-paved streets?' But enough about me. While I was watching all the fun and games, I also noticed that you're still struggling with a few demons of you own. You're pissed off, you're more guilt-ridden than ever and you still have the hots for my child. I figured you might need some help in sorting it all out."

For the next hour, I emptied my mind and heart to a ghostly apparition riding shotgun—Buck and John having switched seats. Although he'd heard it before—probably knew it by heart—I shared with him the shame and guilt that had been building through most of my adult life. I dragged him through one failed marriage after another—a tedious rerun of lust and love, screwing and screw-ups, agony and ecstasy. Through it all he just sat there listening, saying nothing.

Even when it was clear I'd finished my monologue, he remained silent. Then, after twenty miles without a response, during which time I'd concluded I'd put him to sleep with my dreadful story, he suddenly spoke.

"Jesus, Scooter, what a pathetic, boring tale. Please don't take this the wrong way, but halfway through it, I thought about shooting myself. Then I remembered I was already dead. Seriously, it's a wonder you're still alive with a narrative like that playing in your head."

No shit, John. It doesn't take supernatural powers to see that.

"Thanks, John. But telling me what I already know isn't much help. For some reason I assumed you were sent here to enlighten me."

"Sorry for stating the obvious. I'm just not sure where exactly I should begin."

"Why don't you start where it ended."

"Meaning?"

"Your death. My present woes didn't fully ripen until Buck and I found your fucking skull, which, by the way, is now nestled in a sealed evidence bag in the county courthouse. Without that, there would be no evidence, no case, no problems. How did it show up at your ranch, when you supposedly died at Shaman Reverend What's-his-name's Oklahoma burial ground?"

My question appeared to catch John off guard. He started to speak. Stopped. Thought for a moment, then hesitantly began.

"I wish I could tell you, Scooter, but the truth is, it's a long story, some of which I've forgotten. Death can do that to a person—play havoc with one's memory. I know that Indian took good care of me, as promised, and I still had my head when I died, or at least I think so."

He smiled apologetically. "Let's just say that Buck finding my remains was not part of the plan and leave it there. For that I'm truly sorry. I guess I should have thought through my exit strategy a bit more carefully."

"I guess you should have," I said, turning to give him a piece of my mind. "Perhaps . . ." But by then he had vanished.

32

SHORTLY AFTER SUNRISE, we stopped in Taos to refuel. While eating breakfast at a local diner, my phone rang.

"Where the hell are you?" It was Shelia Mae.

"Taos."

"New Mexico?"

"Yeah. I drove down here last night after a run-in with our friends. I wanted to wait 'til morning, Shel, but I was worried that if I stayed, I'd be in jail before the sun rose."

"What did you do, Scooter?"

I told her what happened.

"You made them strip?"

"Yeah. I probably went too far. It was a pathetic picture, the two of them standing there shivering in their tighty-whities. But I wanted them to understand what it really feels like to be threatened, exposed and completely vulnerable to the power of someone else. And I figured it would buy me some time to get out of town."

"Do you think they'll come back to the ranch?"

"I doubt it. I was very clear what would happen if they ever did. But I don't know if they took me seriously. You'll probably get a call from Luke looking for me. I'm sure he's built up a head of steam by now."

"What should I tell him?"

"Tell him I'm traveling on business and will be back in a couple of weeks, and that if he bothers you again, you're going to call the state police."

She sighed. "I miss you, Scooter, although sometimes I wonder about your approach to problem solving. Sure you don't want me to come down there and meet you?"

"Shelia Mae, what I said about traveling on business is true. I have some seriously unfinished business with an old partner of mine. Someone whom I've known since we were kids. We parted ways years ago under some unfortunate circumstances, and I—we—really need to put the past behind us."

"Yet another of your former wives or girlfriends?"

"Actually, it's a guy."

"Please," she interrupted, clearly exasperated, "spare me the lurid details."

I laughed. "It's me, Shelia Mae. My alter ego. My evil blood brother who stalks me during dark times. You've seen him. He's pretty fucked up, an emotional, social, and spiritual train wreck. You should be thankful you haven't seen him up close and personal."

"But I think I have, Scooter. And I like that guy."

"I appreciate your sentiments, Shel, but you really don't know me—not in the lustful, self-centered Biblical way. And for that, you should be thankful."

She laughed.

"Seriously. Talk to my ex-wives. There are several to choose from. Hell, there are enough to do a pseudo-scientific study."

"But Scooter, our relationship is different. We're just friends. Very good friends. After the past month, I'm thinking best friends. But that doesn't mean I want to fuck you."

"And therein lies the problem, Shelia Mae. Sometimes I think I do." The words stampeded out of my mouth before the neurotransmitters in my brain could stop them.

Silence.

Shit. Shit, shit, shit.

"Look, Scooter," Shelia Mae finally spoke. "I take that as a real compliment. Seriously. But I'm not convinced that's what you truly want or need from me. I think what you're looking for is companionship, closeness. Maybe I want that, too. Maybe I need that."

The synapses in my brain fired a barrage of charges that, thankfully, rendered me mute.

"Scooter?"

"I'm sorry," I muttered. "I'm really sorry I said that. Forgive me."

"Scooter," Shelia Mae's voice had the cadence of a pre-school teacher, "I don't need to forgive you, because I don't think that was you talking. I think it was that 'friend' of yours. Am I right?"

"You are. And that comment I made is one reason I need to see him."

Shelia Mae laughed again. "I understand. But this time, you do the talking, okay? As you said, he's one really fucked-up dude. And you're not. So, take care of business and come home. I miss you."

As I hung up, I saw a message from Norm.

"Just bumped into a very pissed off Luke at Mary's. Call ASAP!"

I did, and immediately got an earful.

"What did you do, Scooter?" he said by way of greeting. "Luke's gone ballistic. Says you're dead meat. Told me to stay away from you or I might find myself collateral damage. I've never heard him so angry."

I told Norm of the early morning events at the ranch. "If they didn't catch their deaths of cold, I figured they'd be hot on my trail."

"They are. You still at the ranch?"

"No. Off on a business trip. Will be gone for several days."

"Got it. We'll keep an eye on Shelia Mae and the ranch while you're gone and collect the necessary intelligence to design a secure reentry strategy for your return."

"Thanks, Norm. Just don't play Rambo. Given what I did to them, they'd probably come out shooting next time."

"Don't worry. Remember, I'm former CIA, trained and experienced in the dark and occasionally deadly arts. If they go rogue, they'll never know what hit them."

"That's what scares me. Please don't hurt them, Norm. Just scare them if they get too close."

"Will do. By the way, where are you?"

"Not where they can find me."

"Good. Talk later."

Buck and I spent the rest of the morning wandering around Taos, looking for Dennis Hopper's grave. I'm not a star stalker, but always admired Hopper's quirky obstinance in the face of societal norms. He also had a bit of a dark side, which I could relate to, especially after my call with Shelia Mae.

His large wooden cross, when we finally found it in a small cemetery on the outskirts of town, was festooned with bandanas left by admirers. Buck clearly understood the significance of the moment. As I stood there in silence, he lifted a leg to take a ceremonial piss, and was not happy when I stopped him.

After lunch of street tacos and Mexican beer, I needed a nap, so we checked into an old motel near the town square. I woke hours later to Buck's whining, groggy and disoriented in the darkened room. I flipped on a light, and there was John again, sitting in the lone chair, petting Buck, and reading a magazine.

"The crap they put in motels these days," he said.

"Here, this is more to your liking," I said, opening the bedside table and tossing him a well-worn Gideons Bible.

He laughed. "I haven't seen one of these in years. And, as strange as it might sound, there are no Bibles in Heaven."

"Really?"

"Nope. Holy books are considered human artifacts, well-meant but somewhat pagan volumes, sincere but misguided attempts by man—by that I mean males—to explain their existence and place in the universe. It's not that the Bible is bad, it's how we interpret it. It's really just a Boy Scout handbook for adults. Beyond that it should be read with caution. There are some good, illustrative myths—the story of creation, for example—but much of the narrative is designed by those who wrote it to maintain control and power. It's laced with propaganda, fake news, and purposely distorted bullshit."

"Praise the Lord," I said.

"Don't be snarky. Holy books were written by humans. And every human who has or will roam the earth creates an equally suspect narrative of their own. Take yours for example: The way you tell it, you're a selfish loser who purposely hurts those you love and care about. At least that's the story I heard last night on the road. Hell is what we make it, Scooter, and yours is a doozy."

"Meaning?"

John shot me an exasperated look. "I'm sorry, Scooter. Clearly, I failed you as a spiritual guide when I was living. Or you were too broken to understand."

"Probably the latter," I said.

"More likely a combination," he replied.

"But now you have superpowers, right?"

Another frustrated look. "Let's try this: I want you to spend a few days alone, pondering life and death. Without my holy help. Working it out on your own is harder, but way better—if you can do it. If not, I'll come back in a few days and we'll talk more."

"Okay. But before you go, one more question: Have you visited your daughter lately."

"No. I told you, the time's not right. Why do you ask?"

"That bit about the Bible. It sounded like something she said recently."

"Really?"

With that, he again disappeared.

———————

In the morning we headed south. The weather had warmed considerably, and I decided to look for a campsite on the Rio Chama. We settled on a secluded spot with some good water nearby, and after setting up camp, I put on my waders and went fishing. Buck followed along the bank until he found a sunny spot on a large boulder and settled in for an afternoon nap.

The water was icy, the fishing slow. I spent the first hour making hurried casts, noisily slapping the water and then, before waiting for a fish to take notice, impatiently recasting to what I was sure was a better spot.

But the cold, distilled air and the river's winter rhythms were infectiously relaxing, and before I'd realized it, my body and brain had geared down to a crawl. The fishing picked up a bit and in the next hour I caught three nice browns.

I continued fishing for another hour, but my concentration, along with my mood, began to fade with the winter sun. Suddenly a large fish took my fly and ran with it, pulling me back to reality. I played it briefly but lost it within feet of the net.

The adrenaline rush that comes with such a fish, even one lost, usually keeps me fishing until I land another or darkness falls, whichever comes first. Not this time. Within minutes my focus again flagged, replaced by scattered ruminations on my past. Exhausted and cold, I climbed out of the river and returned to camp. I warmed myself with a small fire and a cup of steaming cocoa, hoping to revive my energy. But within minutes I was in my sleeping bag, Buck curled up against me.

The dreams that visited my tent that night were far less comforting than the pines that whispered above us. A trio of ex-wives stopped by to see me. They spent the night chastising me and arguing with each other about who had suffered most under my ham-fisted husbandry. I struggled, as one does in dreams, to defend myself, but in vain. It was a sad, pathetic and at times weirdly funny nightmare.

I awoke exhausted, as if I'd been playing a never-ending game of matrimonial whack-a-mole. It was still dark, but Buck was on high alert, softly growling. At first, I thought he might have sensed the spirits I'd been wrestling with. But then I heard the slow movement of something large outside the tent.

I reached out and stroked Buck. We lay there for several minutes, both wide awake, but scared and smart enough not to move or make a sound. My guns were still locked in the pickup but would probably have been of little use even if they'd been within reach. Slowly, the sounds faded, replaced by the river's soothing murmur. I peeked out of the tent. A light snow fell in the waning moonlight. I climbed back in my bag and slept until dawn.

The snow was still falling the next morning as we drove into town for breakfast. After clearing my mind with a bloody Mary and a double order of huevos rancheros and buying enough supplies to get us through a couple of days in the woods, we returned to the river and I again went fishing. The trout seemed to be energized by the snow. I kept two for dinner and released the rest.

By the time we returned to camp, the snow had picked up and was beginning to build on the ground. I started a big fire, refilled my lantern and stove, and settled into the tent with Buck, a book, and a tall scotch.

As night fell, I fed Buck, fried the trout with bacon, potatoes, and Brussel sprouts, and under an awning I'd rigged out of an old tarp, opened a bottle of wine and had a peaceful and delicious dinner.

I returned to the tent satiated and ready for sleep. But it would not come. Instead, I kept thinking about my conversations with John and Shelia Mae. Both were telling me to lighten up, get over myself and my faith, get out of my head and move on with my life. I understood their logic, but living it is easier said than done, especially when a chorus of voices insistently whispers another, far darker proverb in your ear: "life's a bitch and then you die . . . and then you die . . . and then you die."

Sleep finally came, bringing with it more dreary dreams—some so bleak they made the Cohen brothers look like Looney Tunes. I awoke near dawn. Outside, a full-blown blizzard raged. Inside, I was seized by a suffocating panic.

Only those who have experienced such moments of darkness know the anguish and despair they bring. Those who observe from outside see them as incredibly selfish, childish behaviors. Both perspectives are accurate.

I lay there most of the next day, trying to read, write, and pray myself out of an increasingly dangerous funk. Life *is* a bitch, I kept thinking. And maybe ending it *is* the best option.

Finally, as night returned, I waded through the foot-high snow to retrieve a gun from my pickup. I started to pull out one of my shotguns but opted for John's pistol. I viewed my guns as pieces of art, beautifully crafted of deeply blued steel and fine-grain wood, too elegant for the task at hand. A handgun, like John's old .45, was what I needed, a simple mechanical tool with no more soul than a hammer or screwdriver.

I climbed back into the tent and curled up with the gun. Buck, sensing something was not right, went outside and curled up in the snow, silently guarding the entrance. I lay there in the dark, listening to the blizzard's howls for what seemed like hours. I kept telling myself to get on with it and finally put the revolver against my head.

―――――――――――

I awoke to a rogue ray of sunlight that had slipped into the tent. As I tried to raise my head, something cold poked my cheek. I reached up and felt the steel barrel of a pistol. Startled, I grabbed it. What was John's gun doing in my sleeping bag? At first, I couldn't remember getting it or even falling asleep. I wasn't even sure what day it was.

"Good morning, sunshine."

I turned over. There was John, lying on his back next to me, staring up.

"How long have you been here?"

"Since you put my gun to your head."

"What are you talking about?"

"Last night when you were thinking about making a grand exit."

My memory flooded back, bringing with it a tide of bleak recollections. "I guess I should thank you?"

"Actually, son, you should thank yourself. It was your decision and yours alone."

"Please stop calling me that," I snapped, my head spinning. "I'm not sure exactly what you are these days—ghost, spirit, whatever. But I know you're not my father or my priest."

John laughed. "Sorry. How about I call you 'dumb shit' from now on. It's a bit pejorative but certainly appropriate. However, you did save your own life last night."

"Would you have stopped me if I hadn't?"

"Nope. Couldn't have. It's against the rules. Ultimately it was your decision. I was here to take you home if you had. I did, however, almost intercede when you selected my old Colt as your annihilator of choice. That really pissed me off. That pistol is . . . was one of my treasured possessions.

My father gave it to me when I took over the ranch. Made me swear to never use it in anger, except when shooting rattlesnakes or coyotes. And then you decided to use it to blow your brains out."

"I'm sorry."

"You *were* sorry," he said, "a sorry mess. But not anymore. You're fine now."

"Thanks for the kind words, but I don't feel fine. What do I do now?"

"Go into town. Get a good hotel—one that takes animals." He reached over and patted Buck. "Relax and smell the roses. Eat, drink, see a concert. And give Shelia Mae a call. She misses you."

"That's it?"

"Stay until I return. Then you can get the hell back home."

He got up to leave. As he did, I noticed he was wearing a beautiful new robe. It looked heavy and warm. He saw me admiring it.

"Camel's hair." He grinned proudly, and then vanished.

33

I MADE COFFEE and cooked up some eggs and bacon after John left and sat under the fly eating and enjoying the bright winter day. I went to the river and waded for an hour, casting occasionally, but mostly admiring the world around me.

It was during one of those carefree moments that I hooked one of the largest trout I'd ever seen, a big shouldered monster that took out most of my line before I could corral him in my net. I relished his beauty for a moment, then carefully released him.

"Maybe," I said to Buck as we walked back to camp, "life really can be good."

————————

After breaking camp, I drove to Santa Fe. While I favor Taos, with its gritty, hippified trading-post persona, after the past few days I needed some glitz. We found a small, elegant hotel near the square that, for a steep fee, would allow Buck to share my room.

After showering and consuming a rich room-service lunch and

a small bottle of wine, I napped the afternoon away. Then I walked Buck around the square, had dinner, and returned to the hotel. I opened a half-finished biography of Thomas Merton and read for the next two hours—the longest period I'd sat quietly with a printed friend in months.

The next day I hit a couple of museums and surfed the stores and galleries, buying Shelia Mae a pair of turquoise earrings that matched John's ring, which I planned to return to her at some point. After dinner (I had honey-filled sopapillas in honor of John, there being no locust on the menu), I wrote a lengthy entry in my journal, the first in weeks, the first optimistic in months. It began:

I've learned an important lesson I should have learned years ago: Just because you love someone doesn't mean you have to make love with them. Also, it's okay to love or at least like yourself.

Buck and I turned in early for the second dreamless night in months, only to be awakened by John's cheery voice.

"Rise and shine, boys. You have a long road ahead of you."

As I sat up, clearing the fog of a night well slept, he handed me a cup of coffee. Starbucks. He had one too, and as I watched he took a sip. I started to say something but stopped. It was too early in the day to attempt unraveling the mysteries of the universe—especially one so tiny and inconsequential.

"What?" he said, reading my mind. "I miss my morning coffee. Haven't had a latte since I passed."

He pulled up a chair and sat facing me.

"Looks like you're in better spirits," he said, watching me carefully while Buck rubbed against him. "Both of you."

"Yes, and I hope I can maintain this pleasant equilibrium for a least a few days."

"Not just a few days or weeks or years, Scooter. For the rest of your life." He grabbed me by the collar and pulled me to the mirror. "Is your evil twin still staring back at you? No. Why? Because by not putting a bullet in your head two nights ago, you put one in his."

He released my collar and took a step back. "Actually, Scooter," his voice no longer that of a railing prophet, but of a trail-weary old rancher, "you didn't destroy him. We never completely vanquish our demons. The best we can do is manage them. And, as I've told you before, we do that by ending our preoccupation with the past.

Our internal rearview mirrors are there for a purpose: to learn from the past. But all too often we find ourselves stuck there, wallowing aimlessly.

"Look at me. Much as I've tried, I can't forget how I treated Shelia Mae about the whole gay thing. I tried to make my peace with her before I died, but I didn't, not really. And even now, I can't get up the nerve to visit her. But I have learned from it, and I try to focus on those lessons—how to apply them going forward and share them with others. Like today. I've come to help you finish cleaning your mirrors, which still have a few shitty spots you missed."

"Sorry, John. I think I understood the first part of your soliloquy, but it sort of unraveled there at the end."

"What I was trying to explain is that you—like all of us—have made stupid, regrettable mistakes. But instead of learning from them and moving on, we keep looking back at them. The lenses we're looking through are cracked and dirty, distorting not only what we remember, but how we remember. Take you: I've known you since you were a little grasshopper—"

"John, please, don't get all *Kung-Fu*ey on me."

He grinned. "I've known you since you were a little kid, and I know the kind of crap people fed you about life and death—especially death. They—including your parents—served you some bad soul food that you've been ruminating on ever since. Sadly, they thought they were saving you, not damaging you for life. They were not bad people, simply well-meaning folk blinded by a toxic faith—a perfectly fine faith, I might add, that had gone bad over time through ignorance, fear, and old tribal ways.

"It's that fear that is the real evil here. Puny little fears triggered by pride, envy, and greed, and big-ass existential fears like loneliness and death. We all have 'em. Part of the so-called human condition. Unfortunately, we personalize those fears through the narratives we create, which are anchored in what we see and are told as children.

"Your personal set of gremlins went far beyond the religion you were taught. You remember sitting with your Daddy in that old, World War II control tower outside of town when you were a Cub Scout, watching for Soviet bombers on their way to destroy our airplane factories on the other side of the state? Remember practicing crawling under your desk in case one of them happened to nuke the grade school? Tell me that didn't do some serious psychic damage to your malleable, little mind.

"Think about it: during the week you worried about being blown up and burned to pieces by the goddam Russians, and on Sundays you were being told that never mind the Commies, God Himself, depending on his mood that day, could very well light you up and keep you burning through all eternity. No wonder you became such a needy, messed up, guilt-ridden man.

"Life is short, Scooter. The way I figure it, you've lived more than half of yours. You deserve to spend the rest of it living a good life and doing good things, so that when you do finally pass, you'll leave a life well lived. That doesn't mean there won't be any rough patches. You'll still hit a few potholes now and then. But they won't throw you off the road like they've done in the past, because you've finally gained the confidence and knowledge to handle them."

John finished his coffee and got up to leave.

"Speaking of potholes, I must warn you: when you get back to Creekmore, you're going to be facing holy hell. You didn't hear this from me, but you and your buddies are in some serious trouble. A warrant has been issued for your arrest. I'm not sure what the charges are, but I hear they're serious, possibly murder or manslaughter. You may want to get yourself a good attorney."

"Is there anything you can do?"

"No, not really. No one in Heaven is allowed to practice law. Especially lawyers. But hey, I'll put in a good word for you."

He started to leave but stopped. "Scooter, this might be my last visit. You're doing well and there are a lot of other 'clients' who need me more than you do."

"You're telling me these therapy sessions are over?"

He smiled sadly. "I'm afraid so."

"I understand," I said. "But if I don't see you again, please do me one last favor. Stop by the ranch and visit your daughter. She needs you."

He gave me an exasperated look, shook his head, and was gone.

———

By midmorning, we were heading north. John had given me a lot to chew on over the long road ahead. His last appearance had been a mixed blessing. Yes, having just dodged a big bullet, a sense of peace and harmony had suddenly settled over me. Perhaps he was right, perhaps I finally had put my terrors—at least the darkest of them—behind me.

But John's final warning had also made it clear that I was not out of the woods yet. I still had to face a real-life demonic sheriff and his deputy back in Creekmore.

I started to call Shelia Mae to seek some succor and tell her I'd be home in a day or two, but instead dialed Norm when I saw he had repeatedly been trying to reach me. He answered on the first ring.

"Bad connection, Jamal. Call me later this afternoon." The phone went dead and them immediately rang again. "Scooter, where are you?"

"It's Jamal."

"No time for smart-ass comments, my friend. Had to go to a secure line. We're in big trouble, and I was trying to throw them off in case they were listening."

"Them who? Andy and Barney?"

"Them, the state bureau of investigation, and more than likely half the population of the county, including your friend Shelia Mae. Word is, there's a warrant out for our arrest."

"On what charges?"

"You've been charged with murder and making false statements in the death of John Marshall. Bobby, Digger, and yours truly are charged with being accessories to the crime.

According to Norm, Luke had turned up the heat on John's death after identifying his skull through matching dental records. He had done a second round of interviews with Bobby, Norm, Dan, and Shelia Mae. A state investigator also had shown up, although Norm didn't know what his involvement was.

"You'd better turn around and lay low until you get lawyered up," he said.

"How much does Shelia Mae know?" I asked.

"I assume everything, Scooter. But for God's sake, screw your head on straight and focus. She isn't the problem. It's her daddy's skull that may well send us all to the state pen."

I assured him that I would call a Texas lawyer friend of mine the moment I got off the phone. But instead, I rang Shel.

"Scooter." Her voice was flat, remote.

"What's wrong?"

"Nothing. Been going through more of Daddy's stuff. Kind of bittersweet."

"Did you find other things that upset you?"

"You could say that."

"Like what?"

"Like the fact that you're a lying piece of shit. You charming, prick bastard!"

She knew. Everything. Or thought she did. And I should have ended the call there. But I plunged ahead.

"What did I do?"

"You know fucking well, Scooter! For starters, you might want to explain how long Daddy's head—his skull for God's sake—has been sitting above your fireplace, like a macabre tchotchke? What the fuck was that all about?"

Before I could respond, she hung up.

I started to call her back but thought better of it. Instead, I called Paul, a tennis partner and respected Dallas defense attorney.

"What the hell, man?" he said, after I laid out the story of John's death, the discovery of his skull, my rekindled friendship with his daughter, and the antics of her jilted high school boyfriend. "You've done some dumb things in your life, but this takes the cake. Where are you now?"

I told him I was headed back to Creekmore after a week of fly-fishing in New Mexico but left out the gory details.

"What's your ETA? I'll fly up and we'll get things cleaned up. Meantime, do not talk to the sheriff or the girl."

I took his advice and continued north. Buck curled up in the back seat and slept. I ruminated, clinging as best I could to the recent optimism I'd experienced and the sage advice of John's final sermonette, while trying unsuccessfully not to replay my conversation with Shelia Mae.

By the time the lights of Creekmore finally appeared on the horizon, my dueling voices of reason had come to a compromise: I had to come clean with Shel, even if it meant never seeing or speaking to her again. After all, if I had learned anything during this ghastly, ghostly adventure it was that I didn't need a woman to make my life complete. It was high time I, like everyone else on God's green earth, faced the music and learned to dance with the one who brung me—my twin in the mirror.

It was time to bring the curtain down on the melodrama I'd both directed and starred in most of my life. And I needed to do it in a decidedly undramatic way—no gunshots, leaps into the ocean, or other life-ending finales. I needed to get out of my head and on with my life.

And then, as I topped a small rise in the blacktop, I saw it: a well-lit billboard with a giant picture of Luke and WD in their boxers. Below it, equally large letters proclaimed:

Welcome to Creekmore—our lawmen are here to serve you.

I slammed on the brakes, pulled over, and dialed Norm.

"What were you thinking?" I demanded.

"You saw the sign," he said. "Some really bad-ass work, no?"

"No. Just dumb-assed stupid."

"Well, it got the desired result," Norm pouted. "Luke is offering a reward for anyone having information on who put it up."

"Oh swell. And your next move is . . .?"

"Blackmail!" he said gleefully. "We'll remove the sign when he drops the charges against us."

"Which will now include attempted blackmail, you idiot!"

"Calm down, my friend, you have nothing to worry about. I have a plan."

"Another plan? Oh great. You going to tell me what it is?"

"Still working out the details. Where are you?"

"In front of your goddamn sign."

"Well, don't go into town. Turn around and head west. I'll call you back in a minute."

As I disconnected, I saw that Paul had messaged me that he had landed. Twenty minutes later, I picked him up at the local air strip. We rolled his plane into an old, abandoned hanger and headed west, having still not heard back from Norm.

I again went over the whole story, this time in more detail, from John's final journey to the discovery of his skull, to my less than truthful conversations with Shelia Mae and my troubles with the sheriff.

"Wow," Paul said, after I'd finally finished, "that's one hell of a tale. What you need is an agent, not a lawyer—someone should make this into a movie, the royalties of which will pay the exorbitant legal fees I'm going to bill you to get you out of this mess. Seriously, Scooter, you're in the eye of a major shit storm, getting out of which will not be easy, or perhaps even possible."

"Thanks for the pep talk. It really makes me feel better."

––––––––––––

Thirty minutes later, as we continued heading west, driving aimlessly through the dark, empty night, Norm finally called. With no introduction, he gave GPS coordinates and orders to "approach without lights, park in the barn, and avoid further communication."

I gave him a smart-ass "Roger that, Bandit One," but he had already hung up.

After another hour of crisscrossing the landscape on dusty, minimally maintained country roads, we pulled into what appeared to be an abandoned farmstead. What had once been a handsome, two-story farmhouse was now a collapsing pile of weatherworn wood. The barn was still standing, but barely.

We parked inside it and made our way to the only sign of life, a battered old double-wide on cinder blocks in a far corner of the property. As we approached it, an armed, black-clad figure materialized from a nearby stand of trees.

"Halt or I'll shoot!" Norm demanded, pointing a banana-clipped assault rifle at Paul. "Who the hell is this?"

"My personal high-powered defense attorney."

Paul walked over and hesitantly shook Norm's hand.

"Welcome to the safest safehouse on the High Plains," Norm whispered, lowering his weapon. "The coffee's on, there's beer in the fridge, and Rapid Deployment Team Bravo is in place, locked, loaded and ready for action."

Once inside the dark trailer, I could make out the figures of three other men seated in the tiny living room. Only when Norm lit a kerosene lantern did I recognize Bobby, Father Tim, and Digger, all but the priest armed and clad in camo.

"Holy shit," Paul exploded. "Are you guys planning on kidnapping or killing someone? It was my understanding that I was enlisted to help plan a legal case, not participate in another crime—assuming there was a first one."

"I understand," Norm said. "But you won't have much of a case if your client is dead. And unfortunately, the sheriff and his deputy are a couple of crazy dudes who would like nothing better than to terminate Scooter and avoid the messiness of what is sure to be Creekmore's biggest courtroom drama in a century."

"Jesus, Norm, they're not going to kill me," I protested. "Luke's pissed at me for trying to steal his high school sweetheart. Misguided as that is, he probably has a solid case for throwing the book at all of us for our role in John's death."

"No shit!" It was an angry, panicky Digger. "I should never have listened to that crazy old rancher, or you misguided idiots. I don't know what I was thinking. Even if I'm acquitted, I'll be ruined. When they hear what really happened, no one's ever going to let me near their loved ones, let alone bury them."

"No one's going to find you guilty of anything, Digger," I said. "We—Norm, Bobby, and I—got you into this. We own it. You were simply the victim of a death wish gone awry.

"Oh, I like that," Paul chimed in sarcastically. "Can I use that line in your defense?"

Father Tim laughed, receiving hostile looks from rest of us. "What can I say?" he shrugged. "As the Bible says, 'Blessed are the ironic, for they shall become standup comics.' Seriously, may I suggest that with the help of Scooter's friend here, this fine and I'm sure rational attorney, we come up with an honorable plan for dealing with and defusing this unfortunate matter."

"A great idea," Paul concurred, "from an equally level-headed man of the cloth, whose presence here, for the life of me, I can't figure out."

"Confessor and friend," Tim replied, "who happens to have a somewhat unique perspective on the incident, but rest assured, was not a part of it."

For the next two hours, over the beer and pizza Norm had picked up on the way to the farm, we discussed John's death and what we really knew of it. We talked about the sheriff's motives for going after me, and how much he really knew about how John had died. Finally, we debated what, if anything, we should do to address the problem. While Norm continued to argue for a confrontation, Paul, Bobby, Tim, and I made the case for a peaceful approach.

"Let me be blunt if I may," Paul finally said. "While I'm sure you were an outstanding CIA operative, Norm, such tactics in this situation might, shall we say, be misinterpreted by the sheriff and his deputy, given your description of their demeanor."

"Amen to that," Tim chimed in.

Norm refused to budge, finally suggesting that we sleep on it and revisit it in the morning. In the meantime, convinced that we might have been followed and were vulnerable to an early-morning raid, he demanded that we post a sentry throughout the night.

"I'll stand the first watch. Scooter, you'll take over at 0400, okay?"

Reluctantly, I agreed, and at the designated hour microwaved a cup of instant coffee and took my position on a frayed old camp chair Norm had hidden in a patch of high weeds near the trailer. It was a beautiful night—clear, crisp but not too cold, and unusually still—a perfect night for gazing up at the stars and into one's soul.

Which was exactly what I did. I thought about John. I thought about Shel. I thought about the people close to me. I thought about what a good life I had: a long and happy marriage and a daughter who was not only beautiful and successful, but also incredibly grounded in her faith and life. I reflected on the two successful careers I'd had, both of which I not only enjoyed but also, I believed, had helped make the world a little better of a place.

So, with all the good, why was it hard to let go of the bad? Why couldn't I just accept myself for whom I was and enjoy this adventure called life? One had only to look up at the night sky and realize that the brilliant engineer, artist, or whatever is behind it all, had created something that operated pretty much like clockwork without our fretting and meddling.

I woke up to the sound of gunfire and electronically amplified demands to surrender lest our hideout be torched, and we all be consumed in a fiery hell. The mix of a threatening, godlike voice serenaded by automatic weapons was so terrifying and weirdly comical, that I first assumed it was just another of my dark, daft dreams, and I pulled my coat tightly around me and tried to go back to sleep.

Then I heard the calming, priestly voice of Father Timothy

admonishing someone to "put down your weapons my sons, we are coming out peacefully," followed by Norm's very angry "like hell we are!"

I grabbed the assault shotgun Norm had given me and peeked around the trailer. There, only a few feet away, were Luke and WD, hiding behind their cruiser.

"Don't move," I calmly commanded, sliding the pump action in a replay of our earlier encounter. "Drop your weapons and put your hands in the air."

Again, they did as they were told. I shouted to Norm to shut up and put down any and all weapons I was sure he was carrying. Then, I called to Tim and Paul, asking them to come out and help me deal with our two "captives."

Moments later they appeared, the priest in boxer shorts, a clerical collar, and a bling-sized crucifix that I'd never known him to wear.

"What seems to be the problem, Sheriff?" he asked, calmly. "Why the gunfire on such a peaceful night?"

"I have a warrant for the arrest of four suspects, one of which is pointing a gun at me and three others I believe are in that trailer," he said, trying unsuccessfully to manage his anger. "I need them to disarm and surrender peacefully, or else—"

"Or else what?" Paul glared at the two.

"Who the hell are you?" Luke asked.

"I am the attorney of the aforementioned suspects. Having just witnessed an unnecessary and, I believe, unlawful effort to apprehend these good citizens, I would suggest you two are the ones who should be answering the questions here."

"Fuck you," WD said, spitting in the general direction of Paul and Tim.

"Duly noted," Paul said. "Now, lay flat on the ground and spread 'em so we can cuff you."

The two looked at him incredulously.

"You heard him," Tim growled, sounding more like a low-country evangelist than a Roman Catholic priest.

After handcuffing the two and locking them in the back of the cruiser, we went inside to figure out what to do next. Bobby and Digger were subdued and clearly scared. Norm, still thirsty for vindication and retribution, was apoplectic. Before he could launch into one of his militant screeds, I suggested that Paul lead the discussion, as he was our attorney and the only objective voice in the room.

It didn't take Paul long to convince everyone but Norm to take a peaceful, somewhat contrite approach. "Scooter and I will drive back to town and meet with the county judge and the local prosecutor. Tim and Digger, you follow in the cruiser with the sheriff and his deputy. Monitor the radio to make sure no one attempts to contact them. Norm, you and Bobby drive home and chill out until you hear from us. Okay?"

Digger, Tim, and Bobby nodded. Norm stared silently at the ground. I felt a huge, albeit fleeting, sense of relief.

34

JUDGE ABBOTT HAD BEEN a close friend of my father. Although I had not seen him in several years, I assumed he would give me a fair shake or at least hear my side of the story. The young county attorney, Nash Brewster, was a question mark. I had never met him, but heard he was a gun-toting neo-conservative and one of the sheriff's drinking buddies.

We met them in the judge's quarters in the county courthouse. The old stone building, which stood on the town square, carried the musty aroma of decaying ledgers and ancient history and the earnest aura of small-town democracy that I had sensed the first time I entered it as a child.

The judge, shockingly old and frail, greeted us warmly and introduced us to Nash, who was decked out in a western-cut suit, bolo tie, and a stainless-steel six-shooter in a hand-tooled holster that matched his boots.

He nodded coolly but remained seated.

"What can I help you fellas with?" the judge chuckled. "I assume it is of some urgency, given it's the Sabbath."

"It's about your sheriff and his deputy," I said.

"Then why aren't they here?" Brewster asked. "Seems you should have called them if you had a problem."

"They are here, counselor," Paul said, pointing to the window. "Handcuffed in the back seat of their cruiser."

The young lawyer jumped from his chair and ran to the window. "What the hell? What happened?"

"I witnessed them using excessive force in an attempt to intimidate and arrest my client here and three other suspects," Paul replied. "They were subdued and disarmed early this morning to avoid any unnecessary bloodshed. They have in no way been harmed, at least physically, although by now I think the sheriff's ego may be shot to hell."

Brewster turned on Paul, his hand hovering over his holster like a wannabe Wyatt Earp. "Like hell they did. Your client here and his pals are cold-blooded murderers. And you, my friend, are nothing but a sleazy, son-of-a-bitching, golden-tongued, big-city lawyer."

"Sit down, Nash, you idiot," the judge ordered with a casual wave of his cane. "You're out of order, not to mention using way too many multisyllabic adjectives. Good thing you weren't an English major or I'd jail you for contempt." He winked at me. "Scooter, is there something you'd like to tell me? Perhaps you and I should have a private little chat."

After sending Paul and Brewster out for coffee and donuts, the judge listened quietly as I shared the story of John's death with as much honesty and detail as I could. I told him of John's wishes, of the trip to Oklahoma, and of the earnest but deceitful story we hatched to cover the truth. Finally, I told him of Buck's discovery of John's skull and the unsolved mystery and suspicion it had created.

When I'd finished, the old judge stared at me solemnly for a minute or two before speaking.

"That mutt of yours," he said, "must be one heck of a bird dog."

"He is, Judge," I agreed. "Maybe too good."

He chuckled and then grew serious. "Does Shelia Mae know this story?"

"No sir. She doesn't."

"You haven't told her?"

I stared at the floor. "No sir."

"Because you don't want to hurt her, right?"

"Yes sir."

"And because, after all these years, you're still sweet on her? Right, Scooter?"

"That's right, your honor, because I'm a goddamn romantic fool."

The judge came over and placed his hand on my shoulder. "That's nothing to be ashamed of Scooter," he said. "I sometimes think the world would be a much better place if we all were romantic fools . . . with good bird dogs."

He called the two attorneys back into the room and asked them to retrieve Luke and WD and bring in the rest of the gang. He then ordered the lawmen into his chambers with the two lawyers and told the rest of us to take the coffee and donuts and go sit quietly in the courtroom.

"Given it's Sunday, perhaps Father Timothy will lead you in some much-needed prayer and meditation. There's a Bible in there somewhere, Father. I don't think it's your version, but feel free to use it, or let Digger here read some scripture. He's done enough funerals, I'm sure he'll do a good job."

For more than an hour, while the judge heard the other side of the story, we sat quietly in the old imposing courtroom. Despite Norm's protests that we were innocent and didn't need spiritual guidance, we let Tim offer up a prayer blessing the donuts and seeking help from God in guiding us through "this unfortunate situation in which my brothers find themselves."

Dan then read a short passage from the Psalms.

Finally, Brewster and the two lawmen returned, looking flushed and grim, and sat on the far side of the courtroom. Except for the county attorney announcing that the judge wanted to see my four friends in his chambers, no one spoke.

Another hour passed, after which the quartet returned smiling. Moments later Judge Abbott, now robed, gavel-wielding, and looking quite the formal jurist, entered. We all rose without being asked.

"Sit down, boys," he said. "Given the unusual nature of these proceedings, let's keep the formalities to a minimum. The information that you've shared with me this bright Sunday morning is indeed dark and bizarre: murder charges pending against an upstanding member of the community, an armed assault on him and his companions followed by their capture and delivery to me of the county's entire law enforcement department in handcuffs.

"Oh, and that god-awful billboard on the highway. Am I to assume that embarrassing photo of Creekmore's finest is somehow wrapped up in this?"

"Damn straight it is, Judge," Luke said.

Judge Abbott's gavel came down hard. "Shut it, Sheriff. As you are well aware, there is no profanity in my courtroom."

"No shit," Norm whispered.

"I heard that, Norm! That goes for you, too. Now fellas, here's what I'm going to do: First, I want everyone in this room to calm down and stop acting like children. Second, I want all of you to think hard about what you did and why you did it. Luke, as I told you when I reluctantly signed the warrants, these are serious charges. Are they justified? If you truly think they are, if you have the evidence, then by all means go forward with them.

"But," here he pointed his finger at the sheriff, "when it comes to Scooter, you seem to have some nonsensical bug up your butt. Whether it's the envy bug or a jilted boyfriend bug, I don't know. But if either is the case, then you may want to reconsider your actions.

"And fellas," he said, turning to us, "if there is something you need to do or say to clear yourselves, now would be the time to do it. For example, some of you may want to remove that disgraceful eyesore out on the highway. Norm, that might be a job for you and Bobby. Scooter, I don't know, but I wonder if you might want to talk this whole affair over with someone besides your three amigos— someone who might have a, shall we say, different perspective."

He gave me a gentle smile. "I'm just saying . . ."

"And Father Tim, you just keep praying for everyone involved in this sad situation, including the soul of my late, great friend, rancher John Marshall, and his sweet daughter.

"Gentlemen, we will meet here next Sunday morning, promptly at nine. At that time, Sheriff, Attorney Brewster, you will let us know whether you are going to proceed with this case. Between now and then, none of you will say anything about this to anyone outside this room. This hearing, or whatever you want to call it, is over."

With that he brought down his gavel.

35

NORM AND BOBBY took down the billboard that afternoon. I spent the day reassembling my ransacked house. As I went through the bits and pieces of my life that the sheriff had strewn about, I also tried to sort the disparate thoughts and emotions scattered throughout my brain.

Part of me was still pissed at Luke, part of me at John, and part at myself for getting into this mess in the first place, and then not being honest with Shelia Mae. And yet, as I put things in order—creating neat piles of both stuff and thoughts—I began to see again how natural and unavoidable the messiness of life was.

None of the players in this shit show I was a part of were bad people. Their—our—intentions all came from our own unique sets of desires, needs, beliefs, and fears. Through these filters, each of us was constantly rewriting and editing the stories we created that allowed us to live with some semblance of pride, purpose, and dignity in a chaotic and threatening world.

Normally, our values and beliefs kept us from losing it when our lesser angels whispered those yarns back to us. But there were times when, our guards down, we listened as they urged us on, and did exactly what our stories told us to do.

While I couldn't vouch for the others, I knew I'd been listening to far too much of my own bullshit over the past few weeks. Come what may, I had to break that cycle. I had to come clean with Shel, and I had it do it now.

I grabbed my phone and texted her: *Back in town. Have missed you. If you're not still angry would love to talk.*

So much for not listening to my own BS. I deleted the message and typed a second: *Shel, I'm back. There are some things I need to tell you about your dad's death that I've kept from you. I'm sorry.* I deleted *kept from you*, replacing it with *lied to you about*, hit SEND, and then realizing my continued cowardice, picked up the phone and called her.

She answered on the third ring.

"Shelia Mae, it's Scooter. We need to talk."

"Why?"

"Because I've been a real shit to you."

"I know."

"I lied to you about my involvement in your dad's death."

"I know."

"I want to tell you what really happened—or what I think happened."

There was a pause. "I'll be honest, Scooter, I believe I now know what really happened. I can't believe I fell for your bullshit. I'm hurt and angry and don't ever want to speak to you again."

The line went dead.

I drank too much and slept very little that night. I kept thinking how badly things had gone wrong, and what—if anything—I might do to make them right. I begged John to return, but he never showed.

Finally, near dawn, I fell asleep, waking up only a couple of hours later, feeling ragged and depressed. After moping about for another hour, I decided I needed a long walk to clear my mind. I made a smoked pheasant sandwich, stuck a couple of beers in my hunting vest, put Buck along with my favorite twenty-gauge in the truck, and headed out.

It was a sunny, windless late December morning, good, I thought, for finding birds. We drove to a small piece of land in a far corner of the county. Buck got birdy right out of the pickup and flushed a rooster and two hens before I could load my gun. He gave me a concerned look but kept hunting. By lunchtime, we had a couple of roosters and three quail. But as the temperature continued to rise, the birds scattered.

"We need a blocker," I told Buck. "Someone at the other end of the field to keep them from running."

Seconds later my wish was granted. An orange-clad figure suddenly appeared in the distance. Buck saw it too, and immediately ran toward it. By then I could see it was John, in sunglasses and a wearing a bright orange hunting vest over his brilliantly white vestments.

He knelt to scratch Buck and greeted me warmly.

"I'd love to block for you guys," he said, "but I don't have a license or a gun. Besides, I'm not sure the birds can see me. As long as I'm here, though, I may be able to corral some of the recent craziness that's still swirling around in that little brain of yours, Scooter. I know I told you that you probably wouldn't see me again, but I thought you could use a little more guidance."

"You're a mind reader, too?"

"Sort of. For example, I know that you missed that last bird because you were thinking about Shelia Mae and the trouble you're facing, and not because it was a difficult shot. It wasn't."

"Fair enough. Let's find a place with shade, have some lunch and talk."

We picnicked under a small stand of trees near a dry creek. John looked on enviously when I pulled out my sandwich and beer.

"A good brew and a sandwich are about the only things I miss," he said when he saw me looking at him. "Even something as simple as a peanut butter and jelly. But go ahead and chow down. I'm just here to listen."

For the next hour he did just that, as I recounted the events that had happened since returning to Creekmore. But unlike past visits, I was unusually calm and focused. I talked about wanting to straighten things out with Shelia Mae so that she could get closure and move on with life. I talked about the pending charges, and how I should deal with them.

"I was the ringleader in our little adventure. You know that. Norm jumped in with both feet, but only because I asked him. Bobby came along because he was friends with both of us. Also, he knew that someone would have to wrangle Norm when he went all 'secret agent' on us. And Digger—he was just being the nice, earnest, accommodating friend he always is. Now, he's collateral damage just because he cared about you and the rest of us."

John listened with empathy, nodding occasionally, sometimes shaking his head.

Finally, he spoke. "If I were alive, I'd take the rap for all of you. Don't forget, it was my idea—my adventure—not yours that started the whole thing. In the end, I used you unfairly, lied to you about my true plan, and left you holding the bag, so to speak—a bag, unfortunately, that now holds my skull. For that I'm truly sorry. If I could, Scooter, I would go down to the courthouse right now, and set things straight with the judge. But I can't. And even if I could, I'd probably give old Judge Abbott a heart attack.

"All that said, I'm also thankful. I'm thankful for you granting me my last wish. Without the help of you and your friends, it wouldn't have come true. And, after listening to you, I now realize that this, like most things, happened for a reason.

"Do you realize that for the past hour you've been talking, you never once have spoken of yourself in a negative way? There's been none of the 'woe is me' crap that has consumed our past conversations. This whole time, you've been talking about your friends and how you can help them."

He grinned. "If I didn't know better, I'd say you've been healed by a miracle. Hell, I don't know, maybe you have. Praise the Lord!"

He stood. "To quote a favorite cliché, I think my time here is done. Just one last thing, Scooter: don't give up on Shelia Mae. She'll come around. Be patient."

With that he grabbed the beer I'd been nursing and downed it in a single gulp. We both looked on with dismay as it instantly puddled around his Birkenstocks, muddying the ground. "Shit," he said, "I should have known. Haven't met an angel yet who could hold his alcohol."

He shook his head, and with a sad smile waved goodbye. "See you on the other side my friend. You too, Buck."

Buck and I remained in the field until sunset. Although Buck found his share of birds, I didn't shoulder my gun once. It wasn't the first time I'd gone on aimless, armed walkabouts. But this one was different. Instead of my usual morose slog, I ambled along with a smile, occasionally humming old hymns and tunes from the sixties and enjoying the day. Buck, sensing the difference, frequently returned to my side to make sure I was okay. "I know," I finally told him, "it's weird. But, trust me, it's good weird."

On the way back to town, I called Norm and asked if he and the guys wanted to meet for dinner at Mary's.

"Clearly," he said, "you've not seen the news."

"No. Why?"

"You're all over it, pal. 'Texan a suspect in pagan ritual sacrifice of local rancher.' Apparently," he continued, "the sheriff is drinking buddies with the news director of our friendly Fox affiliate. Only Luke is dumb enough to violate the judge's gag order, and only that freak show of a station is shameless enough to run with it."

"I can't wait to watch it," I laughed.

"Where's your head, Scooter? Jesus, we're being fed to the wolves."

"I'm done being outraged and indignant, Norm. It is what it is. And it will all come out in the wash—one way or the other."

"Well, at least don't parade it down Main Street. Why don't you and Buck come on out and lie low until all this blows over or the shit hits the fan and they take us away in shackles?"

I hung out at Norm's for the better part of the week. It was safe shelter from the shit storm that was apparently building in town. We got up late, read by the fire, snuck out to hike or hunt in the late afternoon, took turns showing off our culinary skills in the evenings, made a serious dent in Norm's humidor and wine cellar, and ended every evening with an esoteric debate on the existential issue of the night—everything from the future of democracy to Jesus' divinity to the best gun to own if you could only own one.

Unfortunately, any thought of lying low dissipated the first day.

Word spreads quickly in small towns, and soon I was getting calls and visits from supporters and well-wishers, who usually came with gifts of either food or drink. I greeted them warmly, thanked them for coming, and convinced them it was much ado about nothing.

The only trouble came from our self-righteous local lawmen and a few religious zealots. Luke and WD kept around-the-clock surveillance until Norm threatened them with a dummy Russian-made RPG, after which they were reduced to erratic drive-bys. Norm, however, kept his fake artillery near the door, and continued to use it to scare off a few protesters and the Fox news team that ventured out in hopes of a scandalous interview or some outrageous footage.

Brother Leon showed up the second night with a couple of deacons and asked if they could pray with me so that I might come back to the fold and be spared an eternity in Hell. I thanked him but graciously declined his offer.

Unfortunately, as they turned to leave, one of the deacons got in my face and called me a "satanic sonofabitch who deserved to die like a dog," at which point Norm went for his RPG and Buck for the man's leg. Although the visitors escaped uninjured, I gave Buck a small piece of steak as a reward for his bravery.

On the last night of my stay, all the guys came over for a barbeque. While sitting around the firepit, we started talking about the pending hearing with Judge Abbott. Norm was continuing to push his dark and mostly violent strategies, while Bobby and the padre proffered caution and restraint. Digger fretted.

I'd had enough.

"Guys, please. Let it go. It's going to turn out just fine. There's no need to get our shorts knotted up over something we have no control over."

They stared at me.

"What's happened to you, Scooter?" Norm finally asked. "You've changed since you came back from New Mexico. Have you just given up?"

"Far from it. But I'm not going to let it ruin my life. Nor am I going to continue getting all worked up and depressed. I—we—did the right thing in helping John pass to the other side. I'm sure if he showed up here tonight, he'd agree. In fact——" I started to tell them about his visits, but caught myself, knowing it would only create unnecessary distraction and concern for my mental state.

"Look, we've all done some stupid shit over the years. But John's death was not one of those times. What we did was honor an old friend's last wish, and we did it with the dignity and respect it demanded. The fact that John apparently used us a bit, well, I believe he was just trying cover his tracks and protect Shelia Mae."

They continued to look at me as if I'd grown a second head.

"Have you gone off your meds?" Bobby cautiously asked.

"No, Bobby, but I have flushed down the toilet all the religious and emotional crap that has been driving me crazy all these years. Replaced it with faith—in myself, in others, in life."

Norm was not buying it. "Now you're speaking in tongues. You're sounding like Brother Ezekiel, that preacher who used to broadcast his sermons from speakers atop the old Assemblies of God church. You haven't turned holy roller on us, have you?"

Father Tim winked at me. "I think what Scooter is trying to tell us is that he's slain a few demons that have been chasing him for a long time and is finally getting on with his life."

With that, the party ended, and I went to bed.

36

TIM HAD SAID IT WELL. Unfortunately, there are always new demons ready to step in when the old ones die. I still had not heard from Shelia Mae. And, despite John's urging patience, I was getting antsy.

I didn't have to wait long. At three in the morning the phone rang.

"Scooter," her voice was quiet, calm. "You were right. We need to talk."

"Shel...? What...? Now? Why the change of heart?"

"I couldn't sleep, and was going through Daddy's old rolltop tonight, rereading some of his journals. I found a letter he'd apparently written to me shortly before he died. Not sure why I didn't see it before. It must have been right here in front of me the whole time.

"In it, he apologizes for how he says he exited this world. Says he alone was to blame. Said that while some of his dear friends supported him, it was his plan and his alone."

She paused. "It's weird, though. It almost sounds like he wrote it after the fact. Said that I should not believe any unfounded rumors I might hear after he was gone."

Oh, John, I silently prayed, *you beautiful old bastard. Bless your heavenly soul.*

"It's probably good that we talk," I said, trying hard to check my emotions, and not sound overly eager.

Another pause.

"Could you come out in the morning? I'll make breakfast."

———————

I was on my way to the ranch before sunup. So as not to appear too eager, I made a detour to the pasture where John had first appeared to me after his death and walked to the creek where he spent his last moments.

Buck assumed we were hunting until a couple of roosters exploded into the air and I ignored them. He apparently hadn't noticed that I was unarmed. From then on, he ran free, not bothering to stay close by.

I climbed the platform John had built, and watched morning come to life. In the stillness, birds began tuning their voices for the coming day. Coyotes and a few head of cattle joined in. A waning moon was still high in the western sky.

It was a beautiful place to witness the world, to welcome a new day and perhaps one's final earthly night. I wondered if John had witnessed an equally gorgeous dawn of eternity on his perch up here.

A breeze smelling of snow and cow shit kicked up from the north, and a chill set in. It was time to go. Still, a dozen feet or so in the air, I lingered, not sure what questions Shelia Mae might be serving with breakfast.

Finally, as doubt again began to seep into my recently restored psyche, I climbed down and walked the short distance to the ranch house.

I could smell smoke from the fireplace and a hint of bacon by the time I reached the barn. Moments later, Buck and I were on the porch, ringing the old chuck wagon gong that served as a doorbell.

"I didn't hear you drive in," Shelia Mae said, opening the door. "Where's your truck?"

"It's a long story," I said, "giving her a hug. "I hope we aren't here too early."

"Not if you don't mind my rather eclectic dress," she laughed, twirling slowly to show off a gorgeous silk robe, old pair of boots, and equally worn flour-sack apron.

"I missed you," she said sadly. "I'm sorry, but the last few days have been horrible."

Over strong cowboy coffee and omelets, she recounted what had happened since I'd fled to New Mexico.

"Two days after you left, I got a call from Luke. He asked me to come down to the sheriff's office and identify some *property* he thought might belong to me. He and WD acted very official and formal. They asked me what I knew about Daddy's death. I told them very little except what you and Digger had shared with me at the time—that Daddy had died, and based on previous arrangements he had made, was to be cremated immediately, with no fanfare or formal funeral.

"I told them that I had agreed. I explained that I told Digger I was going through some medical issues at the time, which Daddy knew about, and that we would hold a memorial service when I next returned home.

"Then Luke reached in his desk and brought out this skull. He proudly placed it on his desk so that it was facing me and asked if I knew whose it was. I was stunned and confused, and frankly so freaked out by what he'd suddenly done that I almost fainted."

She paused, trying to hold back tears. "'It's your daddy's,' he said, in that cocky, official way of his. 'We found it on your old boyfriend's mantle. Weird, ain't it?' I was speechless—horrified. Repulsed. What I wanted to say was how sick he was for shoving it in my face and gloating about it.

"Luke ignored my discomfort, immediately launching into his theory of what had happened. Said he initially figured that there'd been an accident when you guys had been goose hunting. Somehow, one of your guns had gone off in the blind and killed Dad. Rather than face the scandal and outrage that was sure to follow, you made up the story of him dying of a heart attack. You brought him back and convinced Digger to sign the necessary papers and cremate the remains."

"That's not what happened," I interrupted. "The four of us——"

"Let me finish Scooter, please. After finding and identifying Dad's skull, Luke now believes there was foul play. His thinks you purposely killed Daddy. In his twisted mind, he believes that you always wanted to get your hands on our ranch and in my pants, and that with Dad out of the way, it would be smooth sailing."

Again, I started to speak. Again Shel, her face distorted by sadness and anger, stopped me.

"I know, Scooter. His theory is crazy. I never thought you purposely killed Daddy. But the accident—I could believe that, did believe it until early this morning when I was again going through Daddy's stuff, looking for small signs—happy memories—of his presence."

Here she paused. "I have to admit, Scooter, I was . . . still am, desperately searching for the truth . . . evidence of what really happened to Dad . . . and how, if he really died hunting—whether by accident or heart attack—and was cremated, did his skull—if it really is his—turned up in your house."

She paused again, drying her eyes and grasping for composure. "Anyhow, I found his bone-handled pocketknife, the one he always carried, even to church. I found his favorite fountain pen and a smooth piece of obsidian, a tiny but powerful talisman he carried with him, but nothing that would confirm or dispel Luke's theory. Then, as I was about to close the rolltop, I saw this stamped, but unmailed letter addressed to me, dated shortly before Daddy died."

She retrieved it from the desk and handed it to me. "I think you should read it."

I slowly unfolded the handwritten letter, wondering what John had written, praying his words not only put to rest Shelia Mae's suspicion and anguish, but also exonerated me for my role in helping her father die, in part by explaining the mysterious reappearance of his skull.

> *Shel,*
>
> *You probably will never see this, as I still haven't decided whether to mail it. But if I do, or if you happen to come across it later, I'll be upstairs, dancing with your momma and all the angels.*
>
> *I'm writing this because I want to set the record straight about my death. As I've told you, I am a sick old man, sicker than I've let on. Daily I feel Death stalking me. At first, he was a frightening*

specter. But lately I've sensed he is more herder than hunter, and my fear of him has faded.

While I'm in no hurry to leave my earthly home, I now realize the time has come.

As you know, I've never been big on weddings or funerals. I detest the fakery and fiction that both generate in the name of love and goodness. The fancier the wedding, the more likely it is to be a dark fairytale that will one day end in pain and sadness. Funerals, too, are often equally phony. The grander the speechifying, the bigger the bloviating, the smaller the truth that is spoken.

Which is why I have decided to steal away in the dark of the night and face death alone as our native brothers and sisters sometimes did. Because I don't want to worry or hurt you, as a last wish I've asked Scooter to help me with the "arrangements" such as they are. I've also asked him to not speak to you about this, and if questioned, to lie or at least obfuscate the details.

My only concern is that, knowing our little community, people will talk and rumors will fly. If that happens, don't get sucked into the tiny-minded tittle-tattle. As some point, I'm sure Scooter, the good man that he is, will cave and tell you the truth. When that happens, don't be angry with him. Remember, he did this to honor your old man.

Love,
Dad

I folded the letter and handed it back. For a long time neither of us spoke.

"Just as Daddy predicted," Shelia Mae finally said, putting the letter back in her father's desk. "Creekmore is abuzz with rumors. I've had more than one phone call telling me you killed my father. One came from Brother Leon, who assured me he would continue praying for the salvation of both our souls. I told him he was full of shit and to go to hell. "But I wonder. Honestly Scooter, I don't know who or what to believe any more, and despite what Daddy wrote, I need to hear the truth."

So, I told her.

37

IT WAS EARLY FALL, the previous year, when I first called John. The temperature and humidity in Texas had dropped to manageable levels, and for the first time in more than a year, the suffocating sadness that I'd carried since Anna's death had left me. In its place was a growing need to go home—a need to walk and hunt familiar land.

I'd come to believe that returning to Creekmore would provide the reset I needed to finally move on with my life. The thought of coming back filled me with a renewed but fragile sense of hope that I feared might vanish as quickly as it had come.

So, one night I picked up the phone and dialed the ranch. It rang several times before John picked it up.

"Scooter, good to hear your voice. I was beginning to think you'd forgotten me." He sounded old and tired.

"No, sir," I said, "just have had a lot on my mind since, you know, since she . . . left, and haven't felt much like socializing. But I'm better now and think it may be time to thin out your pheasant population."

John seemed to perk up. "Definitely, Scooter. They're overrunning the place. Can't walk ten feet in the big pasture without stepping on a couple."

We both laughed and spent the next twenty minutes talking about hunting, farming, politics, and who had died in the months since we had last spoken. As we talked, John was overcome with fits of coughing and his voice began to sound like a scratchy old seventy-eight record.

I asked about his health.

"Shitty, Scooter," he said after a long silence. "I'm waiting for the tests to come back, but I think the Big C has final caught up with me for all those years I smoked. To be honest, I don't think I'll be here a year from now."

He went on to assure me that I shouldn't worry, he had good doctors and still felt fine for his age. He also ordered me not to say anything to anybody, including Shelia Mae. "She's going through her own difficulties right now," he said. "The last thing she needs is another distraction."

I started to protest, but he stopped me. "Dammit, Scooter, listen to me. Do not call or email her about my situation. I'll let her know when I need to. Promise me?"

I assured him I would say nothing.

A few days later, John called me back, which was unusual, because like so many of his generation he still assumed any call outside a two-mile radius was a costly, long-distance undertaking.

"I was right," he said when I answered. "It's in my lungs. Looks like this is the big one."

I was saddened and stunned and tried to reassure him that new treatments were available that could prolong his life. But again, he cut me off. "Doc says it's too far gone. Says I probably have six months or less." There was a pause. "But you're still coming up to hunt those colorful chickens, aren't you?"

I assured him I was and joked that if he were still up to it, he could be block for us. He laughed and said he would, but that it would require body armor given the way Norm, Bobby, and I shot.

I even proposed a goose hunt, which I could tell lifted his mood considerably. Moments later, however, he again became serious.

"Before you go, Scooter, there's something else I need to discuss with you if you have time."

I assured him I did.

"Good. Now, you haven't said anything to Shelia Mae, right?"

I told him I hadn't.

"Well, don't. And don't say anything about what I'm going to propose."

With that, he laid out a plan for his last days. Funerals, he said, were no fun, especially for those still living. Nor did he like the idea of spending eternity in a fancy, plush-lined box buried under several feet of black prairie earth.

"I've always thought it was disgusting," he said. "It's one thing to bury a dog you loved, but not a person. Shit, it's just wrong."

I mentioned that Ruthie was buried just ten minutes from where he now sat, in the family plot in the big pasture. But he quickly brushed it aside. "You can't refuse a loved one's last request," he countered. "I tried to argue her out of it, but she wouldn't listen."

"So, you want to be cremated?"

"Hell no!" he said. "Maybe ten years ago I would have considered it, but not today. Not with global warming. There's too much carbon in the air as it is, even out here in the country. Burning my carcass up would just be another contribution to a growing existential threat. I'm certainly not going to live to see it, thank God. But I sure as heck don't want it to be my final earthly legacy."

"So," I ventured, "what are you thinking?"

"I'm going out *native style*, so to speak. Don't worry, I've researched it. It's legal, it's practical, and it's cheap. Only one small problem: it will require your help."

"Given your environmental concerns, I assume we're not talking a fiery pyre, are we?"

"No," he said chuckling. "That would draw attention or worse given the drought we've been having. The whole county is under a fire ban. But you're not far off."

He went on to describe a practice employed by certain cultures, including supposedly some Native American tribes: *senilicide*—the killing of the elderly or elderly suicide.

"When I was growing up," he said, "I remember people talking about old Indians who just walked off to die. They also told stories of early settlers finding Native Americans dead on platforms built above the ground. Apparently, they did that in the winter, when the ground was frozen and they couldn't bury them.

"I'm planning on combining the two—building a platform up in a tree and then going up there to die. "It may sound weird, but I think going out in a warm sleeping bag under a sky full of bright stars is much more appealing that laying down on the cold ground.

"Besides, I've always found God more alive, more accessible, out in the living world He created, among the trees and grasses and critters. What better place to meet up with Him for my final journey, than up in the cottonwoods along the Sawlog."

"You're not serious?"

"Deadly serious," he laughed. "But, if I try to do that around here, someone will discover I'm missing, they'll launch a search, and if they find me, they'll think someone did me in or something. God knows what rumors will be flying around. You know how stories sprout wings in a small community like ours. If it was just me, I could not care less. But that's not the legacy I'm going to leave my daughter."

"So, you're going to . . . what?" I was confused and concerned. John was beginning to sound a bit deranged. "Be captured by aliens? Rise up to Heaven in a cloud, with trumpets blaring?"

I knew I should have been more understanding. Here was an old friend facing death. For all I knew, he was just rattled by the news he'd received and was not thinking straight. On the other hand, John was never one to get spooked by bad news.

"Nope. Shaman Ricky Running Bull is taking me on my final journey," he said.

"Salmon who?" Now I was really worried.

"*Shaman*! An Oklahoman, distant cousin of Jimmy Iron Tail who used to work for Dad. He's the real thing. Been trained as a medicine man and ordained as a Christian minister. He's also an EMT. He'll take care of everything."

"Everything? Like giving you a lethal injection?"

"Nah. We'll go out on his ranch to a remote area and pick a spot. He'll build a platform, outfit it, so to speak. There's a ceremony— dances, prayers, peace pipe, and everything. Then he'll put a remote monitor on me and leave me be, along with a flask of what he calls *friendly firewater*—a medicinal cocktail of sorts that I can down if I so choose, to speed my journey. When the monitor starts beeping on his phone, he'll know I've passed on to the happy hunting grounds."

"And then?"

"For the next year or so I'm left to the vagaries of nature—coyotes, worms, the weather, etcetera. At some point, when the time is right, he'll return, bless and scatter my bones, say a few final prayers, and, well, as Porky Pig used to say, "Th-th-th-th-th'. . . that's all, folks!"

I was horrified. Not only by the thought of John's body decaying in an Oklahoma pasture, but also by the still-living John's apparent conviction that this was a perfectly fine idea.

"Not so fast, John. What are those you leave behind, especially Shelia Mae, going to say when they hear about your plan?"

John chuckled. "That's where you come in, Scooter. With your help, they never will. Remember that goose hunt you invited me on?"

With that, he launched into a complicated plan that included me and, as he put it, "a couple of collaborators of your choice." We would stage a rather benign version of John's demise shortly before his actual tree-top death in northern Oklahoma.

Complicated and far-fetched as it was, John had clearly spent a lot of time thinking it through and was convinced it would work. First, we would go on a real goose hunt. Then, I would drive John to Oklahoma to meet Shaman Ricky.

After leaving John with his spiritual guide, we—who my collaborators would be, I didn't yet know—would return to Creekmore and spread the story that he'd dropped dead of a heart attack in the goose blind.

Somehow—here is where John's plan turned murky—with the help of Digger, we would fake a cremation and burial.

John sensed my growing skepticism before I could voice it. "Trust me, Scooter, it will work. And it is for the best. The only downside is that you must carry the story to your grave. I know it's a big ask. But think of the peace it will provide Shel.

As I told you, she has enough going on right now without worrying about me dying off in some tree in Indian Country. And I can die the way I want to, on my own terms. It's the best for both of us."

I was too busy thinking how I could defuse this dreadful ticking time bomb of a plan to respond. But John could sense that I wasn't buying it.

"Look, Scooter, I know you think I'm crazy. Believe me, I'm not. I watched Ruthie, the love of my life, waste away in the nursing home, suffering far longer than she should have thanks to modern science and a culture that says that even though a beautiful, carefree future awaits us in the next life, we need to cling to this one no matter how shitty it gets. Well, that's not right. Either we believe what we preach and practice it, or we're scaredy-cat phonies. For almost a century, I've been the latter, and it's high time I stopped. Which is why I'm going through with this whether you or anyone else likes it or not."

"Okay, John," I said, my thoughts finally settling into words, "I can understand your wish to go out on your own terms. Honestly, it really does sound better than dying in the old folks home. It has some cool, mystical, and even romantic elements to it. And it's organic in a sort of primitive way––"

"Primitive, hell!" John interrupted. "It's a leading-edge ecological practice."

"Maybe in California," I laughed, "but here in the heartland it still is considered weird and wrong. And I'm pretty sure it's illegal."

"Screw the law. Nobody's going to arrest me when I'm dead."

"No," I agreed. "But they just might come looking for me if they found out I lied about your death. Which reminds me, who's going to sign your death certificate if there is no body? Certainly not the sheriff."

"Digger will do the honors if we ask him."

"We?" This was getting more complicated by the minute.

"You and me. He needs to know that you're handling the details from this end. We'll go talk to him. Sell him on the idea. Buy a top-quality urn from him. Maybe even ask him if he has any leftover ashes we might be able to fill it with."

"Uh-huh. I'm sure the most detail-driven and by-the-book funeral director in the state will be happy to forge your death certificate and give us a big zip-lock bag full of human remains—both of which could cost him his license, not to mention a heavy fine or jail time."

John was beginning to lose patience. "Dammit, Scooter, work with me on this. Dan, his father, his grandfather, and his great grandfather have been burying us Marshalls since we settled this land. Hell, we're even related—sort of. Digger's mom was a cousin of mine. I'm sure he'll see it as his duty to send me off in the fashion I am requesting."

"Well, I guess *you* better ask him," I said, hoping Dan's shock and refusal would end his hairbrained idea.

"*We* will," he said. "When the time is right, we will."

———————

I didn't hear back from John for several weeks and hoped he'd forgotten his bizarre exit strategy. But while I knew I should call him to see how he was doing, I put it off, fearing he might bring it up again.

Then, a couple days before heading to Creekmore to hunt, I spoke with Norm, who mentioned he'd seen the old rancher in Mary's looking sick and forlorn.

"He told me he was 'troubled in body and soul,'" Norm said. "Talked about not being long for this world, about missing Ruthie and Shelia Mae. Said Shel was dealing with some serious problems of her own but wouldn't say what they were. Told me she didn't want his help.

"At one point, he tearfully shook his head and proclaimed that his guilt and regret as a father were going to kill him if the Big C didn't get him first. I thought it was just the ramblings of an old man, but I didn't have the heart to argue. Also didn't ask if we can hunt the ranch, but I'm assuming we can. We always have."

"Later that day John called to confirm I was still planning on coming up to hunt. "It's getting that time," he said.

"I can't wait," I replied.

He laughed. "I was talking about my big finish, Scooter, not pheasants. We have to finalize our plans as soon as you get up here. Time's a wastin'—at least as far as I'm concerned. The birds will have to wait."

I promised him I'd come out to the ranch as soon as I arrived.

Two days later, just as the prairie sun was putting on a spectacular fall finale, I pulled into the ranch. An ancient figure with a cane shuffled slowly out to greet me. I tried to mask my shock and gave him a gingerly hug, fearing I might crush his fragile frame.

He motioned me to follow him into the house, where he'd lit a fire and set out a bottle of whiskey and two glasses. He pointed to one of the chairs, and then all but collapsed into the other.

"I was hoping you'd get here before bedtime," he said, weariness slowing his words. "Glad you made it when you did. As you can see, I'm not in the best shape."

With that, he quickly moved on to the business at hand. "We need to talk to Digger in the morning. I told him we'd meet him at the mortuary about nine thirty. Then we have to go over the details one last time. I told Shaman Rick you'd be driving me out later this week or early next."

"So soon?" I was stunned by his determination and sense of defeat.

"Yep. I'm ready to get it over with."

I started to protest but John cut me off. "Scooter, please just shut up and humor me. I know this is hard for you, but I've made up my mind."

"Have you said anything to Shelia Mae?"

"I called her yesterday. Told her I was feeling poorly, but still able to fend for myself. She was going to cancel a business trip to Italy and fly home, but I talked her out of it. Told her she had enough to worry about and that I was in good hands." He grinned. "Said you were taking me goose hunting as soon as you got up here, and that I was really looking forward to it.

"I think that convinced her I was okay. Oh, and I also told her not to rush back when I did pass. We agreed that she would wait until one of her regular trips home and hold a memorial party for some of my closest friends—the few old ones still around and the young ones like you.

———————————

As soon as I left the ranch, I called Norm and Bobby and told them I was in town and that we urgently needed to talk. Norm told me to drive straight out to his place. He met me in the driveway and directed me to park in his workshop garage.

"There are eyes in these hills," he said cryptically. "Good eyes with very bad intentions."

I assumed it was just Norm's professional paranoia, but when we got inside, he told me he suspected the sheriff was watching him. When I asked why Luke would be staking him out, he was vague—

something about the sheriff and WD having nothing better to do.

Bobby arrived a few minutes later, and over dinner I shared John's plan.

"Make's perfect sense," Norm said. "Elegant, dignified, understated. I'm impressed. But given the deception and trickery involved, why are you telling us?"

"Yeah," Bobby agreed. "It's noble of you to help John, but the fewer people who know the better, and you and I know that Norm is the biggest gossip in town."

I ignored Bobby's attempt at humor. "Because I need both of you to help me. The goose hunt needs to be real. The three of us need to take John on a hunt. I know a good place south of here near the Oklahoma border. We'll get a few geese, take pictures of everyone, and then I'll drive John to meet the shaman."

It took some convincing and most of a bottle of twenty-five-year-old scotch, but they finally agreed. After all, at one time or another, especially when we were younger, John's sage, plain-spoken wisdom had saved each of us from our own folly and made us better, stronger people. We all had our stories, some even too private to share with each other. The least we could do was to grant John his final request.

Convincing Digger was more difficult. John and I met him at the funeral home, ostensibly to plan for John's eventual death, something Dan had been suggesting for several years.

He greeted us warmly and led us to his office adjoining the casket showroom. "Well, John, I'm glad to see you. I was getting worried that you'd never come. I know it is tough to do, but you did the right thing, especially for your daughter. You know, death is a funny thing. Most of us avoid it like the plague. Out of sight, out of mind. But sooner or later it comes. And if, when it does, no one has bothered to plan for it, you're dealing with a god-awful mess."

He handed John a folder. "I don't know what you have in mind, but we have a number of options here, depending on how much you want to spend. The big costs are usually the casket and the vault. State law says you must have both. Now, you can save a chunk of change if, instead of a copper or stainless-steel vault, you go with a concrete or plastic one. I say plastic, but it's really the same material the NFL uses in its helmets. Very resilient and you don't have to worry about concussions."

Dan's attempt at humor, like a big Canada shot at altitude, fell with an earth-shaking thud.

John slowly leaned forward, putting his hand on the funeral director's desk, and looked him in the eye. "Forget both the casket and the packaging, whatever the hell it's made of. Where I'm going, Digger, and how I'm going to get there will require neither."

"You're thinking of cremation then?"

"Not exactly."

A look of horror spread over Dan's face as John went on to explain in detail his final plans: the goose hunt, the Oklahoma road trip, the shaman-reverend-spiritual guide, the rest in the trees.

"John," Dan spoke softly, shaking his head, "that's just not right, not to mention illegal in most states. What would Ruthie think? What will Shelia Mae say?"

"Ruthie would think that she was right after all, her husband was a bull-headed nut. Shelia Mae will never know. "And," he added, "you will be paid in full for the service you provide."

"What services?"

"Signing my death certificate, faking my cremation, taking care of my internment in the family plot and keeping your mouth shut. Oh, and providing some ashes if you have any extra lying around."

The look of horror on Digger's face turned to one of fear and repulsion. "I could lose my license, not to mention my reputation. Besides which, it's just plain wrong. Everything about it is wrong."

"Relax, Dan," I said, trying to keep the conversation from spinning farther out of control. "Think of this not as a sick, sinister plot to rid ourselves of this old rascal here, but rather a novel and somewhat unique homage to a good friend and father figure. You and I have talked many times about the role John here has played in shaping the men we are today. This is a way to thank him for that—a noble and dignified ritual to honor a good man and a lifetime of good work."

Dan still looked skeptical, but I could see he was weighing the arguments.

John saw it too, and quickly jumped in. "How about this? I'll still pay full freight for a first-class service, complete with a high-end casket and a stainless-steel vault. You can donate it all to one of your less fortunate victims."

"Clients," Dan corrected him. "That would be generous, John. Really. But you're still pushing my comfort level, not to mention my ethics and legal liability."

"I understand, Digger," John replied softly. "But know this, I would forever be grateful."

For what seemed like minutes, Dan contemplated the obviously ill old man sitting before him. Finally, he stood, walked around his desk, and shook John's hand. "You are a weird old rascal, John. But as Scooter says, you've been one hell of a friend and mentor. It's a deal."

———————

A week went by, and then one evening John called and told me it was time to go. "The pain is getting worse. I talked to the doctor. He said I should think about hospice care. I told him I'd call him in a couple of days."

The next afternoon, after making final arrangements for our journey with Norm, Bobby, and Dan, I drove to the ranch. As I pulled in, I noticed that John's ancient Indian motorcycle was sitting on a trailer, shining like a new bike. When I asked about it, he said we were going to pull it to the Shaman Reverend's happy hunting grounds.

"I've heard tell that old Indians used to ride off into the sunset on their favorite mount. I just couldn't do that with Felix. That old steed has been with me too long. So, I'm going to take my final ride on my old bike."

When I asked John if I could help him pack for the trip, he shook his head, pointing to a backpack on the dining room table. "Don't need much where I'm going," he said. When I asked what he was taking, he told me it was none of my business. "Just some personal stuff and a little scotch."

He'd also prepared the house for his leaving. In a large binder, he left detailed instructions for a neighbor, who several years earlier, had taken over most of John's farming and ranching. He also left an inventory of equipment that should be sold or given away and a list of household items that should be donated to the Salvation Army.

"Emma, my housekeeper, came over last week," he said, looking around the large living room. "It should not need another cleaning until Shelia Mae comes home. I want it to be welcoming when she shows up—like it should be. It's hers now."

That night after dinner—I'd cooked him a big steak from a cow he'd butchered that summer—we sat and talked.

"I know you think I'm crazy, Scooter," he said as he again surveyed the room, now illuminated only by a small fire. "But I feel more at peace than I have for a long time. My only lingering sorrow and regret is how I've treated Shelia Mae."

With tears in his eyes, he talked about his struggle in accepting her sexuality. "I knew I should have the minute she told me, but I just couldn't. Not sure why. Perhaps it was my religion, what I'd always been taught. Maybe it was just my reaction as a father. In any case, I refused to accept it. Wouldn't. Could never, ever, discuss it with her. Denied it. Pushed it out of my head. And, in the process, pushed her away.

"If you learn one thing from me, Scooter, it's this: Don't ever lock those you love in little boxes. Don't distort your love for them with rigid religious or cultural rules. Don't try to control them or change them. Don't be so goddam selfish. Just accept them and love them.

"You and me, Scooter, we can be real assholes. Shelia Mae calls it the *jerk gene.* She once told me that all men have it, at least all the ones she'd ever met. I think she's right. And most of us can't seem to overcome it."

He stared into the fire.

"Reach out to her if you can, Scooter. She's going to need some help after I'm gone—some strong moral support. Not so much with the ranching or farming. I've already leased the cropland, and she's damn good at buying cattle, if for some reason she ever wants to come back here.

"No, what she needs is emotional support. I know you haven't seen much of each other over the years, but I think you're still one of the few people around here whom she'll listen to, whom she trusts."

Norm and Bobby met us at the ranch shortly after midnight, and soon an oddball funeral procession of two pickups and the trailered old motorcycle were rolling southeast.

We were tucked into the goose blind well before dawn. Drinking coffee and warmed by tiny gas heaters, we comfortably witnessed the unique, unhurried creation of another day.

The distant honking of geese seemed to push a wave of new life over John. He put his ancient, battered call to his lips, answering as if he was their long-lost brother.

"Coming in low from the southeast," he whispered after a few minutes. "Guns up!"

I could see the twinkle in his eyes as he peered through the straw-laced screening, watching the large V steadily advancing with the dawn. I could not take my eyes off his happy, contented sunlit face, even as around me the air exploded in gunfire, falling geese, and excited shouts.

Within a couple of hours, John had his limit. While the rest of us continued to hunt, he sat in a corner of the blind, eyes closed, smile on his face, quietly humming some of the old hymns he knew by heart—"The Old Rugged Cross," "What a Friend We Have in Jesus," and "When the Roll is Called up Yonder, I'll be There."

When the shooting slowed, we took photos of each other with our birds. While I packed our gear, Bobby and Norm said their final goodbyes. As I made the last trip from the blind to the truck, I could see the three of them in a small circle, staring at the ground or praying, I wasn't sure which. When I reached them and they looked up, I could see everyone had been crying.

As Norm and Bobby headed homeward, John and I pushed south into Oklahoma. When we stopped for lunch in one of the small towns that dot the old state highway we were traveling, I asked John how he was doing.

He offered a melancholy smile. "Woeful in some ways, Scooter, but wonderful in others. The hunt was magnificent—glorious. Still hitting me, though, that it was my last. And that a week or so from now, I'll be watching the souls of those geese I shot, circling in the skies of Heaven." He chuckled. "Just hope they don't recognize me and shit on my halo."

About sunset we arrived at the motel where he was to meet Shaman Ricky early the next morning. What I'd assumed would be a small, rundown place was an upscale, big-chain hotel connected to a new casino.

After helping John check in and unhooking the trailer carrying the old Indian, we had dinner, then lingered as long as we could over one last whiskey. Finally, as the conversation began to die, neither of us having much left to say, John rose and said it was time to go.

"Let's not make this sadder or more significant than it is, Scooter," he said, reaching over and giving me a rare and awkward hug. "It's more than a handshake-parting, but it's not forever. We'll be seeing each other again sooner than you think."

He stepped back and looked me in the eye. "Take care of things like you promised. Be good to Shelia Mae. And remember, if that means lying about my departure, so be it. Believe me, the good Lord will understand."

With that he turned and headed toward the blackjack tables. And that was the last time I was to ever see John—or so I thought.

38

FOR SEVERAL MINUTES after I'd finished, Shelia Mae continued to sit silently, head down, as she had throughout my retelling of the story. Then she stood, walked over, and with teary eyes, embraced me.

"As much as I thought I wanted to hate you and hurt you, I can't. If I should be pissed at anyone, it's Daddy. But I can't be angry with him, either. He did what he thought was the right thing, crazy as it sounds to the rest of us. If anyone should be angry, it's you. It had to be difficult, lying to me the way you did. You're too damned honest to be given that kind of deceitful task. And, I think, too fucked up."

She kissed me on the forehead and laughed, but then quickly stepped back and again became serious. "So, the skull Luke waved in my face . . . it's not Daddy's? That sonofabitch, I should—"

"Actually, Shel, it is your dad's. And that's where the mystery begins."

I told her about Buck finding the skull while pheasant hunting and how, later, I discovered the platform he built near the creek, not far from the ranch house.

"Your dad died just a few hundred yards from where we're sitting, Shel, close to home and to your mom, just like he'd planned it. There was no Reverend Shaman Ricky Running Bull or Oklahoma burial ground. It was all a ruse, Shel—a con. Your dad made it all up to throw us off his trail. He was afraid that if we found out what he was really planning, we would stop him.

"So how did he get back home? You just told me you left him at a casino in Oklahoma."

"I did, Shel, and for the life of me I can't figure out how he got back here."

"The Indian?"

"Shel, I told you, Ricky Running Bull was a fabrication. He doesn't exist."

"No, Scooter. Daddy's motorcycle."

"It couldn't have been. I don't think he was up to riding it this far in the middle of winter. And even if he could, the bike was ancient. Both of them were pretty worn out. Besides, I looked for it. There's no motorcycle out here."

"Oh yes there is," she said, jumping up. "You just didn't know where to look. Come on, I'll show you."

She grabbed my hand and a flashlight, and we headed for the barn. There, she pulled me to a stall in a back corner and, sweeping aside the hay and dirt covering the floor, revealed a large trap door. We opened it and headed down a rickety wooden ramp. And there it was, the old bike, surrounded by a roomful of children's furniture and toys.

"I found it the other day. I hadn't been down here in years. It was my hideout and playhouse as a kid. I got to thinking what might still be down here. And there it was. I wondered how it got here. Now I know."

I went over and straddled the old bike. So, I thought to myself, the old bastard had outfoxed us one last time. I couldn't help but smile.

We walked slowly back to the house, both lost in thought—memories too raw even to share with each other. We collapsed in front of the fireplace, still silent, still processing the truth about John's final journey.

"I wonder," she said, finally, "where Daddy is right now. I wonder if he's watching us, and what he's thinking."

As if answering her question, Buck rose from the rug, walked over to the stairs, and looking up, moaned softly, wagging his tail.

"Oh, he's definitely watching us," I said. "And knowing him, he may even put in an appearance before the day is over."

I spent the rest of the day at the ranch. We went through more of her dad's papers—the journals, newspaper clippings, old photo albums. I showed her the draw where Buck found John's skull, and then walked with her to the scaffold along the creek.

"It is a beautiful place to spend the last moments of one's life," she said, after silently circling it several times. "Before I saw it, I was convinced we should tear it down. Now, I'm not so sure. I'm beginning to see it as a monument to Dad, and not the tragic symbol of his death."

"Here's another memory of him that you can carry with you," I said, pulling his turquoise ring from my pocket. "I found it the day I discovered the scaffold, half buried by leaves."

Shelia Mae slid it on her finger and tearfully gazed at it. "Grampa's ring. Dad always wore it. What a wonderful gift to leave me." She smiled. "A much sweeter reminder than what's sitting in the sheriff's desk."

"Don't worry, Shel," I said. "We'll get that back, too, and give your dad a proper burial."

Toward evening, I decided it was time to go, but as I got up to leave, Shelia Mae stopped me. "I don't want to be pushy, Scooter, but after what you've told me today, I need another sleepover."

Reluctantly, I agreed. And after what happened that night, I was thankful I did.

I was in the midst of a rare amorous dream when John shook me. "Shhh! Don't move, Scooter. It's me. I know I said I wasn't coming back. But after today, I had to thank you. "We—you—did the right thing. We—the three of us—needed . . . what do they call it? Closure? You nailed it. And I'll be forever—and I mean forever—grateful. I wish I could stay to help you with your legal troubles since I was the one who got you into this mess. But I can't—dead people can't testify in a court of law. Good luck, son. Whatever happens, I know you'll face it with courage and honesty."

He floated over to Shelia Mae, bent down and kissed her on the forehead. "I love you, child. Forgive me for the horrible wrongs I did to you. Just remember, they were done out of love and ignorance— never out of anger. You're a wonderful person. Don't ever forget it. May your future be blessed."

With that he was gone, the only sign he'd been there a tiny trail of tears.

———————

"Scooter!"

I could tell from the smell of sausage that I was late for breakfast. Downstairs, Shelia Mae was already putting food on the table. "Sorry to wake you, but I wanted to see you before I left."

"Left?"

"Headed to Omaha for my Aunt Janey's funeral. The last of Mom's sisters. I'll be back early next week. We can celebrate then."

"Celebrate what?"

"Your vindication. After you explain what really happened with Daddy, there is no way Luke and Nash are going to move forward with the charges."

I smiled weakly, not having the heart to tell her that the sheriff would still believe he had a lot of evidence in his favor. "Sounds like a plan."

She gave me a hug. "I've got to run. Breakfast is on the table. Stay as long as you like. *Mi casa su casa*. I'll be back sometime Sunday. There's so much more I want to ask you. Oh, and when you see the sheriff, tell him I want Daddy's skull back. You're right, he—it—needs a proper burial."

After breakfast, I walked back down to the creek. It was another cold, windless morning. As I approached, I could see a nice buck and a doe grazing under the scaffold. Shel was right not wanting to destroy it. It was not only it a monument to John, but also a necessary station in his daughter's journey of grief and growth.

Unfortunately, the rough-hewn structure also was evidence, which, as Paul reminded me when I picked him up at the airport early that afternoon, I dare not tamper with.

We drove to Norm's and spent the rest of the day discussing Sunday's hearing before Judge Abbott. The entire entourage was there, and the conversation was what you'd expect given those present. Norm was still of the opinion that a covert operation was the best solution but had moved from an outright violent confrontation to a cyber-attack that would leave the sheriff so ashamed he would never show his face in town again.

We vetoed it when he suggested involving a former Agency colleague who was some sort of double agent-Russian troll.

Dan was still bemoaning the possibility of losing his mortician's license, not to mention his business, which had never been better given the county's aging population. "I'm just reaching my full potential both as a business owner and artisan of the dead," he whined.

We mutely acknowledged his pain.

Bobby, who had personal experience on both sides of the law, was far more objective, noting that given the limited courtroom skills of the county attorney, the odds were in our favor, and any sentence or fine likely would be little more than a slap on the wrist.

The good Father, thankfully, said nothing, but simply smiled serenely and gave me an occasional nod.

Finally, Paul stood and cleared his throat. "Gentlemen," he said, "let's look at the facts—the real facts, Norm. As I understand the hearing tomorrow, it is a formal legal proceeding—very odd, even unique, but still legal. I would suggest you let me lead our side of the proceedings. I would further suggest that the rest of you—yes, Norm, that means you—remain silent unless asked to speak by me, the judge, or the county attorney, and then provide brief, direct responses with no extraneous opinions."

He went on to lay out his approach. He would start by asking the judge to, in absence of compelling evidence, throw out the case. If that failed, he would threaten to file a complaint of illegal search and seizure on the part of the sheriff and his deputy.

"After I get through, I doubt the sheriff will want to pursue the matter further," he said. "We should be out of there in thirty minutes or less."

39

PAUL AND I took our time getting to the courthouse Sunday morning, leaving the house for the short walk only minutes before our hearing before the judge was due to start. It was a beautiful day—bright, cold, a dusting of snow—that, I hoped, presaged an equally sunny outcome.

But nearing the courthouse my hopes began to fade. Cars lined both sides of the street for several blocks, and a crowd appeared to be forming.

"Is there some sort of parade or festival today?" Paul asked.

"Not that I know of. Unless it's for us. In which case, it may be a lynching party."

We looked at each other and quickened our pace. As we neared the courthouse steps, we were met by a large crowd. Upon spotting us, one side started cheering, the other booed and hissed. Shouts of "you get 'em, Scooter," mingled with "roast in Hell, you sick bastard" and "murderer!"

Off to one side a small group of old friends were riffing on an old anti-war chant: "Hey hey, ho ho," they cried, "Luke and WD gotta go!"

Apparently, the two lawmen had heeded their advice. They were nowhere in sight. In their absence, Pastor Leon and Father Tim were trying to keep ecumenical order, but with limited success.

As we pushed and shoved our way toward the entrance, the door opened, and Judge Abbott let us in. He then went out, locking the door behind him, and after finally getting the crowd's attention, spoke.

"Listen up!" he said, sounding more like a high school coach than an officer of the court. "I don't know what drew you here this morning, but there's nothing to see. I'm having a closed hearing on a small legal matter that has come to my attention. Nothing more. So, rather than stand out here in the cold, freezing your tails off, why don't you go home. Better yet, as most of you are good Christian folk, get your sorry souls to church."

"Sorry, Judge, but we're not leaving!" someone yelled from the back of the crowd. "We know what this is about—the murder of John Marshall," screamed another. "Rumor has it Scooter and some of his no-account friends did the old rancher in—killed him in cold blood and took his skull as a trophy."

"That's a lie, and you know it!" someone from the other side of the entrance yelled. "Scooter and his friends were set up by Luke and his cousin. If anyone should be locked up, it's those two."

Now both sides were yelling, each trying to outdo the other. The judge, hands on his hips, watched them for a moment, then shook his head and came back in. "God Almighty," he said, leading us to his chambers. "I'm still not sure what you and your pals were up to, but you've certainly riled up the town folk. Let's hope they get bored and go home while we get to the bottom of this."

Luke, WD, and the county attorney were already sitting stiffly in the judge's chambers when we arrived, looking tense and pale. Norm and the rest of our gang also were seated at the judge's big table.

Judge Abbott began by recapping the events as he understood them, and said he hoped to be able to bring us to a fair and agreeable decision on whether to proceed, and if so, how. Without asking permission, the sheriff immediately started arguing his side, at which point the judge, pointing a finger at him, told him to "shut the hell up!"

The silence that followed was quickly broken by the sound of doors opening and people running up the stairs. Then came loud voices and banging on the chamber doors. The sheriff rushed toward the door before the judge demanded he "sit the hell down!"

The old jurist then grabbed a sawed-off shotgun from behind his desk, told everyone but the two attorneys to hide in a small holding cell behind his office, and stormed out to meet the crowd. Soon the noisy commotion died down, replaced by Judge Abbott's steady, quiet voice.

"I wish I knew what he was telling them," I said. "Hopefully to go home."

"Maybe he's showing them how to tie a hangman's noose," Luke smirked.

"Maybe you should get the fuck home, too," Norm said, his face now inches from the sheriff's.

Just then, the judge returned with the preacher and the priest. "Two of our holy men have a request," the judge said. "Boys, state your case."

Father Tim began. "Given the public spectacle this unfortunate issue has become, Pastor Leon and I suggest that today's hearing be open to everyone."

Brother Leon continued. "The good padre here is right, gentlemen. This has become a divisive matter. We think it would be best to air it publicly—get all the facts out once and for all and end the gossiping and bickering that's consuming our community."

The judge looked around the table, silently considering the proposition. "It's an intriguing idea," he said, finally. "And, it has its merits. But it's also highly unorthodox. What do you two legal eagles think?"

Silence.

Finally, Paul spoke. "It's certainly unconventional, your honor. Sort of a crowd-sourced grand jury. But as long as they just observe, and don't try to testify on behalf of either side, we have no problem. Do we fellas?"

We looked at each other and shook our heads.

"If Luke and WD agree, I have no problem with it either," the young county attorney said. The two lawmen shrugged in silent acquiescence.

"Good," Judge Abbott said. "It sure as hell beats a Sunday morning riot on the town square. Especially given our town's motto: Creekmore—The Friendly City!"

―――――――――

It was another hour before the crowd was seated in the courtroom, quietly chatting over sweet rolls, coffee, and juice compliments of Mary's Café. The judge had personally ordered them, reasoning there was nothing better for soothing the souls of small-town Christian mobs than sugar and caffeine. He also had called in the town's two other ministers—one Methodist, the other Lutheran—to assist Father Tim and Pastor Leon in maintaining order. Both were happy to oblige, given their churches were empty and they wanted to see the show, too.

After banging his gavel loudly several times, the judge called the court to order. "Ladies and gentlemen, this is a hearing to get to the bottom of some serious charges leveled by our duly elected sheriff, against some men of our community—respected men whom many of you count as friends.

"You have been invited to witness this proceeding based on the advice of some of our local clergy, who believe in the healing power of transparency. But a word of caution: This is my courtroom. You are my guests. You will listen and observe. But you will not speak, unless invited to by me. If anyone does, I will throw *everyone* out. Understood?"

Silent nods filled the room.

"Good. Then let's get the show on the road. Sheriff, you're up first."

While Luke slowly approached the bench, Judge Abbott asked Pastor Leon if he could borrow his Bible. He then swore in the sheriff and motioned him to sit in the witness chair.

For the next hour, Luke shared his side of the story. He told about his suspicions on hearing about John's death. He talked about questioning Dan, who, he said, seemed unusually nervous. He spoke of the rumors he'd heard about John being shot to death— accidentally or on purpose, he'd heard both—and not dying of a heart attack as we reported.

Although he never mentioned Shelia Mae, or being made

to undress at gunpoint, he went into detail about staking out the Marshall ranch and my late-night visits there. "I tell you, there was no reason for Scooter poking around out there. It was damn weird." He told of observing "secret meetings" at Norm's place, where the "suspects were obviously plotting how to cover their past misdeeds or planning future ones."

He talked about the "raid" on my home, and how "John's skull was right there on the mantle, like some sick trophy," never mentioning that he'd failed to get a search warrant.

Finally, he described his and WD's ill-fated raid on our remote country hideout. "This armed, malicious gang knew we were coming! They ambushed us, hand-cuffed us, took us hostage, and drove us back to town in our own cruiser!"

This last, angry, and indignant statement triggered a few gasps but mostly giggles from the spectators, forcing Judge Abbott to again bring down his gavel and admonish the crowd.

"While I admit the picture the sheriff just painted may be seen as humorous by many of you," he said solemnly, "such outbursts will not be tolerated in my courtroom."

He turned to Luke and asked if he had anything more to add. "Only that I believe these four men, led by Scooter here, are responsible for the death of John Marshall. At best, they aided and abetted a crazy, misguided old man in carrying out an equally crazy death wish. At worst, they murdered him in cold blood."

This time there were no giggles, only gasps.

Again, Judge Abbott gaveled for order. "I think you're finished, Luke. Please step down. Now, who will testify on behalf of you four men?"

Paul started to get up, but I stopped him. "Better to hear it first from a local boy than a big-city lawyer," I whispered.

He nodded.

As I started for the witness stand, Judge Abbott announced a fifteen-minute recess "for those who need coffee and those like me, who can't hold it." Most of the spectators, however, seemed more interested in how their side was doing than in a coffee or bathroom break.

A small crowd of supporters surrounded us, patting us on the back, shaking our hands, and reassuring us of our goodness and innocence.

A few, mainly older women who had been on their way to church when they'd heard about the other "service" taking place at the courthouse, whispered highly un-Christian opinions about our accusers.

Ina Pearl Simpson, one of the last living church ladies who terrified me as a child with her hellish stories of the underworld, hobbled up to me, grabbed my arm and pulled me close.

"Those two men," she whispered, "are evil bastards—dumb as rocks, too. I don't know why the Good Lord didn't strike them down years ago. If I'd had 'em in Sunday School like you when they was little, they'd have turned out a whole lot better." She winked and gave me a knowing smile. "So, I guess it's up to you to do the Lord's work and kick some sense into their heathen asses. Okay?"

Across the aisle I could see, and at times hear, Luke's and WD's supporters giving them similar encouragement. Another church lady, a friend of Pearl's, but a Methodist, pointed a bony finger at me and spoke angrily to Luke. I couldn't make out everything she said but heard enough to know that she believed I was a pompous, womanizing drunk who had turned his back on his faith and his people. She also noted that I lived in Texas.

When Judge Abbott finally got his court back in order, I took the stand and told my side of the story.

I followed the same, now familiar script I had shared with Shelia Mae. In a sincere and even tone, I explained how John and Ruthie had been like second parents to me and many other local youngsters. I spoke of the solid, nonjudgmental advice both had continued to give me as an adult—much needed and welcomed guidance on everything from college to kids to relationships.

At times, I found myself struggling to cross a tightrope strung between the truth and too much information. Most people in the room, I figured, had heard some version of my history and had made up their minds about me long ago. Sitting in the witness stand, it was easy to see which side they were on based on where they sat and how they reacted to my story.

I didn't mention Shelia Mae. I did not bring up the old rivalry between Luke and me, nor did I speak of his harassment of Shel and his illegal search of my house. I was in Creekmore. My hometown. A usually friendly town with a limited jury pool. There was no need to open old wounds or inflict new ones.

I told of how John had shared with me his plan to manage his own death in a way he felt was appropriate, and his request that I help him. I spoke about the goose-hunting trip, designed to give John one last hunt while throwing off any suspicion that might arise. I talked about leaving him at the Oklahoma hotel where he was to meet a Native American shaman, and how hard it was to drive away.

After a pause and a sip of water, I told them about finding John's skull, and how the skull led me back to the Sawlog and the scaffold in the trees where, I believed, John spent his last hours. I did not speak of the pistol or the whiskey. I shared my theory on how he turned the tables on us, riding the old Indian back home so that he could die on the land he'd loved and worked for the better part of a century.

When I'd finished, I took one last look around the room. "Whether it was right or wrong, I take full responsibility for what has happened in the death of John Marshall. I made the decision to help the old rancher and talked Norm, Bobby, and Dan into helping. "They are my friends," I said. "And, they were John's friends, too. We did what friends do."

The silence hung heavy in the packed courtroom as I left the witness stand and walked back to my chair. I did not look up, assuming I had changed no one's mind and unsure of what would happen next.

Judge Abbott thanked the sheriff and me for our "time, sincerity and honesty." He then asked the county attorney and Paul to approach the bench. For the next ten minutes the three carried on a whispered, animated conversation. Finally, they returned to their seats and the judge spoke.

"Ladies and gentlemen: first, I want to congratulate you. Never on a Sunday morning have I seen my fellow citizens sit so still, with rapt attention, for as long as you have today. No one slept. No one fidgeted. There was very little whispering. Perhaps it was the sermon we've been listening to this morning.

"I think you'd all agree that it was better than most preached to us from the pulpit. It had everything. Good. Evil. Life and death. The only thing missing was a resurrection. But who knows? Maybe John himself will make an appearance before the day is over."

Oh, I prayed, *if only you would, my friend. Just float in quietly and give some of these folks a good what for. Tell them you were sent from the Big Man himself. Remind them of what it says in the Good Book they read so piously and publicly: "Vengeance is mine sayeth the Lord." Then give them a cold hard stare and dematerialize in a tasteful display of heavenly fireworks—a couple of small lightning bolts and a puff of smoke.*

But he didn't. And the judge wasn't finished. "After witnessing this Sabbath miracle, I've decided to do something I've never done before. This was supposed to be a simple hearing to review the accusations and see if these men should be formally charged with a crime, as the sheriff is requesting. But given your obvious interest, and the fact that you're all *good* Christians, I'm going to let you be the judge—actually, the grand jury. I've asked our county attorney, Nash here, to summarize the case for the prosecution. Scooter's Texas attorney friend will then speak for the defense. Each will have thirty minutes. After they have spoken, you will each be allowed to cast a ballot either for or against proceeding with this case in a true court of law. If there are no questions, Nash, you're up."

For a small-town county attorney who'd seldom handled more than simple assault and disturbing the peace cases, Nash Brewster was an exceptional prosecutor. Harvard-trained, he had learned how to meld his natural, aw-shucks, country approach with the sophisticated legal knowledge of a big-city federal prosecutor. For the next thirty minutes, sensing that this could be the first step to a higher office or get him quickly run out of town, he took that art to a new level.

He started by talking about two old friends, "Scooter James and John Marshall, one a well-meaning but misguided soul, the other, his revered surrogate father."

He then went on to review the "tragic crime that Luke, veteran lawman and true professional had described there today."

"I'm sure John sincerely believed in his plan for leaving this world. But let's face it, he was very old, dying, and was no longer thinking clearly. Now, I would like to believe that Scooter did what he thought was right, given the love and respect he had for this man. I would like to believe that he felt an obligation, a duty, to honor John's request. But I'm yet to be convinced. And, sadly, even if it was, this sense of love and duty blinded him to the two greatest tenets in the world—the laws of man and the laws of God."

For the next fifteen minutes he read from the state laws and the Bible, leaning more heavily on scripture than statute. He closed by reminding the spectators, who, except for periodic head shaking or nodding had sat motionless throughout, of their duty as citizens and Christians.

"I know you all would rather be worshiping your Savior this morning than sitting where you are. But the Almighty didn't give you that choice. Instead, he called you here today. And now, listening to His Word and those of our great state, you must do the right thing. Even if Scooter is the good man he claims to be, he and his friends must pay for their sins just as Jesus paid for ours."

With that, he sat down. The silence that followed was discomforting. Even Judge Abbott appeared tongue-tied. Finally, he thanked Nash and asked Paul if he was ready to present his summary.

Paul nodded and walked slowly to the front of the courtroom. He surveyed the still silent spectators and then looked down. He appeared to be studying his notes, but knowing his thorough preparation, I suspected he was offering up his own silent prayer— something along the lines of "Jesus! Please get me out of this holy mess."

After a few seconds, he looked up again. But before he could speak, the old oak doors in the rear of the courtroom noisily swung open, and a voice, that of a woman, addressed him.

"You can sit down, counselor. I'll take it from here."

As the entire room turned, Shelia Mae, in boots, jeans, a western shirt and pearls, strode down the aisle, her head high, looking directly at the judge. She stopped before reaching him and asked if she could approach the bench. Stunned, he nodded.

She did, but then turned and faced the crowd. "As most of you know, I am the daughter of the alleged victim. Like many of you, I also am a friend of the alleged killer, Scooter James."

Here she paused, coldly surveying the room and then staring at Luke and the county attorney.

"As for being a good Christian woman, I have my doubts as I know many of you also have. Indeed, some of you have been kind enough to share those doubts with me. Bless your little hearts."

Suddenly her icy façade melted, and she was crying, shaking with the obvious anger and sorrow she felt.

"I am so sorry," she said softly, struggling to regain her composure. "That last comment was uncalled for. Please forgive me, but I'm a bit distraught. For the past thirty minutes, I've been standing at the door, listening to the legal stylings of our talented county attorney. Nash Brewster, you may be a brilliant lawyer, but you're full of bullshit. And what you said just now stung me to the core and makes me very angry.

"How dare you talk about Daddy that way? He had a better mind than you'll ever have, even with your Ivy League education. How dare you call Scooter a sinner? This man is a good man—a loving, caring, thoughtful man. Sure, he's experienced his share of screw-ups. Don't look so innocent, folks. I know you've heard the stories because I've heard you share them with your friends."

Now, the newly manicured, blood-red nail on her index finger was pointed directly at the county attorney, just inches from his heart. "You pious little bastard! How dare you use the Holy Bible for such unholy ends?"

Nash started to object, but Judge Abbot, suppressing a chuckle, motioned to him to sit down and be quiet. "Please, Shelia Mae, as you were saying."

"As I was saying . . . I do not appreciate the tone of the prosecutor, nor the accusations that the good sheriff and his worthless cousin have been making to everyone who would listen to them. Luke could not care less about my father. What he's really after is me. For some reason, he has the idea that we should rekindle the brief adolescent romance we had in high school. He has been pestering me about it since I returned home. More than once he's showed up the ranch. He and WD even staked out the place to see what Scooter and I were up to. Yes, folks, I've entertained my supposedly murderous friend on several occasions. But, no, it's not what you think.

"What those silly lawmen were really doing was stalking me." Now her finger was in Luke's face. "If you ever do that again, buster, you'll be in for a big surprise—big as in double-ought buckshot."

She again faced the packed courtroom. "Folks, there was no foul play, no murder. Scooter, with the help of his friends here, granted a dying old man his last wish. Daddy had the strange idea that he wanted to die as the Native Americans who once owned this land supposedly had. He'd heard stories from an old Kiowa ranch hand when he was a kid—tales of how the elderly just walked into the sunset, of how the dead were put on scaffolds in the air. He used to tell me about them.

"Apparently, though he never told me, he decided he would end his life in a similar fashion. He made Scooter swear never to tell me because he didn't want to hurt me. But last week, knowing that eventually I was going to hear a very dark and twisted version of what happened, Scooter told me everything.

"He showed me the platform my father built on the Sawlog, and where he found my father's skull, which, by the way, Luke and WD stole during their illegal search of Scooter's home."

She smiled. "Together we solved the mystery of how he returned home from Oklahoma, where he told Scooter he was meeting a shaman who would take him to his final resting place, a story he fabricated to throw Scooter off his trail.

"Yes, your honor, Daddy was crazy—like a fox. And in the end, he outfoxed us all. Sure, I'm sad about Dad's death, and I'm pissed at how he chose to die. But it's time we stopped pointing fingers and placing blame, and instead started celebrating the life of a wonderful man who died a good death."

40

IT WAS ONE of those spring-like afternoons that occasionally bring a warm window of hope to our otherwise frigid plains winters. Shelia Mae and I were making the short pilgrimage from the ranch to her parents' graves, which now contained the last remains of her father.

Two weeks had passed since the courtroom drama that finally put to rest John's soul and the malicious rumors surrounding his death. After Shelia Mae's impromptu courtroom appearance, Judge Abbott had quickly dismissed the case, calling for an end to the rumors and bickering that had consumed Creekmore.

"There's no need for a vote," he told the crowd. "What is needed is for all of us to take a close look at our own behavior, not to mention our beliefs."

He called for a day of prayer and healing and urged his fellow citizens to "return to the church of your choice and pay as much attention to what your minister says as you did to the drama that was played out here today."

The following Saturday was proclaimed John Marshall Day. A

memorial service was held in the high school auditorium. It was officiated by Father Tim and Pastor Leon, who managed to sneak in a Baptist-style alter call at the end, saving, by my count, six new souls.

A number of people spoke publicly about the rancher and his role in their lives and community. Shelia Mae gave a touching eulogy and thanked everyone for their kindness and support. The music ranged from Frederic Chopin to Johnny Cash, ending with "When the Roll is Called Up Yonder," which, surprisingly, even the Catholics and Lutherans knew the words to.

After the three-hour community lunch that followed, Shelia Mae and I, along with Norm, Bobby, and Dan returned to the ranch for a private graveside service officiated by Tim and Leon. The Sheriff and WD had returned John's skull the day after the hearing, apologizing to both Shelia Mae and me for any trouble they'd caused and offering to do an extensive search of the pasture and creek for additional remains.

Shel thanked them but declined their offer. "If bits of Daddy are resting out there, he would want them left there."

Now, I was getting ready to return to Texas before the arrival of the next winter storm, which was creeping in from the northwest. I had come to the ranch to visit Shel one last time before heading south.

We had spent a lot of time together since the "trial," discussing the events of the past month, how they had affected us, and what our futures might hold. Shel had decided to return home for good and take over the ranch. I had promised to spend more time in Creekmore, including, of course, returning every fall to hunt birds.

Now, as we prepared to say our final good-byes, we stood before the graves of John and Ruthie, each of us silently reflecting on the remarkable life and death of the old rancher.

Silently, I thanked him for the love and guidance he'd so generously shared with me over the years, starting with that long-ago spiritual pep talk given to a small boy about to pee his pants in the basement of a little country church. I thanked him for rekindling my relationship with his daughter and promised to continue watching over her as he had asked me to. Finally, I asked if he might continue to drop in from time to time to check on us both.

I don't know if it's possible, my friend, I prayed, *but your visits are always welcomed. Please, don't be a stranger.*

As soon as I'd said the words, I felt a sudden presence at my side. Thinking he'd heard my prayer I opened my eyes. But it was only Buck, returning from chasing a rabbit. He sat there between us, moaning softly, then walked to the freshly turned earth that covered John's grave. There, he lifted his leg, and, in his own way, solemnly blessed the now sacred ground.

Shel and I laughed, hugged, and slowly followed Buck back to the house. As for John the rancher, I never saw him again.

EPILOGUE

MY FATHER NEVER TOLD ME how John died. Nor did he tell me about his occasional "visits" after his death. I only learned the details after discovering this manuscript while going through an old box of papers that had been sitting on a basement shelf for years.

My first recollection of John was much like Dad's. We were visiting my grandparents in Creekmore and had gone out to the Marshall's ranch for Sunday dinner. When we'd finished, John asked me—I was six or seven at the time—if I would like to see his cattle and horses.

Being a city kid, I was thrilled. We climbed into the dusty cab of his pickup, a veritable rancher's mobile toolbox with everything from pliers and a rifle to medicines and giant hypodermic needles and were off. As we bounced across the prairie, John introduced me to an amazing new world of fading wagon trails, barbed wire, prairie dogs, and red-tailed hawks—a landscape of tall grass, green crops, and the ghosts of Native Americans and the buffalo that sustained them until the White men came.

From then on, whenever I went to Creekmore, I always visited Ruthie and John. We talked about everything from school to boys to faith. Unlike my parents—most parents, I think—they never preached or were judgmental.

The day my grandmother died John picked me up at the house—Dad was still at her bedside at the hospital—to tell me she had passed. Driving the same old pickup, he took me to the dairy bar and bought us ice-cream floats. For the next hour we drove through the countryside, discussing death, God and, of course, Gran.

"Your grandmother," he told me, sipping on his straw, "was a good woman. Better than she realized. Like many of us, she was both God-fearing and skeptical, a combination that doesn't play too well in these parts. Pious folk tend to say hurtful things that make us question our faith. I know your grandmother suffered from such remarks, most of which were made out of innocence or ignorance.

"At some point, if you haven't already, you'll have similar doubts," he told me. "Embrace them, roll them around in your mind and your heart, but don't let them eat your soul and destroy your faith.

"Blind faith is as dangerous as it is dumb. God gave you a brain so that you could grow in both knowledge and faith. Don't ever let anyone tell you differently. Your gran knows that now that she's passed. All that doubt and fear she suffered is gone. God bless her."

When I was older, Dad and I used to talk about the importance of Ruthie and John in our lives—how their subtle spiritual guidance helped shape both of us.

"A lot of folks in our little town thought of themselves as good Christians," Dad said. "Some were. Others just talked a good game. John and Ruthie were different. They lived their faith every day of their lives, right up to the end."

Dad moved back to Creekmore after he retired. He lived in the family house but spent much of his time out at the Marshall ranch, which Shelia Mae had taken over, having never returned to Paris. When I was older, someone—probably one of the nosey church ladies—once asked me if he and Shelia Mae had "a thing" going on. I told her it was none of her business and so what if they did, even though I knew they didn't—at least in the Biblical sense. That said, I saw a closeness between them that is lacking in many traditional relationships.

Looking back, the story of John's death explains a strange incident that happened a year or two before Dad's own passing, and a later comment he made that I never understood.

One snowy evening, Shelia Mae spotted a lone, armed figure trudging through the pasture behind her house. Concerned, she called the sheriff. Following the tracks of dog and man, he eventually found Dad and his pointer Shiner, asleep under a towering cottonwood on the bank of the Sawlog. Dad told the sheriff, somewhat indignantly, that he was simply taking a nap after a day of hunting, and to please go back to town so he could get some peace.

Soon after, on Shelia Mae's advice, we moved Dad to the nursing home, where he was surrounded by three of the characters that figured in his story—Norm and Luke who were also residents, and Father Tim, who came almost daily to visit. It was a jovial group—all anger and animosity apparently having been erased by time—who spent their days playing pinochle or dominoes and talking about the past.

One day several months later when I was in Creekmore to check on Dad, I went with Shelia Mae to visit them and smuggle in a bottle of scotch and a pan of fresh-baked cinnamon rolls. It was a late spring afternoon, and all of us were sitting on the patio, which looked out on a tapestry of ripening wheat and prairie grass that spread to the western horizon.

At some point the conversation turned to subject of their failing health, a familiar topic, and they began talking about how they hoped that death, whenever it came, would be quick and painless. It was a benign, almost whimsical conversation until Norm spoke.

"Let's be honest, fellas, I think we all know the best way to exit this life."

"I never thought I'd say this," Luke said, "but for once I have to agree with you."

Everyone smiled and nodded.

"He was a special man," Father Tim said.

"A special dad, too." Shelia Mae agreed.

"A saint," Dad said. "A goddamned saint."

ACKNOWLEDGMENTS

THE STORY OF *ST. JOHN THE RANCHER* would still be a vague notion rattling about my brain had it not been for a number of people who offered encouragement, insight, and expertise along the way. They range from Mr. Trent, my junior high English teacher and coach, who first suggested I forego my dreams of Major League Baseball and instead become a writer, to the team at Koehler Books, which is in a league of its own when it comes to helping writers like me bring their creations to life.

Nor would this book have happened without the support of my family: my wife Jeanne, editor extraordinaire, and my children, Mary Lu, Wilson, and Joel, who provided a goodly share of material and eye-rolling criticism.

Finally, I owe the people of the small High Plains community where I grew up, especially a local rancher, also named John, for providing the inspiration that led to the creation of the story and its central character. Although I have yet to be visited by his ghost, John's spirit lives on in the wisdom and goodness he shared with me and many others.